D1489800

MIDDAY

By David B. Lyons.

PRINT ISBN :- 978-1-9160518-0-5

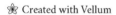 Created with Vellum

WANT TO STAY UP TO DATE WITH DAVID B. LYONS'S NOVELS?

Visit David's website:

TheOpenAuthor.com

or

Sign up here to become a David B. Lyons insider and receive exclusive information on his latest novels

www.subscribepage.com/dblinsider

MIDDAY HAS BEEN GETTING RAVE REVIEWS FROM THE CRITICS

Here's what reviewers are saying:

"A gripping and high-octane page turner that keeps you guessing right until the end." – Irish Mail on Sunday

"Neatly plotted with a devastating twist in its tail." - Irish Independent

"An intense, addictive, and incredibly clever read." - The Writing Garnet

"What an utterly clever book Midday is." – NovelDeelights book review

"I never envisioned the surprises the author held in store for me and my enjoyment intensified towards the truly gripping finale." - ByTheLetter book review

"I had my hand to my mouth, gasping." - RubinaReads book review

MIDDAY HAS BEEN GETTING RAVE REVIEWS FROM THE CRITICS

"Very tense." - Col'sCriminalLibrary book review

"One to ponder after reading. A very well thought out scenario, well written." -NickiBookBlog review

"For me, David B. Lyons is the Tarantino of the book world." – Bookstormer

"A fast-paced thriller that's roaring up the charts." - CrimeFictionLover book review

I included the 'B' in my author name so you can come on this journey with me.

07:00

Vincent

As soon as I wake up I let out a sigh that probably sounds as if I'm disappointed to be alive. There used to be a time when I wouldn't care if I woke up or not. But not now. Not with the excitement that envelops me these days.

I tap the screen of my iPhone to put an end to the beep. I purposely chose the most annoying alarm tone so it would force me to sit up when it goes off. There's no need to look at the clock. It's seven a.m. – the same time the alarm sounds every weekday morning. I wipe my hand over my face before throwing my feet over the side of the bed. I always rest them on the carpet before mustering the energy to lift my body to a standing position. A shower will refresh me. I open the Spotify app on my phone and pause for a moment. Some days, this is the hardest decision I make.

What will the soundtrack to the morning be?

I scroll until I see Beyoncé's name. This is nothing new. Her songs have so much energy in them that they are the perfect tonic for a wake-up call. 'Love on Top' begins as I shuffle my way to the en suite. I don't even look behind at what I've left in the bedroom. It's the same scene every morning. A crack of light forms from a gap in our blinds and casts itself over our king-size bed. Ryan will be curled up in foetus position, contemplating what to do with himself today. He'll be well aware that I've got up, but turning over to wish me a good morning won't have crossed his mind. It's way too early for him to talk.

The sensors turn the light on in the en suite for me as I head straight for the mirror. I don't know why it's the first thing I do every morning. I look my worst at this time of the day. Everybody does. My eyes are swollen and my face appears puffy. I check my hairline again. If I stare at it every day I don't notice it receding too much. But who am I kidding? I'm going to be a bona fide bald man soon. I've trimmed my hair as much as I can. It's long enough to look like I have some hair on my head but short enough to look like I'm not trying to hide the baldness. I turn the shower on and decide to dance my way into the spray. 'Love on Top' is a great song. The tempo builds and builds. I contemplate the day ahead before getting annoyed with myself. I shower for two reasons – to wash and to refresh. This cubicle doesn't entertain thoughts about work. To distract myself, I imagine I'm on stage at the 3Arena prancing around in high heels in front of twenty thousand obsessed fans. I snatch at the blue bottle of body wash and use it as my microphone. I love these lyrics. It's one of those songs that you can really put everything in to.

Now I'm awake!

I stop singing when I get out of the shower. I know it annoys Ryan. I think I've got a decent singing voice, but I've noticed him wince every now and then when he hears me harmonising around the penthouse. Instead, I pick up my iPhone again and, having turned off the music, I turn the kettle on. That's my favourite use of the iPhone – the fact that I can turn the kettle on in my kitchen, while in another room, through a Bluetooth device. It's hugely pointless, but it brings me a little joy. I wrap the towel around my waist and make my way through the bedroom towards our open-plan kitchen and living room. It's the perfect time of the morning to wake up on an April day in this old town.

The sun has just risen and thin rays of gold are beaming their way into our penthouse. We have floor-to-ceiling windows all around the living quarters of this place. The living room and kitchen are flooded with light in the daytime. I love these two minutes to myself. I use them to stare out onto the rooftops of the city. The disorganised mess of architecture appears silhouetted at this time of the day. I love Dublin. Well, I used to love Dublin. It's lost its charm for me a little, but there's no getting away from the fact that it's ruggedly handsome. It shouldn't be, but it is. We can make out a lot of the iconic buildings around the town from our vantage point. The top of the Spire creeps its way above everything in the distance. I think it's a deadly sculpture. It's striking to look at – isn't that what art is supposed to be? I can't get over the fuckwits who moaned about the cost of the Spire. We were always a population of easy-going jokers in Ireland, but we've turned into a right crowd of moaners in recent times. We adopted a lot of traits from the Brits over the centuries, but we always stayed clear of their miserableness – up until we got money. Now we're just a tiny replica of our big brother across the Irish Sea – a bunch of moaners and groaners. I don't like to moan. I always try to look at the positive. Such as this view. I can never get enough of it.

What does Dublin have to offer me today?

I stay at the window until a click confirms that the kettle

has boiled before I pour both myself and Ryan a fresh mug of coffee.

'Mornin', gorgeous,' I call out as I re-enter the bedroom to place the mug on his bedside table. I get a grunt in return.

Some mornings I feel like throwing the hot coffee into his pretty little face.

07:00

Ryan

I HATE THAT FUCKIN ALARM. I'M CERTAIN VINCENT CHOSE THE most annoying tone on his phone just to make sure I start every day in a miserable mood. He takes his time turning it off each morning too.

I lie in bed contemplating another long day stuck in this penthouse. At least I used to wake up with aspirations for the day, a year or so ago, even though I knew that I wouldn't go on to fulfil them. But now I can't even bother to lie to myself. I'm going to get out of bed, not long after Vincent brings me my coffee in about ten minutes' time, to watch morning television with him over a bowl of Corn Flakes. He'll leave for work at about seven forty-five and I'll climb back into bed. I'll probably stay here until midday with only the urge to masturbate at least once disturbing my lie in. I agreed to get up with Vincent at seven every morning when I left my job almost two years ago. Vincent thinks I spend eight hours a day on my laptop writing a future bestseller. I can't bring myself to tell him that I've written one page of notes in the past twenty months. That's it. I've lost my ability to write, but more annoying than that is the fact that I've lost my passion to write. I was always full of great ideas. I had a strong imagination when I was younger, but my creativity receded so much as soon as I started to work in media. My writing was forced to become formulaic. I use the laptop Vincent bought for me to scroll through Facebook and to watch porn. I'm useless. I do nothing with my days and I'm no longer afraid to admit that to myself.

I'd fall back asleep contemplating my failing life if it wasn't for the fact that I have to put up with Vincent singing in the shower. He thinks I can't hear him over the noise of the water, but I can. His voice is genuinely shit. There's only about three-quarters of an hour left until he heads off. Seven forty-five is my favourite time of the day. In fairness to him, he stops singing once the shower is turned off. He does that for me. I love him and loathe him in equal measure. Sometimes I just wish he wasn't successful. That way, we'd both be useless together and I wouldn't feel so inadequate. But then again, we wouldn't be living in a place like this if Vincent wasn't so brilliant at what he does. I constantly have to remind myself that I shouldn't blame him for my depression. It's all on me.

I can hear him pour coffee into our favourite mugs and I know he's coming to wake me up. He loves me so much. His dedication to our relationship has never diminished. He does all the right things. I feel really grateful when he places the mug of coffee on the bedside table beside me and I know it's cute that he still calls me 'gorgeous'.

But some mornings I just want to throw the hot coffee back into his ageing face.

07:05

Darragh

I'VE BEEN LOOKIN' FORWARD TO THIS DAY FOR MONTHS. BUT now it's all about to go down, I'm nervous – or anxious. Maybe both. I don't think I know what the fuckin difference is between those two feelings anyway.

I stand at the corner of Blood Stoney Road and Horse Fair, leaning against a lamppost so I can stare up at their apartment. It looks like a pretty cool place to live in. This building's seven storeys high and made entirely of glass. The sun's just popped up in the sky and the reflection from the windows is starting to blind me. I know I have everything in me bag because I checked it at least five times before I left me bedsit an hour ago. But I tap the inside of me jacket pocket to assure meself that the gun is still with me. Then I rub at me jeans pocket to feel for the mobile phone JR handed over to me last week. I'm good to go. I'm just waitin' on that phone to ring.

Me mind flashes through what could happen throughout the morning. Part of me hopes I don't have to kill again and that everything goes according to plan. If that's the case, I'll be a millionaire by midday. But another part of me won't be bothered at all if I do have to shoot Ryan. That'd be murder number three for me. I really am turning into a proper fuckin gangster.

A light turns on in their apartment and I know for certain that the fags are awake. JR has this down to a T. These jammy fuckers must have a lot of money to live in a place like this. The first two floors of the building used to be a warehouse but were turned into a marble lobby on the ground floor, and a posh bar and restaurant on the first. Some investor, about twenty years ago, pumped a fair few quid into this area of Dublin. He musta made a fuckin fortune. They're all pretty cool-lookin' buildings around here now. It looks like a mini New York City. But there's no doubt that this is the most jaw-dropping mini tower round the place. And these pricks live at the very top of it. JR knows everything about these fags. He even knows everything about their neighbours. Fat Barry and Ugly Janice, who live on the sixth floor, spend most of their time in London and won't be around this week – this is just one of many apartments they have around Europe. Keith and Sean, who live on the fifth floor – and who we also believe to be fags – will both be in their art studio further down the street on Clare Lane. I watched them leave about ten minutes ago. They don't normally come back until around five o'clock. I'll be grand anyway. The noises I make will be minimal. There'll be no raised voices and I have a silencer for the gun. There isn't a need for me to worry. JR and I have done our homework. This will be a walk in the park for me. I've hardly any work to do. It's Vincent who will be doing all the hard graft after all.

I'm glancing around the area again for no other reason but to pass some time when the phone finally buzzes.

'All good?' asks JR.

'All good, boss. Beautiful morning, isn't it?' I reply.

'You in place?'

'Been waiting on your call. I've had a good look around. Everything is as we said it would be. It's ten past seven, do you want me to make the move now?'

'Go ahead. Don't take the lift.'

'Of course I won't take the lift.'

JR's amazin'. He's taken me under his wing over the past few months and taught me so many things I've always wanted to learn. But sometimes he treats me like I'm an idiot. Of course I won't take the lift. That's been drilled into me as part of the plan for months. There are cameras in the lifts. There are also cameras in the reception area of the building, but we figured out a way to get by them. Besides, with this disguise on, nobody would be able to recognise me anyway. I walk slowly towards the entrance of the building and pause for a minute until I see the receptionist face in the opposite direction. As soon as she crouches down, I quietly push at the big glass door and make me way into the lobby – staying to the left as planned. I stoop low to crawl behind the wide leather couch before entering the jacks. There's two doors immediately inside the jacks: one that leads into the urinals and another that has a sign on it, which reads 'Staff Only'. I take out the library card from me back jeans pocket and wrestle with the second door handle before it releases. Another door faces me now I've walked into this pokey room which isn't locked and allows me access straight to the stairwell. I trip over a bucket as I make my way towards the stairs, causing a racket to echo through the room. Me heart races for a few beats. I wait until there's absolute silence before heading towards them. The receptionist didn't notice me entering the lobby and I dodged all the cameras. Job done. I'll be able to climb to the fags' apartment from here without any fear.

07:10

Vincent

I turn on the light in the living room so I can jot down some notes. I have a touch of OCD when it comes to work and I need to know where I am going to be at any point during the day. My work life used to be stressful, but I've managed to take control of my routine and have everything and everybody in line. My career is at a stage now where I just observe all of my staff stressing on my behalf. If I'm brilliant at anything, it's delegating.

Ryan is draped on our couch watching the adverts between *Good Morning Britain* segments. I like the fact that he has a small crush on Piers Morgan. People tell me I look a lot like him. I can see it. We're almost the same age and happen to have the same shaped head. He probably has a little more hair than I do, but we share a rosy complexion. Both of us scrub up well, too. I wonder if Piers looks as dishevelled as I do first thing in the morning before he puts his suit on?

I finish my notes as *Good Morning Britain* restarts and notice Piers is wearing a midnight blue suit with a blue tie. That's what I decide to wear today too as I make my way towards the bedroom. I find my iPhone on our bed and press play on Spotify. Beyoncé is back! 'Halo' begins to play, but fuck that. I want something more upbeat and scroll through the playlist until I find 'Freedom'. I bizarrely have my own dance routine for this song that I can somehow still pull off as I dress. My moves aren't bad for a forty-nine-year-old. I act like a straight bloke everywhere except in my own bedroom and en suite. I can really ham it up in the comfort of my own home. I take a crisp white shirt from a hanger in the wardrobe and dance my arms into it. Just as I fasten the top button I'm certain I hear a knock at the door. That's unusual. I mute Beyoncé and squint my eyes in surprise.

'That you, Ryan?' I shout out.

'It's the door,' he replies.

He can be so fuckin' lazy. He heard the knock for certain and is still slouched on our couch purring over Piers Morgan with a bowl of Corn Flakes resting on his chest.

'I'll get it, I guess,' I say sarcastically as I pace past him towards the front door.

I look through the peephole to see a young guy with an ugly haircut staring back at me.

What the hell does he want?

As soon as I open the door a wave of panic hits me. I'm shoved straight back into the hallway and bounce off the wall before landing face first on the floor. I blink my eyes open in shock to find the ugly prick pointing a gun at me. His other hand is lifted to his mouth, with his index finger stretched up to his lips, signalling that I should shut the fuck up. I hear Ryan's heavy breaths as he sprints towards us. It must be the quickest he's moved in a couple of years. The ugly prick points the gun at my boyfriend before back-kicking our front door closed behind him.

'Not a word, you two. In the sitting room, now,' he orders, motioning the gun up and down. I crawl to a standing position, my body trembling with disbelief.

'Sit down!' he orders again once we're at the couch. The stranger grins at us before dropping his gym bag to the ground. He reaches inside and takes out a reel of duct tape. I stare over at Ryan. He looks petrified.

'Is there anything …' I begin to say before being told to shut up by virtue of the gun being shoved back into my face. My heart races as I try to take in what's happening.

'You,' screams the stranger, pointing the gun at Ryan. 'On the fuckin' floor, now. On your stomach. Spread your arms and legs out as wide as ya can.'

He has the strangest mongrel accent. I'm pretty sure it's half Cork, half Dublin. I'd bet any money that he grew up in Cork but moved to Dublin half his lifetime ago. I stare at his face. He has a bizarre blond hairdo that would have even looked dated in the eighties. You can tell by looking at him that he's had a hard life. I can see it in his bloodshot eyes. Yet he's still only a kid. About eighteen or nineteen, I'd guess. He can barely grow a moustache, but he is trying. And his face is still producing fresh acne. Ryan does as he's told while the kid waves the gun back at me, motioning that it's my turn to get up. Sliding one hand over a chair in our kitchen, he nods at me to sit in it. I notice my hands shake while I slip into the seat. I'm afraid to say anything as he wraps the thick tape around my wrists, fastening them to the arms of the chair. He keeps an eye on Ryan as he's doing this, but my boyfriend is clearly too afraid to try anything. He'll do as he's told. When the kid's finished taping both of my wrists, he slaps me across the face. That boils my blood more so than having the gun pointed at me. He then reaches for the back of Ryan's neck and pulls him to his feet.

'Sit in that other chair, fag,' he says, grinning.

Fag? Have we just rewound the clock by a decade?

The prick ties Ryan to the chair in much the same manner he tied me, but then proceeds a little further. Ryan's ankles are also taped down and I figure he must have missed that part of the process with me.

'We'll cooperate with you,' I finally manage to say. 'We'll do whatever it is you want, just don't hurt us, please!'

He walks over to me with a grin gurning across his face.

'Too fuckin' right you'll cooperate with me. Whether I hurt you or not. Now shut the fuck up.'

Turning his back on us, he reaches further into his bag. My eyes widen. I have no idea what he has in store for us. I look over at Ryan again. He looks like a rabbit caught in the headlights of an oncoming truck. At this moment I am more worried about him than I am for myself. And that's unusual. My default is normally selfish. At least I can admit that. Ryan's much weaker than I am. I'm relieved to see that the kid has only removed an old mobile phone from his bag.

He walks towards Ryan and wraps more tape tightly around the back of his head and across his mouth at least eight times. Ryan keeps his head still, but he can't help grunting in fear. When he's done, the smug fucker strolls towards me.

'This is for you, big boy,' he says, shoving the phone into the breast pocket of my shirt before falling back onto our couch.

'Here's what's gonna happen,' he says.

Ah ... I know what's going on.

07:20

Jack

I TAKE A QUICK PEEK AT MY WATCH AS I LEAN AGAINST A lamppost on Horse Fair across from their apartment. It's less than five hours until the deadline. I know it's still early but I'm agitated. I take the mobile phone out of my jeans pocket and stare at the home screen again. Still no missed call. For some reason I don't believe the phone and click into the call history to double check. I notice a strange number that makes me squint for a second before I realise it was me who dialled it. It's the number for the reception on the ground floor of the apartment building. I rang there ten minutes or so ago asking for a form that I knew would make the receptionist turn around. But since then there's been no activity on my phone. I hope everything has gone as it's supposed to. I can't stop worrying. More things could have gone wrong in the first ten minutes of this morning than I believe they will over the next five hours. My mind races through all possibilities.

Did the receptionist see Darragh? Did he fail to open the staff door? Is he still making his way up the stairs? Did Vincent or Ryan get the better of him after he pushed his way into their apartment?

I dismiss these notions and conclude that I'm just being way too impatient. Darragh will ring me when he's ready. I wish I was a fly on the wall up there. I'd love to see Vincent and Ryan's faces as Darragh explains to them what a tiger kidnapping is.

I check my watch again and sigh loudly. Only one minute has passed since I last looked at it. I decide to take a slow stroll around Sir John Rogerson's Quay to try to relax. I catch a glimpse of myself in a car windscreen as I cross the street. A beard suits me. I don't like the black wig so much but it's amazing how many years the beard has taken off me. I thought it would have made me look older. I might grow one for real, but I suppose that would defeat the purpose of why I'm wearing one today.

Checking out the Sir John Rogerson's Quay area over the past few months has made me dig deep into my memory bank. I was eight years of age when we moved out of this place. It looked a lot different then. My da used to work in a bakery on the corner of Lotts Road, near the dog track. His boss rented us the small flat above it. Every time I smell cinnamon, it brings me back to my tiny bedroom; just enough room for the bed itself and a tiny cabinet. This area has changed so much in the four decades since we lived here. It's a nice modern area of Dublin now, but back in my day it was quite rough. At least I was led to believe it was rough. I don't remember seeing anything bad happen around here. My ma did her very best to make sure we didn't become friends with the Luciano kids. Their father was supposedly involved in the Italian mafia. I'm pretty certain that was just a rumour. They were the only Italians in the neighbourhood, so they were just labelled 'mafia'. They may well have been the nicest family around, but nobody knows because nobody got to know them. My parents would come down hard on me if I wasn't improving at school. They both took a big interest in anything I did. When my da forced me to join the local underage GAA team, he made sure I didn't miss one training session. It wasn't that he thought I was going to be the next Kevin Heffernan or anything like that, he just wanted to make sure I wasn't mixing with the wrong kids. My folks spent hundreds of hours of my young life making sure I'd grow up to be a respected member of the community. I was always grateful for that. I wonder what they'd think of me now, if they were looking down from whatever heaven my ma pretended to believe in, as I orchestrate the greatest bank robbery in the history of this old country of ours.

During my stroll around the block of City Quay and Grand Canal Street, and making my way back towards the penthouse, I manage to calm down. Morning fresh air is a remedy for almost all head-fucks. Darragh's not a bright lad, but he's determined and loyal. He'll do exactly as I tell him. He's loyal to a bad cause. If he thinks it's criminal, he's in until the end. He's a weird little boy. I couldn't have a weirder little boy on this job. He'll see it all through for me, I'm certain of that. I've been anxious over the past month or so and didn't really sleep last night; I was rolling around in bed desperate to get back to my dreams. Ironically, today is the type of day I have dreamt about for years.

07:20

Darragh

I CAN SEE THE TERROR IN BOTH OF THEIR EYES. RYAN LOOKS the most frightened though. He doesn't know whether to stare at me in fear or at Vincent for help. Neither of them has any idea what I'm up to. It's hilarious. They nearly shat themselves a few minutes ago when I went searching in me bag for the first time. I was only lookin' for the tape. Fuckin idiots. Vincent keeps trying to speak up but I'm keeping control. Ryan is too stunned to open his mouth. Whatever he'd try to mumble wouldn't make sense anyway. He's all taped up now. But I need to talk with Vincent. That's why I've only taped his hands to the chair. I reach back into the bag and take out the second mobile phone.

'This is for you, big boy,' I say, shoving it into the breast pocket of his shirt. At least this gay fucker is dressed. The other fag only has his boxer shorts on. It's actually a bit sickening to look at. I take a moment, on purpose, to sound as cool as fuck as I fall back onto their couch.

'Here's what's gonna happen. Vincent, you're going to withdraw two million euros from each of the four branches of ACB you run and return to me here with all eight million by midday. If you don't, I'll kill your little fuck buddy here.'

I deliver my lines perfectly, just as I've rehearsed hundreds of times over the past few weeks. Vincent looks stunned. His jaw is practically on the floor.

'But … but … I, eh,' he stutters. I don't have time for this shit. Well, he doesn't have time for it. Time ain't on his side.

'Shut the fuck up, ya little cunt,' I demand, as I sit more upright on the couch. I need to get angry. 'I know for a fact that you are authorised to take two mill from each bank so don't even pretend you can't or I'll shoot you both dead right now.'

Perfectly delivered again. That stopped Vincent in his tracks.

'You need to get this all done within the time frame, d'ye hear me? You have until midday. Not one minute past. Any wrong moves and he'll get a bullet straight to the head. And then we'll come back for you. Do you understand me, fag? If this doesn't go according to plan you'll both be killed. Tick, tock!'

I'm delighted with how cool I'm handling all of this. This is the first time I've ever carried out a kidnapping. JR calls it a tiger kidnapping. I'd never heard of it before. It makes perfect sense. JR is a fuckin genius. That's the hardest part of my morning over. I have both of these fags in place now.

I've tried to play out how the morning would go in my head countless times but there's not much I can predict. I'll be sitting here keepin' an eye on Ryan until I'm told otherwise by JR. While the two fags are taking in everything I've told them, I take a look round their apartment. It's pretty cool, I have to say. They've got one helluva massive television screen. I guess that's what my eyes will be on all morning. JR has been drilling into me for months about not lettin' Ryan get into my head. But what can he do? He looks a lot more terrified than Vincent. I was told this would be the case. Vincent already seems like a bit of a smug cunt. I bet he's one of those fuckers who just thinks he knows it all. I hate that sort of prick. Ryan just looks like a little rent boy. That's all he is now anyway. A kept little fag. It's almost sad. What a shitty life that must be. They're both surprisingly silent as I pace round their couch. They don't know what to do. I go over everything in my head again, one final time. I'm pretty sure I've explained it all perfectly. Vincent knows full well what he has to do and he hasn't flipped out. I get the impression he feels he can do this. The excitement seems to be getting the better of the anxiousness in my stomach at last. It looks like me and JR are gonna be millionaires in just a few hours' time.

07:25

Vincent

I GET INTO CHARACTER STRAIGHT AWAY. THE CULCHIE IS STILL mumbling some big-man bullshit but I'm just thinking of the task in hand. I need to get around each of the four branches of ACB in the next five hours and take two million euros from each of the vaults. I have access to those vaults, of course, but I can't get in there alone. They can only be opened with a double key card system. I have one key, being manager of all four banks, while my assistant managers – who work at each of the branches – have the sister keys. I know for certain that three of them won't even question me, but I'm wary of Noah Voss, who is the new assistant manager of Church Street. He was appointed about three months ago against my wishes; the board felt his experience as head of a successful branch of Barclays in London made him the ideal man for the job. I still haven't figured him out. He asks a lot of odd questions. Plus, he's a Christian. I can't stand Christians. How can you trust somebody who believes in fairy tales?

I've totally calmed down since the prick smacked me across the face earlier.

'Any wrong moves and he'll get a bullet straight to the head,' I was told as our captor nodded towards Ryan about five minutes ago. 'And then we'll come back for you. Do you hear me? If this doesn't go according to plan you'll both be killed.'

I've figured in the past few minutes, after the shock receded, that I can handle the task at hand. I just need to get into character. I'm playing myself like it's any other day. That can't be hard. I just need to keep calm despite the surreal situation. If I stay cool, I can do this. There should be no need to worry.

'Is there a route you want me to take?' I ask our captor to his surprise. He was just pacing around our couch muttering to himself at the time.

'Well … what's the quickest way?' he asks me as an answer.

'Nassau Street, Camden Street, Church Street and then back to the IFSC branch,' I reply rapidly. I've been thinking about it.

'Alright,' he says, looking a bit flustered. 'That makes sense. Work your way around that way. I don't really care what way you work it once you come back with all the cash. But I don't want any mistakes, d'ye hear me?' he asks, his Cork accent coming through the angrier he gets.

'I'll be back with the money before midday,' I assure him. 'Just please don't hurt him. I promise I'll be back.'

'If you're not back at midday … boom!' he says, mock shooting Ryan.

I stare over at my boyfriend. His eyes aren't as wide as they were a few minutes ago. I think he's been calmed by the fact that I seem confident I can do this. A tear that I noticed running down his face earlier has dried into his skin. He hasn't been able to say anything, but what could he say that would interest our captor? This is all in my hands. I'm the one who has to carry out the robbery. I'm acting composed because I want to be in character. If I give anything away to any of my employees then this will all fall apart. I'm also selfishly thinking that there is no immediate threat to my life. I will be getting on with my day, free as a bird, as if it were a normal Tuesday morning. It's Ryan's life that is directly at stake this morning, not mine. That sounds harsh but it's an honest feeling. My stomach may be in knots, but I won't let that be known on the surface. Not to Ryan, not to our captor, and certainly not to anyone in ACB.

'What time is it?' I ask.

'It's almost half past. You leave for work in about fifteen minutes, right?'

Wow, this fella knows my routine off by heart. I nod a reply before eyeing my taped hands. He gets the gist. The kid walks over to me and bends down to undo the tape. He begins the process with the pistol still glued to his left hand. But after struggling for a few seconds he decides to leave it on the ground beside him. It's about a yard away from my left foot. Once my hands are free, I'm pretty certain I can make it to the gun before him. The possibility races through my mind as he releases my right wrist before turning his attention to my other arm. I stare up at Ryan. He knows what I'm thinking and shakes his head in a disapproving manner. He's right of course. Our captor still has an advantage over me. The gun is nearer to him even if I genuinely feel I could get there first. I have no intention of doing it, though. He unties my left wrist and reaches for the pistol straight away. The only muscles I move are in my hands to ease some of the numbness. Then I stand up.

'Calm down, big boy,' I am told. 'Where you off to?'

'To finish getting dressed for work. I assume that's why you untied me,' I reply smartly.

'Yeah, of course,' he says. 'But on my fuckin' terms, okay?'

I figure our captor isn't that bright. It disappoints me somewhat. How could the two of us have been turned over by this loser?

'I'll follow you. Where are your clothes?' he asks.

I point towards our bedroom. I already have my shirt and trousers on. I just need to knot my tie and throw my jacket, my shoes and my glasses on before I'm all set. I stare at myself in the bedroom mirror as I slide a dark blue tie under the collar of my shirt. I can see my captor behind me pointing the gun at me. He appears nervous. But he's also unpredictable. Trying to take him on wouldn't make any sense. He could unload the barrel of that pistol into me without hesitation. I finish the process of getting dressed and turn to him.

'How do I look?' I ask, surprising him again.

'Like eight million euros,' he replies, making a tiny laugh shoot out of my nose. Not a bad retort. Perhaps he isn't as stupid as he looks.

07:35

Ryan

I CAN'T BREATHE. MY NOSE CAN'T TAKE IN THE AMOUNT OF oxygen it needs right now. I have to get this tape off my mouth but nobody seems to be listening to my muffled screaming. I wonder what those two are up to in the bedroom. I'm not surprised how calm Vincent is acting while I'm all tied up. That's his character in a nutshell. Some little prick has broken into our home and is pointing a gun at us, yet Vincent is still going on like he's in control. I decide to stop focusing on my breathing and think this whole thing through. I stare at the digits on the microwave oven that I can see from where I'm sitting – 7.35. I do the maths in my head. Vincent has four and a half hours to go to his office, make some phone calls and then visit the four banks he plans to rob of two million euros each. My breathing becomes panicky again. My head shakes back and forth frantically. I need to calm down. I think of the yoga classes I used to attend years ago before I even met Vincent.

Breathe in slowly, visualise each breath coming in through the nostrils, filling the back of the throat and drifting slowly down the chest cavity before it enters the lungs. Feel the lungs expand. And then visualise the air going in the opposite direction as you breathe out.

It seems to be working. I miss yoga. I miss a lot of things from my years gone by, even if my past was mainly a huge struggle.

Every time my breaths get panicky, it brings me back to the afternoon I sat in my bedroom determined to tell my folks that I fancied men. It was about time I told them. I was nineteen years of age and I'd known I was gay for at least five years. I'd sat on the end of my bed with my head in my hands, breathing just as I had been seconds ago, too heavy and too panicky. My chest ached but that wasn't going to stop me. I stood up and walked down the thirteen stairs of our terraced red brick house before entering the sitting room. Me da was watching horse racing, annoying me ma with tuts and sighs as she tried to read some tabloid rag. Our sitting room was the same scene every Saturday afternoon.

'I'd like to talk to you two,' I said in a way that already spelt out drama.

'In the middle of the fuckin' racin'?' me da asked.

'Dessie!' me ma said sternly. It didn't matter. Me oul fella ruled the roost.

'Wait till this race is over!'

I sat beside me ma on our shabby couch and felt her stare inquisitively at me as she folded the newspaper to put away. She knew something wasn't right. I looked up at her, fully aware I was putting on 'pity me' eyes.

'Ah, fuck ya!' me oul fella shouted out, cursing that his horse didn't win. He jumped off his armchair in a rage and clicked the television off.

'What do you want, son?' he said, standing over me. He was peering down at me as if I'd already ruined his day. He had no idea what was coming next. I knew it wouldn't go well. Me da called gay people 'queers' when he saw them on

TV and he genuinely thought homosexuality was a disease. It was a generational thing, I suppose. Telling him his only son was gay was no easy feat. But he didn't say a thing when I finally got the words out. Me ma didn't either, but she leaned in to me and wrapped both of her arms around my shoulders. She was trying to hide it, but I could tell she was crying. She was worried about what the neighbours would think. I knew that would be her only concern. It's the only concern of any Dublin housewife. Me oul fella spun around and lashed at the TV standby button again, turning the horse racing back on. Then he sat down in his chair as if nothing happened over the past two minutes.

'Give me that newspaper, Anne, will ye? I wanna see who I've bet on in the next one.'

My sexuality was never mentioned again in that house. I only ever spoke to me ma about it when she came to see me in the bedsit I'd rented in Mount Brown. She didn't quite understand what being gay meant but to her credit she tried to learn about it. It turned out that coming out to my parents wasn't as painful as coming out to me mates. I thought people of my generation would be more understanding, but I noticed my so-called pals slowly but surely drift away from me as weeks and months went by. I'd visit gay bars in town to try to generate new friends but I found it very difficult. I was used and abused by some I'd hoped to become pally with, and genuinely contemplated suicide on two separate occasions. They were just thoughts back then, but I was so depressed. So down. I really didn't like my life at all. That was until the bank manager I had met a few times to discuss a loan suggested we meet for a bite to eat outside office hours.

I watch Vincent walk out of our bedroom in his favourite navy-blue suit. It would look like any other morning but for the gunman behind him. My boyfriend winks over at me to suggest everything will be okay. He can be a bit arrogant, but heroes normally are the arrogant type. I trust him implicitly. I am the weak character in our relationship. But I know more than anyone that Vincent isn't as clever as he thinks he is. I know he will feel confident he can get back here in four hours with all the money in tow. But I am sure it's a more difficult task than he will feel it is. He walks over to me, shadowed by our captor, and kisses me on the forehead.

'I'll be back, baby,' he assures me. 'Please just relax. I can get this done.'

I swing my head from side to side in the hope of getting the gunman to remove the tape from my mouth, but he doesn't even react. He just watches as Vincent holds my head still to kiss me again.

'I love you,' he says. I nod and blink some tears out as a response. I want to tell him I love him too.

'You guys are fuckin' sick,' says our captor, pulling Vincent away from me. 'Now, go get me my fuckin' money.'

07:45

Jack

When I hang up the phone, adrenaline rushes through my body. Darragh has done exactly as asked. Vincent should be coming down the elevator and out of the building any minute now. I was worried about the first part of the day because it was the only part I didn't have full control over. It was all on Darragh. But the boy's done well. Now it's all back in my hands. I haven't had a rush like this in years. And even back then I wasn't enjoying it as much as I seem to be right now.

Before I married Karyn I was inducted into the Dublin gang scene. I didn't like it, but I loved her. Karyn's whole family were involved in organised crime and if I was going to be part of the Ritchie family, I'd have to get involved too. I'll never forget her da wrapping his arm around my shoulders on the first tee at Deer Park golf course one freezing morning back in 1985. He was puffing on one those ridiculously oversized cigars he used to smoke for show. It felt like something you'd see in a mob movie. That's the thing with these guys, they try to live up to the stereotype

Hollywood invents for them. The movies aren't a retelling of organised crime, organised crime is a retelling of the movies. And the Irish newspapers do their best to glamorise it as much as they can too, just to jump on the bandwagon. I find it all quite cringeworthy, to be honest.

'Now listen here, kid,' he said, exhaling rancid cigar smoke. 'Ye gotta do what you gotta do. But if you wanna be part of this family then you gotta do a little of what I want you to do.'

It felt like I was an extra in a parody of a poor mob movie but I didn't dare suggest that. Instead, I nodded in agreement and acted like a puppy dog around Harry Ritchie. Everybody did. He was actually a very friendly guy and quite warm, but he was assertive and strict when I first met him. He was probably laying down a marker, but he had an amazing ability to get everybody on his side. I made it quite clear to him that his daughter was my main concern in life, but if there was anything he needed from me, I'd never let him down. He respected my honesty and for that reason, I was always on the periphery of affairs and not fully involved in the heavy-duty stuff. For the first couple of years, I was used as 'body' – that was it. I'd visit restaurants and bars, that my brothers-in-law or other members of the 'family' would break into, to demand protection money. I've always been a big guy. I was six foot three inches tall at just sixteen years of age, and I have always had broad shoulders. I was known as the Friendly Giant through the last couple of years of secondary school and often wondered what those kids would have thought if they'd seen me hanging around with The Ghost. I just stayed in the background as those braver than me would smash a bar manager's face in until he handed over every penny he had in the tills. I didn't get involved in the physical activities for the first eight months or so but after a while, some of the landlords decided to fight back and

I'd be called on to sort them or their friends out. I think I'd only ever thrown one punch in my life up until that point, which was aimed at my old best mate in a school corridor when we were both in fifth year. I enjoyed the thrill of the fights because I always knew we could handle them. But I'd go home at night and feel sorrow for what I'd been involved in. Karyn hated the fact that I'd got involved in her family's business. But she knew all too well that I had no choice. Besides, the money was good. I'd personally take home around a thousand pounds in one week, which was huge money back then. I once calculated that Harry's empire was collecting close to a hundred thousand a week. And that was only in protection money. He had loads of other activities on the go at any one time.

I hide behind a parked Rav 4 as I watch Vincent push open the glass door to exit his apartment building. He really likes that blue suit. I've seen it on him several times recently. His face appears paler than normal but I have no doubt that he will be able to carry out his orders. He has to. He is mainly based at an office at the IFSC, on Harbourmaster Place, which is a twenty-two-minute walk from here. He doesn't order his driver to take him to work. He likes to take in the fresh River Liffey air, for some reason. He'll walk straight over Sean O'Casey Bridge and continue past the two moats in the IFSC until he turns slightly left onto George's Dock. Once there, he'll be only a few hundred yards away from his office. He normally arrives between 8.05 a.m. and 8.15 a.m. By the looks of things, he'll be there at the earlier time this morning. His chauffeur-driven car will be waiting for him in the car park under his office. He'll certainly be using it today. The banks he'll rob won't open until nine o'clock, but he'll spend the guts of the first hour of his morning organising access to the vaults through four phone calls.

I'd already decided that I'd head towards Nassau Street

after I'd watched him cross the bridge towards his office. I know where I'll be standing when he walks out of that first branch with two million euros. I've been spending the money in my head for the past few months. We've already planned our perfect life together as millionaires.

08:00

Darragh

I DON'T HAVE MUCH TO DO UNTIL VINCENT RINGS ME TO confirm he's organised his visits to the banks. He'll be arriving at his office in the next ten minutes or so. It will probably be another half an hour or forty minutes before he gives me the go-ahead that everything is set up. From what JR has told me, none of this should be a problem. Vincent is the boss of ACB.

I pass some of the time by taking a stroll around the apartment. I want a place like this when I'm rich. The living area is somethin' else. It's one big, bright large space with a huge L-shaped leather couch taking up the middle of the floor. It faces what must be a fifty-inch TV screen. Just off that is a pretty cool kitchen. I think it's the biggest kitchen I have ever seen. A big floating table thingy separates the living room and the kitchen. The colours wouldn't be to my taste, it's all creams and whites throughout the whole space. I like blues and blacks. Dark colours. Probably because I have a dark mind. A faggoty perfume smell fills the place. This has the look and feel of a gay couple's apartment except for the sports magazines and newspapers that are thrown across both the floating table thingy and the couch. It's a clean home but it's untidy. Ryan mustn't be doing his job properly as a little fairy housemaid. According to JR, this little fag hasn't worked in a couple of years.

I stare over at him as I walk around his table thingy. He no longer looks petrified. He looks depressed. Maybe he doesn't trust that Vincent will get the job done. I imagine shovin' the gun into Ryan's face at midday and blowing his brains all over the massive window behind him. Part of me wants to kill him, but what we really want is Vincent to get round to all four banks in time to give me and JR a payday we could only ever dream of. If he does, Ryan will survive. JR is tailing Vincent all day; I'm certain the job will be completed without fuss.

I'm not all bad. I do have pangs of guilt every now and then, especially with regards to the first young fella I killed. He didn't deserve to die, but Bob did. He was a sick fuck – a rapist! JR came up with a plan for us to confront Bob with all the information we knew and demand money from him. Take it, then shoot him. Bob was adamant he hadn't raped anyone, but JR had it on good authority that it was true. He has great links with the Dublin mob and they have allowed him to take the lead on a new arm of their gang, of which I am the first newbie. It's a dream come true for me. Most young guys want to be professional footballers or rock stars, Hollywood icons, or some shit like that when they grow up. Me? I always wanted to be Henry Hill. *Goodfellas* has been my favourite movie since I was twelve years old. I must've watched it at least a hundred times by now.

My job was to have the sick rapist empty his safe of cash before blowin' his head off. Everything JR said to me came true. He knew the cunt would deny the allegations and he knew he'd have about fifty thousand euros in the safe. We split it down the middle.

'You have the wrong guy, you have the wrong guy,' he kept repeating. I didn't have the wrong guy. JR's research is always spot on. I shoved the gun into his mouth and asked him a question.

'Any last requests?' I said, not giving him time to answer before pulling the trigger. I figured that could be the line I mutter before I kill people in the future. I could become known for it. It could be my catchphrase. I looked at the hole in the top of his head and licked my lips. I unscrewed the silencer while standing over his body and placed both the silencer and the pistol in my bag before slinging it over my shoulder and making my way out of his tiny gaff. I could hear the soundtrack to *Goodfellas* playing in my head as I strolled away from the garden. I allowed myself a smile. Since then I've had feelings of guilt, but there are also times when adrenaline rushes through me, knowing full well that I am a real-life hitman.

As far back as I can remember I always wanted to be a gangster.

I often repeat that line over and over to myself in Ray Liotta's accent.

Good Morning Britain is still showing on the TV I muted earlier. I notice Susanna what's 'er name is wearing one of those low-cut tops she likes to tease us with every now and then. She's a dirty lookin' bitch. I bet she's savage in the sack. How sexy can one woman be? She is big where all women should be big: lips, tits, hips and ass. She's not great without make-up on, I saw that when she did that celebrity dancin' shite on the BBC a few years back, but there's something in those eyes that screams 'fuck me now'. The white dress she has on today is makin' me dick twitch. I reach for the TV remote and unmute the volume. I instantly hear her voice. That husky British accent was designed for men's ears. Well, most men. Not this fag tied up in the chair just ten feet away from me.

'How can she not turn you on?' I say, looking at Ryan. He doesn't even respond with a head nod. He just sits there feeling sorry for himself. I snigger through my nose when an idea crosses my mind. It's equally funny as it is sick. I unbutton my jeans and slide them down past my ass. I begin to rub on the outside of my boxers, making my dick stiffen.

'See how sexy I find her?' I say, pointing me dick at Ryan. Susanna continues to talk about some British education bullshit but I'm not hearing the words, I'm just hearing that husky voice. She's often awoken my morning glory. I giggle to meself as I walk over to Ryan with my hand wrapped round me whole package.

'See that, fag, bet you never had one that big, did ye?'

I'm not even sure whether me dick is big or not, to be honest. It's seven and a half inches long when hard. I measured it once with a ruler. I think that's a decent size. Google says the average size of a penis is just over five inches when on a boner so I must be fuckin well hung. But when I watch porn I end up a little bit confused. My dick is tiny compared to the guys that fuck on camera for a living. Maybe the camera adds length.

'Oh yeah, mutha fucker,' I say to Ryan while grabbing at my balls. I stare over at the TV screen. Susanna what's 'er name has turned into Piers Morgan. That's one sure-fire way to lose an erection. But for some reason I'm still turned on. I don't normally get this horny this quickly, but I think the strange environment for wanking has added to the excitement. I've never had somebody in the same room as me while I whack one off. Within a minute I spray a load of cum all over the screen, laughin' as I do it. When I'm done cumming I stare over my shoulder at Ryan. His chin is resting on his chest looking down, but I'm sure he had a peek up just to see if I finished the job all over his fifty-inch TV screen.

'That's what real men do, Harkness,' I say to him. He allows himself a look at me, perhaps in surprise that I know his surname. 'You're missin' out on pussy and tits, you little freak.'

I fall back on the couch and sigh deeply, just as I always do after a wank. The thrill of whackin' off is deadly but I always get a depressed feeling instantly afterwards. I don't know if all men get that. I pull my boxer shorts back up over my dick and button my jeans back up just in time for the phone to ring. I answer, expecting to hear Vincent's voice, but it's not him.

08:05

Ryan

I WISH I LISTENED TO VINCENT MORE OFTEN. I'VE NO IDEA what time he gets to work. But if he leaves at seven forty-five each morning I'm guessing it only takes him about twenty minutes to walk there. He should be arriving at his office about now. This morning is the first morning in ages I wish he hadn't left me. I've been a lot more nervous since he headed off.

I've refused to stare over at this spotty prick but he's just turned the volume back up on the TV and I can't help but give him a glance.

'How can she not turn you on?' he asks, pointing at Susanna Reid on *Good Morning Britain*. I answer by looking away again. But I can't help but draw my eyes back to him when I notice he's pulling his trousers down.

What the fuck is he doing?

He begins to rub at his dick right in front of me. This guy is fuckin' insane. My eyes widen as I see him take his dick out of his boxer shorts. I don't look but I know he's tugging away at it. He must be just trying to freak me out. If he is, it's working. But after a few seconds of being disgusted I will him on in my mind to complete the job.

Cum, you stupid prick. Go on, spray a load.

He strolls away from me towards the TV, giving it everything. This is weird for a million different reasons, but none more so than the fact that he's now jacking off to Piers Morgan's smug face. He's not relenting. I hear his spunk slap against our TV screen and I almost laugh to myself.

Way to leave your DNA at a crime scene, you fucking idiot!

I can't believe somebody would be that stupid. It begins to frustrate me that Vincent and I were held captive by somebody with such a low IQ. I think the whole thing through. This can't be for real, can it? I look at his face for the first time since this morning as he falls back into our couch sporting an ugly grin, and realise that he must be some form of retard. And that's when I get really frightened. This guy is so unhinged that he will have no problem blowing my brains out as he promised he would if Vincent doesn't arrive back here by midday. I immediately think of my yoga breathing techniques again as the panic attack resurfaces. My yoga instructor used to always start by saying 'breathe in through the nose'. Right now, I have no fuckin' choice.

Just as I'm calming my breaths, his phone rings. I assume straight away that it's Vincent, as he is supposed to give this guy the okay after he's contacted his assistant managers. But I can hear the screech of an unfamiliar voice on the other end of the phone and I know it's not my boyfriend.

'Good, good,' says the freak next to me. It gives nothing away. 'He's a little tied up at the minute,' he then says while looking over at me. He thinks that line's hilarious, which probably proves again how dumb he really is. 'Great stuff. He should ring me in about twenty minutes then, I guess, like?'

He already told us somebody would be keeping a close eye

on Vincent to make sure he's looking after everything from his end. This must be that guy on the other end of the line. His partner in crime. I wonder if they are as stupid as each other. I also begin to wonder how two stupid people could come up with such a plan, and immediately feel that this has to be an inside job. Somebody Vincent knows must be in on this.

'That was my man,' says the greasy prick to me after he hangs up the phone. 'Your pussy-ass boyfriend is in his office. All's going on time. Your life could be spared yet.'

I try to think of people Vincent works with and immediately get frustrated that I zone out every time he opens his mouth about work. I know there's a guy called Jonathan, who he mentions quite a lot and then there's Michelle, of course, who I know quite well. But neither of them would be the type to get involved in this sort of thing. Vincent also has a secretary called Belinda but as far as I'm aware she's as innocent as they come. It must be somebody I've never heard of. Some low-ranking official from one of the banks or the head office. There's no way they're going to get away with this. Certainly not with this dumb fuck leaving his baby-making juice all over our living room.

I notice him walking around the apartment, taking it all in. I'm willing him to leave more DNA around the place, but in truth he's probably already delivered enough.

'What the fuck do you do around here all day, Harkness, huh?' he shouts out to me. 'I mean it's a nice place, I wouldn't mind hanging out here myself all day, but you must get bored.'

That's the second time he's mentioned my surname. He knows everything about us. This is a well-planned job. I don't answer him. I can't answer him. Instead, I feel justified in knowing that this is an inside job. How does he know I sit around the apartment most days? This guy is leaving me clues every two minutes. He is so stupid that by the time Vincent comes back I may have this case solved.

'Lover boy keep you, does he? You don't have to work because he brings home enough bacon, huh?'

I continue to ignore him. He's right in his assessment though. I haven't had a job for twenty months now. Vincent and I were only dating for about two months when he asked me what my dream job would be.

'I'm a good writer,' I said. 'I enjoy writing. I always wanted to write books but I don't have the discipline. There's also no money to be made from writing unless you pen a masterpiece.'

'There are plenty of ways to make money from writing,' replied Vincent. 'What about creative writing in an advertising agency or something like that? Journalism?'

'I'd love to be a journalist. I just don't have the qualifications.'

With that, Vincent whipped out his laptop and started searching on Google.

'Here ye go,' he said, turning the laptop towards me. 'DCU do a specialised journalism course. Let's see if we can get you on it this September.'

'Nah, I … I …'

'You … what?' he said, looking at me with a raised eyebrow. I just shrugged as an answer before smiling back at him. Within eight weeks of knowing him, Vincent was already an inspiration to me in more ways than I ever thought possible. He leaned over to kiss my smile and I knew right there and then that I was in love with him.

My eyes refocus towards the clock on the microwave. I panic slightly. 8:15. The last quarter of an hour has flown by. I hope the minutes tick by slower throughout the morning. My heavy breaths begin to consume me again and the tape feels tighter around my mouth. I allowed myself to get carried away assuming we were dealing with Ireland's dumbest criminals, but maybe dumb criminals are the most dangerous kind to be dealing with. I can't keep my eyes off the blinking colon in the middle of the 8 and the 15. There is no noise, but I can hear it inside my head. *Tick, tock. Tick, tock.*

08:15

Vincent

I'M ALWAYS THE FIRST PERSON TO ARRIVE AT THE OFFICE. I sit here alone until about quarter to nine almost every weekday morning. I've often remarked how quiet and peaceful these few minutes are to my colleagues when they finally arrive in. But today I can hear the ticking of Belinda's clock just outside my office door as if it's ringing right next to my ear.

Tick, tock, tick, tock.

It is literally a timely reminder. I need to get a move on. I take a deep breath to refocus and get back into character before picking up the phone. I must remain cool. *This is an ordinary Tuesday. This is an ordinary Tuesday.*

'Hello, Vincent,' screeches Michelle as she answers after just one ring. I don't normally call her this early.

'Hey, Chelle,' I say in a friendly tone. We've been close for years. Well, she thinks we're really close but I just play along. I think she likes the fact that I'm gay. She likes telling her friends that she has a gay friend. Whatever floats her boat. I've never played the gay card at all, except when I'm listening to Beyoncé in my own home. I don't want to be any woman's gay best friend. The idea repulses me. I never have been, nor ever will be, the sort of person who will sit around sipping coffee whilst bitching about people who aren't in my company. Fuck that! That's for people who have nothing going on in their own lives. I've got plenty of things going on in my own little world that I don't have much time to dissect other people's. And even if I did have the time, I'd fill it in a more productive way. The one stereotype that annoys me most about gay men is the one that says we're all bitches. It's simply not true. I've known quite a number of gay people in my lifetime and have socialised in gay circles for years. I'd say a low percentage of gay men meet that stereotype. But Chelle thinks I'm a cute accessory to her life and I'm happy to go along with it once she toes my line professionally. She'd do anything for me.

'Nassau Street are low. Just a miscalculation on Jonathan's part coupled with a monumental number of big withdrawals last week. We'll need to shift some notes from your vault.'

'No problem,' she says breezily. 'How much do you need?'

'Two mill,' I reply, while holding my breath.

'Jesus, two million? Wow! That's more than you've ever asked me for before.'

'I was thinking that this morning after Jonathan rang me,' I say, backing it up with a confident giggle. 'But I'll have it back in your vault within forty-eight hours. It's just one of those strange coincidences. There was over one point five mill withdrawn from Nassau Street alone in the past five days,' I lie. 'That's three times the regular amount. They're just really low at the moment.'

'Okay, well I'm about fifteen minutes from the bank. When will your guys be coming to collect it?'

'I'll be transferring it myself,' I say. This is the tricky part. I shift massive amounts of notes between the branches on a regular basis but Securicor, our security firm, normally looks after the transfers for us. Especially the big ones. I've personally shifted some small amounts here or there but nothing coming close to two million euros. I grind my teeth during the silence between my saying that and Chelle's response.

'Really, two mill all by yourself?'

'Ah, he needs it as soon as possible. It's no problem. I have the cases here and will use my car. I'll get to you around nine, just as you open.'

'Okay,' she replies slowly.

I hang up and let out a small sigh of relief. Chelle will be the easiest to get around today. I know Jonathan and Ken will play ball too, even if better explanations are required, but I'm still worried about Noah. I rest my face on my forearm, leaning on the desk. I was thinking of how to approach things with Noah as I walked to work this morning and feel I should just be assertive as his boss. Rather than ask him for the transfer, just tell him it's happening. Who's he going to go complaining to anyway? I'm his only superior. He doesn't have the contacts for any of our bank's board members and, even if he did, they wouldn't have the time to get back to him in any urgent manner. It takes them at least forty-eight hours to return any of my calls and I'm in charge of all four of their Irish branches. I should be fine. I need to channel my acting skills and get in the zone. I can't give anything away. I'm a method actor anyway. Playing myself is a walk in the park.

Jonathan is next on my list of calls. As I pick up the receiver to call him I notice the time on the digital screen on my phone. The flashing colon in the middle of the 8 and the 21 makes me hear Belinda's wall clock again. *Tick, tock.*

Jonathan hasn't answered. I play around with the idea of leaving him a voicemail as his cheesy message plays, but I hang up just before the beep sounds. He'll get back to me when he's ready. Jonathan is always on the ball. I lean my head back on my swish leather chair waiting for Jonathan's call. I'm taking a moment to myself when I immediately sit back upright and reach for the phone. A quote I have lived by professionally for decades enters my head:

If you have to eat more than one frog, eat the big one first.

Get the toughest job done early.

I puff out my cheeks as I hear the ringing tone. He's one of those chumps who answers the phone by saying his full name. I can't stand those sorts of people. What is the fucking point of that?

'Noah Voss …'

08:25

Jack

THE SOLES OF THESE SHOES ARE GOING TO BE WORN OUT BY the end of the day. It's no big deal. I'll be able to afford a walk-in wardrobe for shoes alone soon enough. I'm annoying myself by pacing back and forward on the pathways of Westland Row. I've been lacking patience all my life. I surprised myself by holding off on this heist as long as I could, though. I needed everything to be perfect. And today is ideal. Even God would be telling me so, should the fucker exist. The sun is belting down on Dublin's city centre and I find myself in a jovial mood despite the fact that I am in the midst of the biggest bank robbery in the history of our country. I begin to whistle the tune of 'Under the Moon of Love' by Showaddywaddy and it takes me back to my youth. I must have been eighteen years old when that song was a big hit. It would have been just before I met Karyn. I was a really nice guy up until that point, even if I do think so myself.

I grew up in a tiny detached bungalow on Carpenter's Road after we left town when I was about eight. We used to say our address was Castleknock, but I'm not sure it really was. It was outside Castleknock, really. Anyway, our post always found us and our house price was slightly higher than it should have been. Our gaff was only a five-minute drive to Elm Green golf course. My old man was a member and we used to bond over eighteen holes every Sunday morning. We were huge golf fans. We'd watch as much golf as we could on the TV at the weekends, too, annoying my ma. I was always my dad's favourite for that reason. My old man used to cheer on all the Irish golfers, but I was struck by Gary Player. I just loved the man. He seemed like a movie star playing golf to me, such was his aura through the screen. I used to have posters of him on my wall. Sounds fucking pathetic now. A golfer? When I was in my early teens, Gary Player replaced Jesus Christ as my hero. Like everybody else in the whole of Ireland, I fell for the bullshit that is the Bible for the first fourteen years of my life. My parents were happy for me to toe the conventional line, but there was no way on earth my father ever bought into the nonsense. My ma died believing that crap, my da certainly didn't. My old man was such a great guy, looking back. He worked his ass off to provide for the three of us. Like almost everyone, I hadn't a clue how great my old man was until it was too late to tell him. He was probably more obsessed with golf than I was. It's such a shame – the Irish golfers were pretty shit through his entire lifetime and these days they can't stop fucking winning. If an afterlife exists, then I'm sure my old man would be looking up from hell delighted at the country's successes since the turn of the century. But, of course, there is no afterlife. There is no proof of an afterlife whatsoever, which is why you have to make your years on earth count. That's what I'm doing today. I'm going to make sure the rest of my life is as enjoyable as it possibly can be.

My da passed away after suffering a heart attack in his bedroom aged just fifty-eight. I'm seven short years off that age now. I somehow managed to get over his passing quite rapidly due to my fascination with Karyn Ritchie. My mind was on a new life, not my old one. I think it hurt my ma even more that I dealt with the tragedy quite well and for that reason alone I don't think she ever took to Karyn. I, on the other hand, was obsessed with her from the moment I saw her across the room at Trolli's Dance Hall. I could tell straight away that her eyes were green. I don't know how, she was about fifty yards away from me in a low-lit room, but she stood out in such an obvious way. It was almost as if it was meant to be. I don't believe in any of that bullshit but I'd be stumped to explain with words just how much I was drawn to her that night. I couldn't understand why every other man in the room wasn't staring at the brunette in the blue dress. I'd always been labelled a handsome guy but I found it difficult to find a girlfriend. People used to tell me I was just too shy. I think I was just too picky. It was unusual I'd really fancy a girl. My standards were high. But I distinctly remember the urge I had to speak to Karyn that night. I thought I was being pretty cool by throwing my cigarette in front of me, stamping on it and making my way over to the girl in the blue dress. It was like it all happened in slow motion.

'Fancy a dance?' I asked, feeling a little Clarke Gable-esque for the first time ever.

'No thanks,' she said, embarrassing me in front of all her friends. 'I have a boyfriend.'

I smiled for years afterwards thinking about that moment. I'd never known what fancying somebody felt like until that night in Trolli's. The only thing I could relate it to was my fascination with Gary Player.

I whistle 'Under the Moon of Love' again through my smile when I feel the phone buzz from the inside pocket of my jacket.

'How a ye, JR?' says Darragh in an upbeat tone. It always

amuses me how he pronounces the R with his West Cork accent – as if he's saying 'are'. 'Vincent rang me there. Everything is good to go. He said he has authorised to take the money from each of the banks. He'll be setting off in about twenty minutes or so to get to the first one for nine o'clock. He's going to Nassau Street first, okay?'

I can't really make out what he's saying due to the noise of the traffic so I ask him to repeat himself. Plus, my mind is wandering through the possibilities of the rest of the morning. The excitement builds in my stomach as I realise Darragh is telling me all is in order.

'Great work, Darragh,' I say, ending the call.

I look at my watch. 8:35. If I stroll from here to Nassau Street I should arrive just before Vincent and his chauffeur pull up in their BMW. I can't wait to see the look on Vincent's face as he walks out the front door of that bank with two million euros cuffed to his hands. A rush of adrenaline hits me. Instead of whistling, I sing quietly to myself.

'Let's go for a little walk ...'

08:30

Vincent

Jonathan Reilly has always been easy-going. I can't believe he questioned me so vigorously about the money transfer. I transfer money to and from his bank on a regular basis. Besides, it's not his bank. It's my fuckin' bank. Fair enough, I've never asked him for two million, but I'm a little annoyed that he went against the grain. He usually bows to my every demand. Noah Voss also surprised me. He did bow to my demand, without question. My phone call to him lasted about three minutes with him concluding he would have everything ready when I popped by at around ten thirty. Strange. Everything this fucker does is odd to me. He's a Christian, after all. I can't stand believers of faith. They're so bloody arrogant. Imagine having the arrogance to think you know the answer to life's greatest questions.

Where do we come from? What happens after death?

These fuckin' idiots walk around with a smug persona thinking they know it all. They know as much as anybody else. In fact, they know less than non-believers. Non-believers like to research and seek answers to these questions, believers don't. They are stuck with an answer – a wrong answer – and as a result are totally narrow-minded on the whole issue. Believers are the last kind of people you should listen to when it comes to life's biggest questions. Christianity bothers me more than any other religion probably because I'm surrounded by it in Ireland. I bet most of these guys have never even researched the book they believe to be the word of some creator. The Bible is actually a book filled with plagiarism. The story of Jesus Christ coming down to earth is a total rip off of the story of Horas that was written decades before. Horas, like Jesus, was born miraculously to a virgin, they were both the son of 'God', an angel came down from the skies to inform the mother of her pregnancy, their birth was heralded by a shining star, there is no telling what happened to both between the ages of twelve and thirty, they both had twelve disciples, both performed miracles. Oh yeah, and both were crucified to death before rising again three days later. And then there are stories of other gods such as Attis, Dionysus and Mithra who cover the same bloody plot lines that were written before the Bible. You couldn't make it up. Actually, you could. They did. How can anyone of sound mind believe the Bible is a unique book when the Bible is plagiarised from fictional tales? The truth is, Christians aren't of sound mind. They are liars. They lie to themselves. I don't trust them. I don't fuckin' trust Noah Voss. He's a snake. I didn't like him in his initial interview despite the fact that he had a perfect CV. He had an arrogance that made me instantly dislike him. He told the story of how he grew up in Nigeria before he and his twin sister took refuge in London when they were just thirteen years old, leaving the rest of the family behind. They had not one single penny to their name. He was determined to make a success of himself and managed to obtain education to degree level before becoming a bank clerk. The board members of ACB fell for his sob story. I didn't give a shit.

We've all been through our own difficulties. Appointing him as assistant manager of the Church Street branch wasn't my decision but I was outvoted. He hasn't caused me any hassle since he was appointed but I know trouble is on the horizon. I bet this prick is eyeing my job. The feedback I'm getting from our employees in Church Street is that Noah is quite a fair boss, but I'm sure they'll see through his 'pity me' bullshit in time.

I pick up the phone and dial two. That's the quick way to get hold of John. He is the most loyal man I know. We share the same sense of humour. He's been chauffeuring me for the past decade.

'You're gonna be busy this morning, John boy,' I inform him. 'I'll be visiting every branch. I'll head down to the car park around ten to nine-ish and we can head straight to Nassau Street. Is that okay?'

'No problem, boss,' he says to me. 'I'm just arriving at the offices now. I'll give you a call in about fifteen minutes and you can come down to the car.'

My heart rate quickens up. Fifteen minutes. Wow! In fifteen minutes' time I'll begin a robbery that will be all over the news tomorrow morning. According to the spotty little shit who broke into my penthouse this morning, I have a little over three hours to get back and save my boyfriend's life. I stare at my iPhone after taking it out of my pocket and think about leaving it here throughout the day. I can't be distracted. I suck on my teeth while I stew the thought over in my head before deciding to just turn the power off and bring it with me.

Then I take out the cheap-ass mobile the ugly prick gave to me this morning and ring him with the good news.

'All is in order,' I tell him.

'Good little fag,' he snarls back. That was it. He hung up.

'You look like you've seen a ghost, Vincent, are you okay?'

Belinda asks as she enters my office. I hope she didn't hear me on that last phone call. But then again, I didn't say much.

'Yeah, fine,' I say, smiling back at her.

'You're white.'

'It's the blue suit,' I reply. 'I shouldn't wear it. It flushes my colour out.'

'Will I make you a coffee?' she asks, fake laughing at my retort. 'It might redden those cheeks a bit.'

'A quick one, please. I've to head out in a few minutes.'

'Oh yeah, Jonathan said you were calling over to him in an hour so, you want to take two million from him to transfer?'

The sneaky prick. He got on to my secretary to make sure everything was legit? He shouldn't be discussing any bank business with Belinda without my saying so.

'Belinda,' I say, agitated as I stand up. 'I need you to stay off the phones today. My office is a mess and I'll be out all morning. Could you organise these files into alphabetical order for me and clean up my emails? It won't take long. Just up until lunchtime.'

'Sure thing,' she replies as she walks back out of my office to put the kettle on. I lift up a number of paper files from the shelves behind my desk and shuffle them around. I always have everything in perfect working order so messing these up causes my temples to sting slightly. But I need to keep Belinda away from Jonathan while I visit the banks this morning. When our apartment was broken into just over an hour ago and this robbery was forced on me, I had a number of reservations about how it would go down. But Jonathan Reilly fucking it up never crossed my mind.

08:35

Darragh

IT WAS ONLY A SHORT CONVERSATION BUT I COULD FEEL JR wasn't his usual self. He seemed quite nervy or somethin', almost as if he wasn't listening to me. Everything is goin' as planned. Vincent has got the green light from all four banks to take the cash so I'm not sure why JR would have been off. He kept askin' me to repeat meself. His nervousness is making me a bit tense now. I'd been doing okay up until that call. I'm sure he'll be alright. JR knows what he's doing. I pick up the TV remote control and start flickin' through the channels. There's fuck all on to watch. These pricks have the full deal – around two hundred channels in all. I didn't know fags were into sports, but they must have every sports package ye can get. I manage to click through each channel twice before blowing out me cheeks. I'm bored already. I've only been here about an hour and a half but it seems a lot longer than that.

Suddenly the apartment doesn't seem so big anymore. Ryan hasn't lifted his chin from his chest since he caught me whacking one off to Susannah what's 'er name about twenty minutes ago. I think about removing the tape from his mouth so I have somebody to talk to. At least it'll keep me entertained for the morning. But I know it's not the right thing to do. I'm desperate to not reach inside me jacket pocket. I promised meself I wouldn't, but I just don't think I can get through the morning without doing it. I obviously brought it with me for a reason. I knew in the back of my head that I'd want it. Ryan's eyes almost pop out of his head as I brush by him to make my way to the kitchen table thingy where I'd tossed me jacket earlier. Me fashion choices, if you can call them that, haven't changed since I was twelve years old. I was wearin' a very similar black leather bomber jacket the day I arrived in Dublin.

I miss Cork a little bit. Everyone keeps telling me West Cork is the prettiest place in the world, but I don't remember it that way. I grew up in a red-brick estate. Maybe me memories of the whole area are sketchy, but I remember the neighbours really well – Cork people genuinely are a more straightforward bunch. I had some great friends when I was younger. I would have even considered me da to be one of me best friends until I walked in on him beatin' me ma to a pulp one Friday afternoon. Despite protests from me ma I didn't hesitate in ringing the cops as soon as me old man left the house to go back to the pub. I learned over the next few weeks that beatin wasn't a one off. Me ma pressed charges under pressure from some family members and me old man was sentenced to fifteen months in prison. Within a matter of days of him going behind bars me ma had all our bags packed. We were off to Dublin. Me Uncle Mick had organised everything. He'd been living in Dublin since I was one, and looked after his little sister by arranging' work and a small flat for her and her three kids. It was just off the main Cabra Road. Me ma, me two sisters and meself were cooked up in a tiny two-bedroom flat over a newsagents on the Fassaugh Road. I liked the fact that we were livin' in Dublin for about two months before boredom set in. I had no friends. I hung out with me older cousin, Michael Junior, and his gang of fuckwits for the first few weeks but they soon lost interest in me. The novelty of me Cork accent only bought me so much time with them. They were fifteen and sixteen years old and were too cool to hang around with a kid like me. I didn't make friends in school. I was too new to join any gang. I know most kids say they don't like school, but I really fuckin hated it. I used to ditch it on regular occasions to sit at home watching movies while me ma was out working in a launderette in Glasnevin. *Goodfellas* is two and a half hours long but I learned every single bit of dialogue in that film within a couple of months of being in Dublin.

I've only really had one friend in my nine years in this city – Piotr Simienksi, who I met about four years in. I think we found comfort in each other having gone through similar stories. Me family and me arrived in a car from Cork to escape our past life, Piotr's family arrived on a plane from Poland to escape theirs. As luck would have it, me only mate in the world could barely speak a word of English. He had learned enough to get by, but his accent was so thick that we ended up communicating through actions most of the time. We had our own language, I suppose. When we were both seventeen we managed to get our hands on some really good fake IDs and after a day spent knocking door to door in the estates close to where we lived, offering to do odd jobs around people's homes, we would spend our evenings and the money we earned knocking back warm beer in The Hut on the Phibsborough Road. We used to laugh a lot but I didn't know what we were laughing at most of the time. Neither did Piotr. I think we were just both relieved to have a friend. I sometimes miss those days.

I reach inside me jacket pocket and pinch at the small

plastic bag. I fuckin love cocaine. Piotr gave me me first line of the stuff about five years ago and I can barely get through one day without getting high now. I thought I might have the patience to get through this morning without it as I need a clear head, but the boredom coupled with the nervousness is proving too much for the sober me. I grab one of the sports magazines scattered on the kitchen table thingy and bring it over to the couch with me. Ryan's head cocks up when he hears me choppin' at me coke. Choppin' coke is the only reason I have a library card. But just as I'm about to roll up me five-euro note to snort the line, Ryan starts making bizarre noises. He's fuckin shaking. It looks as if he's havin' a fit.

08:40

Ryan

I ONLY MOVE MY EYES TO CATCH THE TIME. 8:40. I'M NOT SURE if the morning is going really slow or really fast. I seem to look at the clock every two minutes to subtract the difference between what it says and midday. Three hours, twenty minutes is the current calculation. I puff out my cheeks quietly and rest my chin further into my chest. I'm not the only one in the room puffing out their cheeks. This little prick's been agitated ever since he made that phone call a few minutes ago. I wish he'd stop flicking through the channels. It's so bloody torturous hearing one-second snippets of TV shows. He's just skimmed by the start of an old Champions League match that I'd love to watch again. It would help pass the time. He leaves the TV on a music channel that's blaring out one of the most ridiculous songs I've ever heard by a female artist I've never seen before. Then he abruptly stands up. I feel a waft of dread shoot through my body as he brushes by me. He paces over to the kitchen where I hear him fumble around in his jacket. What are the chances he's packing it in and going home? Zero. He just got a phone call from Vincent ten minutes ago saying everything is on track before ringing his partner in crime to inform him of the good news. I wonder what Vincent is up to now and how much he's worrying about me. I get distracted when my captor sits on the couch and begins pouring what I can only describe as the lumpiest looking line of cocaine I've ever seen onto one of my sports magazines. There can't be much money in kidnapping thefts. That is nasty, cheap-looking coke. I should know. In PR you need three things with you at all times; a notepad, a phone and bag of coke. Every PR representative and journalist I know snorts a line or two to get them through the day. PR reps have the biggest egos. They're all like Patrick Bateman from that movie *American Psycho*. They think they're much more important than they actually are. It's cringeworthy.

I tried to get into most newspapers when I graduated from DCU but it was difficult to find employment in that specific area. I wanted to work on a sports desk, but so did the other thousand journalism graduates from that year and every other year before that. I did the odd shift at the *Evening Herald*, but I could never nail down a position. That's when I decided to turn my attentions to PR. I harassed the MD of Wow PR in Harcourt Street until he eventually invited me in to talk to him. I began as an intern but soon found myself climbing the ladder somewhat into an account management position. Wow PR specialised in sport so I felt I'd reached my goal in some way. It was great hanging out with people such as Brian O'Driscoll and Robbie Keane for press calls in the early days, but that soon lost its charm. I was earning little or no money at the beginning but Vincent didn't seem to mind. He moved me into the apartment he was renting in Ringsend while the new penthouse he had just bought from the plans was being built. PR – as I began to find out after a few months in the industry – is full of arse lickers. I can't be that kind of person, my sexual activity aside. The industry is full of pretty little people who will fuck anything that moves – sports stars, sports journalists, other PR staff. It's a horny industry. That wasn't necessarily the part about it that bothered me. I just couldn't stand the fact that PR is full of self-centred pricks. You are either hanging out with PR reps who are too full of their own importance, or worse, journalists. Journalists are a law unto themselves. I swear most of them think they're celebrities in their own right. I found it all a little bit mortifying to be honest. Though I have to say, the one good thing about working in media is the fact that the social life can be pretty epic. I didn't get along with most of my colleagues but that didn't stop me snorting line after line of coke with them in almost every nightclub Dublin's city centre has to offer.

As I watch my captor roll up a used five-euro note to do a line of his own, an idea crosses my mind. I call out to him as loud as I can, mumbling through the duct tape. I manage to lift the chair up and stamp it to the ground. I catch his attention in seconds and flick my head as if calling him over.

'What the fuck's wrong with you, fag boy?' he asks, lifting my magazine from his lap to head towards me.

I eyeball him and mumble further in the hope that he'll remove the tape. It works. He yanks at it, taking most of the facial hair from my cheeks with it. The loop of duct tape loosens and falls around my neck. It allows me to breathe properly for the first time in over ninety minutes. I pant heavily before speaking.

'That's cheap-ass bullshit coke you got there, man. Go into the bedroom and bring out the silver box from the bedside drawer. The one on the far side of the bed. I've got some proper powder for ya.'

08:40

Vincent

I'm rarely stern with Belinda but, as she places a mug of coffee on my desk, I give her a look that I hope suggests I'm deadly serious.

'Be, I really need these files in alpha order by lunchtime today. It's imperative. I just haven't been keeping them in file order these past couple of weeks and I need to use them for reference later today.'

'Sure, that's no problem,' she replies as expected. Belinda has always been a very professional secretary. I've managed her really well. I've nailed that fine line between fear and fawning. It's called respect. She has a ton of respect for me.

'Don't worry about the phone. Let everything go to voicemail and we'll go through any outstanding work between us when I get back, okay?'

I'm concerned that she's aware I'm taking a huge sum from Jonathan's branch. If she gets one more phone call about the withdrawals from any of the other assistant managers she would have every right to be suspicious. It's important she stays away from the phones. I do worry that Jonathan can reach her through her personal mobile phone.

He's a happily married man, but he's had a huge crush on Belinda for years. She's way out of his league, of course, but she seems to enjoy the fact that he drools over her. I hope their flirtatious relationship doesn't fuck all of this up. Their immature dalliance could be responsible for Ryan having his brains blown out before midday. I emphasise to Belinda what I expect from her over the next few hours before I head out of my office door, leaving the mug of coffee she poured for me cooling on my desk. She knows what I've asked her to do is unusual, but she's in no way suspicious that anything extraordinary is going on. I take a moment to refocus when I'm in the lift. I have to act normal when I see John. He probably knows me better than anybody at ACB. But acting comes easy to me. I thought I was coming out to my parents when I told them I wanted to be an actor, having achieved mediocre Leaving Cert results from Saint Brigid's National School, but they didn't quite understand my ambition.

'Acting? That's not a career,' me da would tell me over and over again. 'Ninety-nine per cent of actors are unemployed right now.'

I knew he was right, but I felt I was so talented that I would ease into the one per cent without much bother at all. Neither of my parents had one iota of a clue that I was gay. Nobody really did. I am as straight a gay guy as you could meet. I always have been. I loved acting as soon as I took my first drama class in school. During the final year of school, I used to stay back two days a week with Mr Hanrahan to perfect my acting techniques. He had praised me for my lead performances in some of the school plays. I even landed a professional role in a production of *Who's Afraid of Virginia Woolf?* in the Pavilion Theatre within months of leaving school. Mr Hanrahan had arranged an audition for me and I nailed it. I had decided I was a method actor and took my role as Nick so seriously that I lived as the character for the full eight weeks of the play's run. This annoyed my folks somewhat as they now had a stranger living with them, but I didn't shrug Nick for one whole minute of those two months. The local newspaper's review was admittedly average but everyone I knew was largely complimentary of my performance – except me da of course.

'You were decent, but can't you get a good steady job like your old man?' he said to me. 'I can get you a job in our bank.'

I had zero interest in working in banking for the rest of my life. I was a method actor. The planks of Broadway and the hills of Hollywood were waiting for me.

Today is the first day I've acted in decades. If I can nail Nick from *Who's Afraid of Virginia Woolf?* then playing Vincent Butler on a normal Tuesday morning shouldn't be a problem at all. I have to rid myself of the tension I'm feeling and forget about any outside influences. I have to take two million euros from each of our four banks, acting as if it's a normal procedure, and then I have to return to my apartment before midday. It can't be that difficult.

I am not nervous. I am not under pressure.

I repeat that into the mirrored wall of the lift over and over again as it takes me down to the underground car park. I let out one big sigh before the sliding doors open and I make my way towards a smiling John.

'Mornin', Vincent,' he says, tipping the peak of his cap at me. His Dublin accent as thick as ever.

'All good, John boy?' I ask, as composed as I am every other morning.

'Yes, sir.'

'Can you pop the boot for me? I've a few withdrawals to make today and I need to make sure I've enough cases.'

I do. I look inside the boot of the car and see eight cases. There are always eight cases. That's exactly how many I need. They each pack up to a million euros. Hopefully they'll all be full in the next few hours. I don't have to worry about John. He has absolutely no idea how the banking system works. It's unusual that I'd drive around all four banks to withdraw money in one morning, but John will barely notice. He's just always happy to be out and about rather than sitting around a small office sipping coffee while waiting on me to decide to go somewhere. He's been driving me around for over a decade and has actually been employed by ACB longer than I have. There used to be fourteen bank branches in Dublin before the crisis hit in 2008. I was manager of the Drumcondra branch before it closed and was given John as a chauffeur when I first took the job in 2004. When we restructured in early 2010 the board decided to cut some of the large wage bill by closing down the ten branches that were scattered around the Dublin suburbs, leaving just the four that operated in the city centre. They were the only ones making money. They let go all thirteen of the bank managers, leaving me to run all the four remaining branches. They would hire assistant managers on lower wages to assist in the everyday running of the banks, but I would be the man mainly responsible for the entire Irish operation. The restructure saved ACB almost three million a year in wages and expenses and the Irish branch of the company just about managed to survive. You would think that being the manager of four branches rather than just one would have meant a huge pay rise for me. Not so. I was told I'd be taking a salary cut. I didn't mind, initially. I was just so proud to be the only manager kept on. I felt valued. I hadn't felt as proud of myself since I won the audition to play Nick all those years ago.

'So, where we off te?' asks John as he opens the back door for me.

'Church Street first, John, please,' I reply before I realise I'm making a mistake. 'No, Camden, no, Nassau Street. Yeah, Nassau first, John, thanks.'

'Y'alrigh', Vincent?' he asks, staring at me through the open door. 'You don't seem yerself today.'

I nod my head in response before breathing heavily. In the time it takes him to walk around to his side of the car I feel panic setting in. Maybe I'm not as good an actor as I always assumed I was. I look at my watch and grind my teeth. It is genuinely the first time I've lost my composure since leaving the apartment. The digital clock on the car dashboard just blinked to 8:50. Time to start robbing some banks.

08:50

Jack

WATCHING TEENAGERS HANGING AROUND THE BOTTOM OF Grafton Street makes me wonder what other people are up to today. It's the mid-term holidays. Most kids are enjoying their break from school. Most adults are probably cooped up in some office or factory in a job they hate. For almost every one of the million people in this city, today is just another Tuesday morning. Dublin has no idea that the subtlest bank robbery in the history of this city is under way. Bank robberies used to be a big deal in Dublin. If one occurred, it would make national headlines. But that's hardly the case anymore. They estimate that thirty-five bank robberies happen in Ireland every year. It's not a huge number, but it's significant enough to not have news editors drop their jaw each time one happens. This will be a different story altogether though. Nothing like this has ever happened in this country. It'll go down in folklore. Mostly because the guys that did it got away with it.

A brunette pushing a pram past the side wall of Trinity College reminds me of Karyn. They share the same shaggy, curly mop of brown hair. I twist my neck to take a peek at the baby and notice she must be only a few months old. I think it's a girl. She has a bright yellow bib on. That's all I can go on. Karyn never pushed a baby that young.

A week after my failed attempt at asking her for a dance at Trolli's Dance Hall, my father informed me on my return home from work that some girl had phoned looking for me. He squinted as he tried to make out his own handwriting.

'Karyn Ritchie,' he said, as butterflies swarmed around my stomach. He handed me the small note and I immediately ran to the home phone under the stairs. I didn't hesitate in dialling the number.

'You asked me for a dance last week,' she said smartly after I had told her who was calling. I rang so quickly that I didn't give myself the opportunity to get nervous.

'Yes, I did,' I responded, unsure what she would say next.

'Well, I don't really like to dance, but I do like Italian food. In fact, I really like the Italian food in Pirlo's restaurant on Dame Street. And I would particularly like their food this Friday night at seven o'clock.'

I was stumped. I wasn't sure if the confidence in this girl made me fall in love with her or feel intimidated by her. Either way, I was fascinated.

'Don't you have a boyfriend, Karyn?' I asked sheepishly.

'I might do by Saturday,' she responded, before hanging up.

How bloody cool is she? I couldn't compete with this shit, could I? It turns out I could compete with it. I had a few days to play it cool and managed to gain a pinch of confidence before I met her for our first date. We bounced off each other as if we were an experienced comedy double act. We literally fell into each other's arms laughing. It was as if the script for our first date had been written by Billy Crystal for some Oscar-winning romantic comedy.

Karyn lived about a half an hour from my parents' house

and I needed to take two buses to see her. I didn't mind. When I wasn't working in the print factory I would be hanging out with Karyn. We were each other's best friend immediately. The relationship wasn't very physical. She was a strict Catholic girl but it genuinely didn't bother me that we weren't having sex. The relationship wasn't about that, it was about finding somebody who mirrored me and who I knew I could spend the rest of my life with. We shared the exact same sense of humour and brought the best out in each other. A successful relationship isn't about finding someone you can't live without, it's about finding somebody you can live with. I was working extra shifts at the factory just to save enough money for us to afford a flat together, but in order for that to happen, we would need to speak to her father first.

'That's no problem, he can't be that strict, can he?' I distinctly remember asking her after we'd been going out for three months. 'I mean, we're both nearly twenty, we're adults.'

'You know I told you his name is Harold, right?' she said, arching an eyebrow. 'And you know my second name is Ritchie?'

I nodded, hanging my bottom lip out in confusion.

'Harry Ritchie!' she emphasised.

'Holy shit!' I responded before dropping my mouth open in shock. 'You're Harry Ritchie's daughter? Well, that's it, we need to break up. Break up now!'

We both laughed. This was the kind of stuff that made us giggle, but behind the wide grin on my face lay a deep fear. I only knew about Harry Ritchie through stories lads would tell down the pub. It wasn't really a secret in Dublin that the gangland boss – who the tabloid newspapers nicknamed The Ghost – was Harry Ritchie from Crumlin. It was just sorta known by everyone. The papers couldn't name Harry for legal reasons. So they nicknamed him, just like they nicknamed anyone else involved in gangland crime. The cops couldn't get near him. He kept his hands too clean. I never bothered to read about gangland crime in Dublin. The subject never really interested me. But now it would have to. If I were to get my one true wish in life, which was to get this young woman to accept my ring on her finger, I would literally be marrying into the mob. That would be some transition for somebody who used to be an altar boy in St Peter's Church.

I'm not sure if it's nerves or excitement that hits me when I stroll onto Nassau Street. Rather than walk by the ACB building, I stop at the wall of College Park where I can glance over at the entrance to the bank without looking suspicious. I perch myself against the brick wall and play with my phone. I could easily be waiting on one of the many buses that pull in here on a minute-by-minute basis. There are no CCTV cameras pointing in this direction. I'd planned to sit here when the Nassau robbery was going on. In fact, I know where I'll be for each of the four thefts today. I've sat here on quite a few occasions over the past months, imagining Vincent walking out of the bank with two full cases. I'll be watching that image for real in the next half hour or so. The bank's still not open, but I notice that there are two parking spots available directly outside and I expect John will be pulling up to park in one of them very soon. I look at my watch. 8:58. There's three hours left. It should take Vincent at least half an hour in each bank to go through the procedure required to withdraw money from the vaults. Taking driving time between branches into consideration, we really have given him a tight deadline. But we did that for a reason. The longer this process goes on, the more likely it is that somebody will notice something odd is going on. Plus, I want the deadline to be tight. I need it to be tight. Vincent isn't supposed to complete the task we've set him. I'm mentally trying to play the full morning out in my mind once again when I notice a black BMW indicate right and pull into one of the empty spaces in front of the bank. I know John to see. He climbs out of the far side of the car before walking around to open the door for his boss. I watched Vincent walk out of his apartment earlier this morning looking quite composed; I wonder if he still feels the same way. But the fact he doesn't instantly get out of the car worries me. He seems to be in conversation with John. I hope nothing funny is going on. When I finally see Vincent emerge from the car he doesn't look right. He's really pale. He seems faint. As he and John walk towards the back of the car to retrieve the cases Vincent collapses to the ground on all fours.

What the hell is going on?

08:50

Darragh

I HOLD A FINGER TOWARDS ME NOSTRILS AS I WALK INTO their bedroom just in case I can smell the gay sex. It's a big bedroom but I know the waft of bum fuckin must be floatin' round here somewhere. I step over some old clothes at the edge of the bed to get to the far side of the room where Ryan told me his coke was. I don't get angry with him when I can't find it in his big-ass bedside cabinet. I know it's probably just me. Any time I have to look for something in a drawer or a cabinet I somehow manage to see everything in there bar the one thing I'm lookin' for.

'A silver tin,' I whisper to meself over and over again as I root through old newspapers and gadgets. This fucker must collect watches for a living. There must be at least a dozen old watches in this cabinet alone. Me mind gets distracted by a black Hublot that has the coolest lookin' face. Everything on it is a different shade of black: the face, the hands, the numbers, the date scroll. I throw it round me wrist. It suits me.

'What the fuck are you talkin' about, boy?' I scream out of

the bedroom towards Ryan. Me accent goes all Cork when I'm cursin'.

'The silver tin,' he shouts back.

I slam the cabinet door shut, get up off my knees and storm out to the fag. I reach for the gun resting on the table in front of him and point it straight into his face.

'If you're fuckin playing me for a fool I'll end your life right now,' I snarl at him. He's practically shitting himself. 'There's no fuckin silver tin in there,' I snap.

'It's there, it's there,' he stutters back.

I've no doubt he's telling the truth. I probably wouldn't have noticed a beach ball in that cabinet if it was the one thing I was looking for. I don't know what my problem is. I guess me mind just likes playing tricks on me. I crouch down and yank at the tape strapping Ryan's legs to the chair and, after a struggle, I free both of his ankles. I then pull at the tape round his wrists and set him free. He doesn't budge an inch when I release all the tape. I have the gun resting in the waistband of my jeans behind my back. I reach for it as soon as I'm done with the tape and point it at him again.

'I'm stayin' right behind you, fag,' I say. 'Go get it for me.'

I was in his position once. Piotr and I went a step further with our addiction to coke about three years back. We managed to do a deal with our drug dealer who introduced us to his boss. He talked us into taking five kilos of coke that we were expected to sell over the course of a month on the streets of North Dublin. We were given our own little patch to work on. I was super excited about the deal because I worked out that we could take in around two and a half grand profit each week. Piotr and I drove out to an old warehouse on the way to Enfield to pick up our package. It was explained to us how we should chop it up into sellable sizes that would bring in around €120,000 in total. We'd just have to return in four weeks' time with a hundred thousand euros to The Boss, pocketing the extra twenty thousand for us to split between ourselves. Easy dough.

'We're trusting you to deliver,' we were told. 'Any false moves and you'll both be dead before you even realise we're in the same room as you.'

Dublin gangsters are kinda funny but they're also scary as fuck. They all seem to wear tracksuits that are too big for them. Big, grey, baggy pants with a massive bunch of keys in the pockets. I've never worked out why Dublin people carry around massive bunches of keys. Despite looking a bit like clowns, gangsters are genuinely intimidating. But me and Piotr were really happy to get involved with them. We drove away from the warehouse with a trunk full of coke and talked for ages about what we were gonna do with the money. It was when we were driving through Lucan on our way home that Piotr pulled over and reached for the glove compartment. I genuinely thought he was joking when he grabbed a gun and pointed it at me. I think I laughed out loud.

'Get out,' he said in his thick Polish accent.

The smile dropped from my face when I realised he was serious. He followed me out of the car and walked behind me with the gun held against my spine for about three hundred yards into a small forest. I heard the gun click in his hand.

Is my best friend about to kill me?

'I'm sorry, Darragh,' he said before spinning on his heels and sprintin' back to the car. Lanky prick. I never saw him again. I don't think anybody did.

I hold the gun to the back of Ryan's head as he leans his left arm on the bed to crouch towards his cabinet. He pulls out a tiny casing that looks more green than silver to me. It's decorated with some sort of Scottish tartan. I remember brushing past it as I repeated the words 'silver tin' to meself just a few minutes ago.

'Here,' he says, taking the lid from it.

I take a look inside and see a massive bag of fluffy powder that forces a wide grin across me face.

'Good lad,' I reply before nodding at him to walk out of the room. I keep the gun at his back but I can't keep me eyes off the coke. It looks like snow. This guy certainly buys straight from the mixer. The fag is mumbling something, along the lines of, 'Please don't hurt me', as I force him to sit back down on the kitchen chair again, but I'm not listening. A thought crosses my paranoid mind that this powder may be something other than coke and that this little prick is tryna poison me. Had he somehow planned that somebody would kidnap him so he thought of hiding a bag of poison in his bedroom to pass off as coke to his captor? Course not, but I'm gonna play it safe.

After re-taping both of his legs, but just one of his arms, to the kitchen chair I pour out a small hill of coke onto the magazine before givin' it a little chop of me library card. I don't need to chop this stuff up much. This is as fluffy as it could possibly get. I reach for my old five-euro note and offer it to Ryan.

'You first,' I say, eyeballing him. It's the first time I've seen a glint in his eyes all morning.

08:55

Vincent

I PULL AT THE COLLAR OF MY SHIRT TO ALLOW SOME OF THE cold air circulating in the car to creep inside. I am sweating everywhere: my armpits, my neck, my chest, my back, my forehead. I never sweat like this. I have the air conditioning turned up so high in the back of the car that it sounds as if a small aircraft is flying by my ears.

'You sure you're okay, Vincent?' John shouts back again, eyeballing me in the rear-view mirror. I don't answer him this time. I pretend I can't hear him. Instead I concentrate on my breathing but I'm sure I'm doing it all wrong. I'm breathing way too quickly. I wish I'd accepted Ryan's constant requests for us to go to yoga classes together over the years. I try to calm myself by thinking in the same selfish manner I have been thinking in this morning.

My life is not immediately under threat.

But it's not working. The calm, composed figure I managed to portray back at the penthouse in front of Ryan's kidnapper is proving elusive. I catch a glimpse of myself in the reflection of the car's tinted windows. I can make out a glistening across my forehead. I remove my glasses and wipe my whole face with the sleeve of my expensive suit. Just as I'm dampening down the sweat on the back of my neck with the other sleeve our car pulls right and comes to a halt. Holy shit. We're outside the Nassau Street branch already. That was quick. I stare up at the windowed building and try to force myself to calm down.

This is my bank. I am in complete control. Relax!

I am trying to slow my breathing down when the car door opens.

'Here you are, Mr Butler,' says John.

Since I've known him, I've suggested that he should call me Vincent at all times, but when we are on official duty in the office or at any of the branches he insists on being formal. I find it funny because he doesn't pronounce the 't' in Butler.

'I'll be one moment, John, I just … I seem to …' I stutter.

'Mr Butler, will I take ya home? You clearly aren't well.'

'I'll be okay in a second, John.'

I take three deep breaths before swinging my legs out of the car and rising to a standing position. I assumed I'd be fine once I got outside of the car, but the brightness of the morning sun seems to affect me instantly. My head feels a little dizzy. I try to shrug it off by following John to the boot, though I keep a hand on the car just to ensure my balance. But just as he's about to hand me the two cases I've requested the dizziness proves too much to bear. I feel myself falling to my knees in slow motion. The path I'm staring at seems to be changing colour and a humming sound pierces my ears. I can hear John calling out to me but it sounds as if he's way off in the distance.

'Mr Butler, Mr Butler,' he repeats.

'I'm alright, John,' I finally say when the humming seems to suddenly stop. After a few seconds I manage to sit up on the kerb, staring at John's kneecaps.

'I can call an ambulance, or I can drive ya straight to the hospital?' he says in a worried tone.

'John, trust me,' I say, raising my head to look him in the eye. 'I am genuinely okay. I jogged to work this morning and it was too hot for that kind of exercise. It's my own fault. I'm just a little dehydrated,' I lie.

John disappears, and within a few seconds reappears with a bottle of water. I laugh at him.

'You're always on hand, John boy,' I say before taking a swig from the bottle. The water's warm but I don't mind. I'm much warier of Chelle coming out and catching me sitting on the kerb. She's more likely to cause a fuss over my dizziness than John is. I twist my neck to look behind me and notice that the branch is now open. I stare at the ACB logo etched on the glass doors and feel relieved that nobody has come out to greet me yet. Sometimes Chelle can be out front waiting on me with open arms if she's privy to my arrival. I guess I gave her very short notice this morning. She's probably ordering her staff to have every area of the bank spotless, telling them Mr Butler is on the way. I need to get to my feet before she comes out. John offers me his right forearm and helps lift me up just in time. As I stand and face the bank I make out Chelle's figure caught between the first glass door entrance and the second. She has to wait for the initial door to close before the next one opens. I don't think she saw me sitting on the ground. As she's staring out at me, John is tapping at my ass as if he's a dog desperate to get my attention.

'What the fuck are you doing?' I ask, half laughing.

'Your pants are filthy, Mr Butler,' he retorts. We both giggle. It puts me at ease.

'Vincent, good morning,' bellows Chelle as she paces towards me in her high heels. We kiss on both cheeks as if we're better than everyone else. The fact that she loves me so much kind of annoys me. So much of it is pretentious.

'I'll wait here, Mr Butler,' says John, handing me both the cases and a wink. I tap him on the shoulder and wink back. He's so loyal that he won't give anyone any hints that two minutes ago I almost had a full-on panic attack. As Chelle and I walk towards the entrance of the bank, I'm aware a slight grin is etching itself onto my face, knowing that John will be staring at my assistant manager's ass. He's mentioned his fascination with her figure to me before. Michelle Dewey is forty-four years old and, while you would guess she is around that age, there's no denying that she looks superb for it. She's given birth to two kids and her body has bloated somewhat as a result. But it has bloated in all the right areas. Her hips and ass look like they belong to another body compared to her waist. Her chest is over-voluptuous too. John's often remarked to me, in the privacy of the car, that he thinks she's the hottest woman he's ever known in all his sixty-five years. I have to give it to him. If you are into hourglass figures than they don't come much better than Chelle's. If I was being bitchy I would say that her face isn't a match for her body, but I'm no bitch.

I've known Chelle for seven years. I hired her as a bank clerk for our Drumcondra branch and she impressed me so much that she was promoted four times in her first five years of service. When the board of directors at ACB brought me in to discuss the restructure I had no hesitation in nominating Chelle as one of the assistant managers. Her appointment has been justified since. Our Nassau Street branch is operating like clockwork in comparison to the other three. I know it's in safe hands. Even though we've always had a professional partnership, Chelle has never been shy in trying to double it up as a personal relationship too. Even in the early days she would insist that I'd keep at least one lunchtime free per week just for her. She would obsess about work over a Panini and would pick my brains for any hints or tips on how to improve her role. She's an impressive, hard-working woman. I had to hit the brakes on our social outings though. I felt it was going beyond a line. I did it subtly. I remember sitting on a kitchen chair in her Terenure terraced home with Ryan, celebrating her twin boys' fourth birthday one Saturday afternoon, thinking *what the fuck am I doing here?* I hate kids. Ryan had been asking a similar question on the way over. Enough was enough. Chelle and I still do the odd lunch but that's as far as our social activities go these days. I just make excuses that I'm too busy or want to spend more time with Ryan any time she asks me to do something involving her family or circle of friends. I do like Chelle a lot, and I have a ton of respect for her – she's been through the mill, her daughter went missing what must be fifteen or sixteen years ago now, so she'll always have my sympathy - but I felt our relationship was turning into a gay-guy, straight-gal cliché. We're both better than that.

'Now, you want two million euros?' she asks, squinting, as we stand inside the first door waiting on the second one to buzz us through. 'Is Jonathan alright?'

It's typical Chelle. She'd love it if Jonathan's branch was failing. It would make her look even better.

'He's fine,' I say. 'He just had a substantial amount of withdrawals last week. Holiday season, I guess.'

The bank floor is empty but for the nine staff who all stand in their rightful positions smiling over at me as if I'm going to take note of their smiles and reflect my impression in their next pay review.

'I really must do this quickly,' I whisper over to Chelle, letting her know I have no time to stand around small talking to her staff.

'Of course,' she responds before shouting over at her

personal assistant. 'Janice, do you have that paperwork for me?'

Janice looks petrified.

'Sorry, Mrs Dewey, but the printer is out of ink.'

I almost laugh at the ridiculousness of it all. There is zero chance of me withdrawing any money from this branch without all the necessary paperwork being filled out. If I even remotely hint at that, Chelle would call in either the cops or some mental doctor – and rightly so, too.

'It should be just another five or ten minutes,' Janice says, fidgeting.

'Fuckin' typical,' I mutter softly as I walk away from Chelle and Janice towards the assistant manager's office at the back corner of the bank floor. I shake my head and smile at the thought of Ryan being killed due to a lack of ink in the office printer.

'I'll just wait in here,' I shout back out to the floor in an impatient tone before I slam my arm on the desk and my forehead onto my arm. I sigh deeply and begin to think things through.

What the fuck am I doing?

Earlier on I was somewhat intrigued by what I was being forced to act out. I walked to the office this morning thinking about how I could secure the money and strategising about getting back to the penthouse before midday. But ever since I set out in the car to begin the robberies I have felt nauseous. The more involved in this I'm getting, the less confident I feel. Maybe I am all show and no action. I take out the cheap mobile phone from my jacket pocket and stare at it. I'm trying to think what I can do before I start these robberies when it suddenly buzzes in my hand.

'Now you fuckin' listen to me, cunt hole …' roars the mongrel accent.

I OPEN UP THE TIN AND TIP IT SLIGHTLY SO IT SHOWS HIM what's inside. He beams like a little kid being offered his favourite sweets.

'Good lad,' he says to me in such a patronising tone that it makes me wince.

He's let his guard down somewhat. The gun he's gripping in his left hand isn't his main concern right now. I think about trying to knock it out of his grip by punching at his hand, but I genuinely have never thrown a punch in my life. I could be dead in one second if I attempt to take this prick on. He takes the tin from me and nods towards the living quarters of the penthouse. Pointing the gun in my back, he leads me towards the same kitchen chair I'd been sitting on for the past couple of hours. He shoves me back down into it and turns around to reach into his bag. After removing the duct tape again, he wraps my ankles to the chair legs. He follows that up by taping my left wrist to the arm of the chair but for some reason he leaves my right hand free. The stupidity of this guy is really wrangling with me. I can't quite get my head around somebody trusting a guy this dumb to take charge of an eight-million-euro theft. I watch the smug fucker pouring my cocaine onto one of my magazines before he rolls up his dirty note.

'You first,' he says, handing me the bill. I stare at him, confused. 'Go ahead, fag.'

He holds the magazine with two thick lines of coke under my face and I lift the five-euro note to my nostril before snorting the smaller of the two lines. As I'm doing this I allow myself a look at the microwave clock. 8:59. This is early, even for me. I don't normally take my first line until after midday. I've become a bit of a bum, but I'm a disciplined bum. The rush of cocaine is instant. I love it. You can feel it burn the back of your nose within a split second before the rush makes its way to the brain. After I snort a line of coke I like to dab my finger into the remains of the powder and rub it around my tongue and gums. The instant numbing of the mouth is a great sensation. I don't get to do that this time though. My captor grins into my face as he pulls the magazine away from me and sits down on the couch. He is about to re-roll the five-euro note when his phone rings. I can feel my heart rate rise significantly but that could be down to the coke as much as the phone call. I wonder if it's Vincent calling. I hope he's okay.

Vincent doesn't like me doing coke. It's a bit unfair considering he used to enjoy a line himself. I'm eleven years younger than my boyfriend, but when he was my age he liked to use the drug on regular nights out. He thinks that's all I use it for now – the odd session. He has no idea I snort a couple of lines every day just to get me through the realities of life. The last time Vincent used coke was at our penthouse warming. We moved in four months later than scheduled due to some unexpected mishaps with the building work, but it was so worth it. The penthouse looked just as good in reality as it did in our imaginations. Vincent had worked so hard and deserved an amazing place to live in. I was really chuffed for him and immensely proud. When we first moved to the city centre I was still studying journalism at DCU. I promised that I would pay my way some day, but Vincent seemed content with being the main provider in our relationship. Even when I was earning decent money he made sure I spent it how I pleased. After all, he was earning six times the wages I was. I couldn't believe the size of the penthouse when I first walked into it completed. I had taken walks through the building while it was being renovated but I didn't have a good enough vision to realise how it would be once the kitchen was installed and all the rooms were painted and decorated.

Vincent got so high the night we opened the penthouse up to our friends. He hid in the bathroom to do line after line of coke so his work colleagues wouldn't know. But they must have noticed something was different. He was not only strangely full of energy but he was wiping and snorting his nose at any given opportunity. I remember giggling to myself as he spoke to Michelle and her husband Jake at the kitchen table while constantly fidgeting with his right nostril. If Michelle or Jake knew anything about the use of cocaine it would have been plainly obvious that Vincent was on it. I chuckled constantly thinking about it the next day but Vincent wasn't in the mood for laughing. His cocktail of coke, whisky and wine had his head throbbing. I had to leave a bucket beside the bed for him to puke into as he moaned and groaned his way through the day.

'I'm never fuckin' doin' coke again,' he screamed on several occasions in quick succession while pinching at his temples.

'Try giving up the whisky and the wine,' I roared back at him. 'It's not the coke that has your head splitting.'

He kept to his word. He's never taken any drugs since that

night. He wouldn't even take a drag of a joint these days. The fun seems to have snuck out of his being. I've often thought it's just his age. Vincent is a middle-aged man now. He's only six months off half a century. Yuck!

'Relax. Sorry,' my captor says, startled, into his phone. 'I was in the bedroom … I was … I was just walking around the apartment. I left the phone on the couch. Everything is alright here. Chill out.'

I can't make out what his accomplice is saying on the other end of the line but I know there's panic in his voice due to the raised volume. He's treating this greasy little fuck like a kid. I guess he is a kid.

'But what … he what? What are you saying?' my captor mumbles. He seems really confused. 'What do you mean, he collapsed?' he asks after another moment of silence.

My breathing starts to get panicky again. I'm not entirely sure if I'm initially worried about Vincent or myself. If Vincent has had some sort of panic attack and can't get on with the job, am I going to be shot right now?

'So he's in the bank now – everything must be okay?'

The person on the other end of the line seems to have calmed down. So too has my heart.

'Okay, okay. I'll ring him and make sure he's not up to any funny business. I'll give you a shout back in a minute or two.'

I've no idea what Vincent is playing at, and I'm concerned. He doesn't have a history of fainting. But then again, he doesn't have a history of robbing his own banks of eight million euros, either.

My captor and I eyeball each other when he hangs up. He seems worried. As he lifts the phone to his ear again he holds my stare. That's my fucking black Hublot he has on his wrist!

'Now you fuckin' listen to me, cunt hole,' he snaps down the phone.

JOHN SEEMS TO BE SLAPPING VINCENT ON THE ASS FOR SOME reason. He must be just shaking off the concrete dust. At least I hope that's all that's going on. That's some service.

I watch through a gap between two parked buses as Michelle greets Vincent. He finally looks to have steadied himself. But I'm still a little shook up about him collapsing onto all fours. I remove the phone from my jacket pocket and speed-dial Darragh. My teeth grind as the tone rings out. My panic begins to grow. What the hell could have gone wrong at the apartment? Three minutes ago, everything was going perfectly; now it all seems to be falling apart. I have one collapsed man who is supposed to be taking the money and one accomplice in charge of the kidnapping who can't answer his bloody phone. Huffing, I spin on my heels to take my frustration out on the grey brick wall I had been leaning against. It's kicked repeatedly before I try to compose myself. I need to stay calm. I can't draw any notice to myself. I'm staring at my phone willing it to ring back when, in my peripheral vision, I notice Vincent entering the bank with Michelle. I'm worried about him cracking up once he's in there. Maybe he isn't as strong as we both think he is. I'm desperate to find out what's going on. I speed-dial Darragh once again. This time the spotty prick answers within three dials.

'Where the hell have you been?' I scream down the line. He mutters some response about walking around the bedrooms. The little shit has one job to do – keep a gun on Ryan until midday. How hard can that be? Suddenly he's telling *me* to calm down.

'Listen,' I say sternly. 'Vincent bloody collapsed when he arrived at the bank.' I can tell Darragh's in shock. 'He fell to the ground. He got up, though, and is in the bank now. But I need you to call him straight away and make sure he's not breaking down in there and ruining this for us. Tell him you're going to kill his little boyfriend if there's any more messing.'

I wait for Darragh to hang up but he's still breathing down the line.

'Bloody ring him!' I shout so loud that a pedestrian walking by glances at me.

I'm not too bothered. My disguise really is so good that I can't imagine anybody would recognise me. There is no way any witness could conjure up any sort of photofit that would look even remotely like me. The sun is out in all its spring glory, which allows me to wear my sunglasses without any suspicion whatsoever. Most people on the streets are wearing sunglasses today. Coupled with my wig and false beard, my whole face is covered up.

I only ever had a real beard for about six months in my early twenties. It was about two years into my marriage to Karyn. She claimed she liked the look of it but didn't like kissing me with it. That was fine by me. Our relationship never really took off in a physical sense. I was dreading having the conversation with her but managed to sit her down before we got married to explain I was impotent. Some days we would try to fool around and I would climax but it was a very low percentage of the time. I still pleased Karyn on occasion and we would be intimate in some small way almost every night. We often fell asleep in each other's arms. But I was ashamed and stressed out that my dick didn't work. She was very understanding. It didn't become an issue at all until we wanted to have kids. We read a lot of self-help books and visited doctors about my condition. But after four years of frustratingly failing to conceive, we had to admit defeat. Karyn had looked into adoption for almost eighteen months before I accepted the idea. I didn't know anybody who had been adopted and thought it would be an admission to all our family and friends that my dick didn't work. But Karyn had talked me around and even introduced me to a few people who were either adopted or had adopted. I realised there was no stigma attached to this type of thing in the nineties.

Karyn's family connections helped us to skip some of the dragging protocol when we applied for adoption. That's almost unbelievable. A life of crime got us to the top of the queue to be responsible for a baby. I felt it was totally immoral but not to the extent that I said it to anyone. We'd only have to wait around six months to get our child, not the usual two to three years it took everybody else. We got a phone call one Monday afternoon on the tenth of September in 1993 to tell us we could pick up our son. He had been born four months earlier and was in Sacred Heart in Cork. His mother had been a heavy drug user but we were assured everything was fine with Frank. We named him after Karyn's grandfather. It wasn't forced on me. I'm a huge Sinatra fan and calling my kid after the Chairman of the Board was A-okay with me. Karyn and I were like two hyper kids on the three-hour drive to Blackrock. But we instantly grew up as soon as we met him. My life changed in that instant. I'd never known love like it before.

My mind continues to race, thinking of what Vincent could be doing inside that bank. Even if he has composed himself and is doing as asked he will be at least a half an hour in there. I know the protocol and exactly what's required for him to take the money out of the vaults. I decide to take a little walk and head towards Merrion Square. There's a casual little walkway down there that could help calm my mind while I wait on Darragh to get back to me. If Vincent doesn't pick up, we'll have a big decision to make. The heat forces me to take my jacket off for the walk. I make sure to remove the phone from the inside pocket and cling on to it in my left hand while my right hand holds the neck of the coat over my shoulder. My strategy for something going wrong at Vincent's end is to exit as soon as possible. I'd walk east away from all the banks towards the 3Arena before hailing a taxi back west towards Drimnagh where I'm supposed to meet with Dinah later. I would ask the taxi driver to leave me past my destination at the Luas Stop on the Naas Road, meaning I'd have a twenty-minute walk back on myself. I have it all worked out, but this is not a strategy I want to use today. I have to trust that Vincent is okay, but part of me thinks he may have confessed everything inside that bank. I'm starting to feel a little sorry for myself when the phone eventually buzzes in my hand.

'NOW YOU FUCKIN LISTEN TO ME, CUNT HOLE,' I SHOUT DOWN the phone before he even has the time to say hello. 'If you keep messin' I'll blow your baby's head off.'

I walk over to Ryan and hold the barrel of the gun against his forehead.

'Scream for your sugar daddy,' I order.

'Vincent, Vincent, are you okay?' Ryan screeches down the line.

I have the gun pointed at his brain yet he's more worried about his boyfriend. I'm obviously not gonna kill him, not yet anyway. I'm aware that the safety is still on.

'Vincent, Vincent … he's gonna shoot me. He's gonna shoot me,' he cries. That's what I wanted. I take the phone back up to my ear and grin.

'Did you hear that, lover boy?' I say. 'Any more messin' and bang! Now what the fuck went wrong?'

'I-I just felt a little overcome by the whole situation but I'm fine. I just needed to lie down and get some air before I got on with the show. I'm meeting with the assistant bank manager now. Everything is going as you want it to go. I'll be filling out the paperwork to take the first two million out in the next few minutes.'

'Good girl yerself. Call me as soon as you're done,' I say before hanging up. 'Relax, boy,' I tell Ryan, who seems to be putting on the crocodile tears just to please me. 'Here, have this line as well,' I follow up with, and hold the magazine under his chin while handing him the five-euro note. He doesn't hesitate. 'We'll have some fun while your fagotty boyfriend robs us some money, huh?'

As Ryan is getting his nose dirty I speed-dial JR. He'll be delighted I'm returning his call so quickly.

'It's all good,' I say to him. 'He's in the bank now and is meeting with the branch manager. He's fine. He just said he needed to take a little time out. He's gonna ring me as soon as he's done, like. He's just about to sign the papers to get the cash. There's no funny business goin' on.'

'Great stuff, Darragh. That's a relief,' replies JR. I can hear in his voice that he seems much calmer. 'Thanks, buddy. You're doing a super job.'

I'm always chuffed to receive praise from JR. I look up to him so much. My relationship with him is vastly different to the relationship I had with me first boss; it didn't take long for his gang to catch up with me. It was literally within ten minutes. They had been tailing Piotr's car and watched on as he walked me into the forest before spinning on his heels. I was shoved into their car and taken back to The Boss. I sat, just as Ryan is now, with me hands tied to a chair in the old warehouse I'd left just an hour before when The Boss walked towards me.

'You two have to be the dumbest mutha fuckers I've ever come across,' he barked. 'Within an hour you fuck yourselves right up. Did you think we wouldn't be following you and keeping tabs on our merchandise?'

'Please, sir,' I said, tryna sound polite. 'I had no idea Piotr was going to rob me. To rob you. My intentions were always to make you money. To make me money. I want this. I don't know what happened. I'm as surprised as you are.'

I received an open-handed slap across the face from The Boss before he put me at ease.

'I believe you,' he said. 'But you still deserve a slap. We watched it all go down. What the fuck were you doing teaming up with a guy so fuckin stupid that he would try to rob me?'

'I don't know,' I replied, shaking me head. 'We've been friends for years. I ... I ...' I stumbled. I'm sure The Boss could tell I was being genuine. I should have been filled with fear having one of the most notorious drug lords standing over me, but I was mostly feelin' heartbroken. I was devastated that me only friend tried to rob me and left me for dead in the hands of these gangsters. I couldn't get Piotr out of me mind.

'We caught up with your friend,' The Boss told me. 'The deal is still alive. He's not. We thought the two of you had concocted some sort of plan but he told us right before we dealt with him that you had no part in this whatsoever.'

This caused me jaw to drop towards me chest. Did they kill Piotr? After a moment of silence, I looked up through my wet eyes at The Boss.

'Good,' I said. 'Fuck him!'

'We're gonna spare your life. But your life is ours now, do ya understand?'

I stare over at Ryan. I can tell he is as high as a kite. His eyes are starting to redden and he's constantly wrinkling his nose. I want to join in. I reach for the plastic bag of coke that I'd put back into the tin and pour a thick line onto the magazine for meself. It looks so good.

'That's some good shit,' I say, smiling over at Ryan after I snort as much of it up one nostril as I can. 'You and I could become good friends.'

09:10

Vincent

I'VE BEEN SITTING UPRIGHT IN CHELLE'S OFFICE CHAIR WAITING on her to come in with the paperwork for the past six minutes. I know it's exactly six minutes because I haven't stopped looking at my watch. I need to get this job done. I'm not committing a crime here. I am acting under duress to save my partner's life. Ryan sounded petrified when he called down the phone to me. But I need to put his cries out of my mind. I'm just going to do as his captor says. No messing about. I need I get back into character.

'I'm so sorry about this, Vincent,' Chelle says from the doorway of her office.

I wonder how long she's been standing there.

'I'm so embarrassed. Janice has had to run out to get some ink. She shouldn't be long.'

'What?' I reply a little too dramatically, slapping the palm of my right hand against her oak desk. It stings. Chelle looks stunned. I feel I need to justify my reaction.

'I told you Jonathan needs this money as soon as possible. He's very low, Chelle.'

'How about I give him a quick call myself to apologise and tell him we'll get it over as soon as we can?'

'No. Jesus, no. Listen, I'll look after everything Jonathan's end. You just get me the paperwork as soon as you can. Where has Janice gone to?'

'There's a place that sells ink on Frederick Street. She'll be back in ten minutes. I'm mortified we've run out of ink. I don't recall this ever happening before.'

I look at my watch. Janice probably won't be back until around nine twenty-five. This is a terrible start to the morning.

'Chelle,' I say, rubbing my forehead. 'Just get me a coffee will you, please?'

I stare around her office and notice her qualifications framed on the walls. She actually has more certificates than I have. I fuckin' hated studying. I auditioned for at least forty roles after landing the part of Nick in *Who's Afraid of Virginia Woolf?* but didn't land one of them. After that play, I spent eighteen months unemployed and living off my parents. My da was getting tetchy. I was the only one of my friends that wasn't moving on to pastures new as we were turning twenty-one. Bennett, one of my closest friends through secondary school, moved to London to take up an internship with a tech company called Black Castle. My very best friend, Keith, had been studying in Galway since we left school and still had another two years of his marketing masters to go. They were literally going places while my life seemed to be stagnating. I just had to get out of my parents' house but the only light at the end of that tunnel seemed to come from accepting my father's invitation to work at his bank. I hated the type of work I was doing from day one, but I somehow got talked into studying accountancy at night to ensure I could be on the big bucks in the future.

It amazes me that not enough people follow their dream. We only have eighty years on this planet, on average, yet most of us spend forty hours of our weeks working on something we fuckin' despise. How does that make sense? Why would we do that? Yet I'm one of those dumb schmucks who spends half the time I'm awake doing something I don't like doing. As soon as I received my degree in accountancy in 1992 I left TSB. I didn't want to be working with me da. He understood and saw to it that I got a great reference, which helped me get through my interview for a banking official's position with ACB. I've never liked banking but I have to admit that it suits my natural skill sets. I'm very straight up and immensely efficient. My brain is also dialled up to deal with numbers. I've learned over the years that I don't have a great creative brain. That disappoints me so much. All through my teens I figured I was one of the creative types. I guess I was wrong. I was only twenty-eight years old when I was appointed assistant manager of ACB's Drumcondra branch, having worked at the company for less than five years. I was the youngest person ever to reach that position. The board of directors thought highly of me and the feeling was mutual. Unfortunately, the old guys have either retired or passed away since then, leaving their spoilt little snotty offspring in charge of decisions they just don't care enough about. They are so clueless that it stuns me on a regular basis. ACB is back running a healthy business in Ireland. I know for sure it's because of me. I think the board assume it's because of them. Fuckin' idiots.

Chelle is full of apologies again as she returns with my coffee. I don't budge off her big-ass leather chair, leaving her to sit in the more uncomfortable visitor's seat. I huff a bit of puff to remind her how frustrated I am, but we soon get talking about our lives. Chelle has always been fascinated with Ryan. She can't wait to read his novel.

'It's coming along well,' I lie to her.

I sometimes wonder if Chelle only asks me about Ryan so that I return the politeness by asking about her perfect little family. I don't this morning. Instead, I allow an awkward silence to fill the room after I'm done lying about Ryan's book. She's clearly aware that I'm upset with her. This must be killing her inside.

09:10

Darragh

THIS COKE IS SO FUCKIN GOOD. I ROLL UP THE NOTE AGAIN TO take another small line and promise meself as I'm doing it that I shouldn't get too carried away. I'm only supposed to be taking this to relieve the boredom and to help me relax. This isn't about partying it up. I shake me head with delight as the coke hits me brain again.

'Where do you get this stuff from, fag?' I ask Ryan.

'I know a guy,' he answers. 'I can sort you out. I can keep you in this type of pure coke every day for the rest of your life if you just let me go.'

I stare at his face and fake laugh as loud as I can.

'Dude, in about three hours' time I'm gonna have millions to me name. Why the fuck do you think I would give that up for a little splash of your coke every now and then, like? Where I'm goin' and what I'm gonna be able to do will give me the best of every world. Don't have any fears that I won't be enjoyin' life after I leave here today, boy.'

'What's your plan?' he asks.

He must think I'm stupid. 'Now why the fuck would I tell you that, fag boy?'

The truth is I don't actually have a plan. JR and I have been obsessing about this robbery for months but I never really got to the point where I figured out what I want to do when it's all over. I just want to stay a gangster. I want to be a hitman for JR. The money is insignificant to me. Once I have enough cash for a few beers and a few lines of coke every evening, that's enough for me. I get me real kicks out of carrying out thefts or killing people. I'm not sure why I haven't thought it through, but the coke is helping to open me mind further. I start to wonder about JR and what he'll do after we steal this eight mill. I hope he's not planning on retiring. As far as I'm concerned, we're just getting' started. I know JR has never pulled off a heist that brought in this amount of money before, but I never thought to ask him what he plans on doing with the cash once he has his hands on it. JR's been a gangster most of his life. I'm sure that's not gonna end today. Once a gangster, always a gangster. Me old boss must've had millions to his name but that didn't stop him continuing in his job.

I was just a common street drug dealer for him but I always figured it was my first rung on the ladder to gangland fame. I was lucky they believed Piotr's story about me and that my life was spared. I was grateful that Piotr stuck up for me but me mourning for him didn't last too long. According to The Boss, I owed him big time so I was forced to sell his merch on the streets of north inner-Dublin for little or no profit comin' in my direction. I'd have to prove meself trustworthy before the initial deal offered to me and Piotr would be put back on the table. But once it was, I would be pocketing the full twenty grand profit every month for meself. Sounded good to me. I had to work up a load of contacts in the area to sell to, but despite a slow start I began to talk to the proper lads in the area. They were intimidating at first but once they understood I was selling for The Boss it earned me an awful lot of respect. It also kept rival drug dealers away from me. They didn't want to start a patch war with my gang. It made me feel like I was finally worth somethin'.

In each of the first three months, I returned to The Boss having sold around eighty per cent of the drugs. He'd rant and rave, saying it wasn't enough, but I'm pretty sure he was impressed that I could shift this much in an area I didn't really know that well. I was delighted to be a drug dealer but passing small bags of coke to guys outside bars and through car windows wasn't really pushing me buttons after a while. I was involved with a feared gang, and I wanted to get my hands really dirty. While my eyes were on bigger prizes I was determined not to get complacent. I'd learned through me new mates that the cops could smell complacency from miles away. Durin' one shitty evening I was cornered by two guys waving their Garda badges at me. I had sold a lot of my merch already that day but I was still left with a few small bags in the boot of the car. I felt confident they wouldn't find it when they searched but the younger of the two cops lifted my spare wheel with one hand and checked inside the tyre.

'Looks like you're fucked!' he said to me and grinned. 'Get inside the car, now.'

The two of them spoke to me for about an hour, insisting they wouldn't arrest me if I gave up some bigger fish. They wanted me to rat out me mates in order for me to be set free. Fuck that. I'd learned from *Goodfellas* that you never rat on your friends. As it turned out, I was talking to two of them. I'd no idea. They were friends of The Boss and had set me up just to check out whether I could be trusted or not. I passed with flyin' colours. It was some relief. I was shittin' it sitting inside that car but I never wavered. Not for one second did I think about dobbin' the boys in.

'Can you twist my chair around so that it's facing the TV straight on?' Ryan asks.

It makes me laugh. Probably because I'm super high. Ryan laughs along with me. This genuinely is some super-hot coke. We both sit in the plush apartment laughing loudly before we realise the ridiculousness of it all.

'Why not?' I say, having calmed down. I lift my ass up off the couch and twist at the legs of his kitchen chair so that he can see the TV clearly. 'Here ya go, boy,' I say, handing him the TV remote control. 'Throw on what you want.'

'You like football?' he asks me.

'Ah, I used to,' I reply. I did. I used to watch a tiny bit of football back in Cork, but I haven't seen a game in years.

He flashes a TV guide menu onto the screen before scrolling down to some sports channel. When he turns it on I notice the words 'Man U' in the score line up on the top left-hand corner.

'That's Man United, right?' I ask him. Ironically that was the team I used to support as a kid. Me old man was mad into them.

'Yep, they're playing Bayern Munich. This is the Champions League semi-final.'

'I know of Man United but that's about as far as my football knowledge goes, fag,' I say.

'Well watch this, you might as well. We have the time. Let me tell you how the game works.'

I look at him, confused, but I'm also aware that a wide smile is starting to spread across my face. It's the coke. Picking up me phone from the arm of the couch I press at a button just so the face lights up and I can make out the time. 9:16. Fuck it, I'll watch the game. What else is there to do?

09:10

Jack

I watch a young girl leave the bank and head in the direction of Grafton Street. I don't find it suspicious in any way but I decide to keep an eye on her from across the street. I feel so relieved since I hung up the phone. I was seriously thinking of implementing my exit strategy and cursing my luck, but Darragh has assured me everything is okay. Vincent should be filling out the paperwork about now. The excitement has returned to my bones. I'm confident once again that we will be millionaires in just three hours' time. I stay about a hundred feet behind the young girl but she's walking at a brisk pace and it's not easy to stay on her tail, given the fact that parked buses are obscuring my view of her. Having followed her along the wall of the college, I notice her turn onto Frederick Street. I figure she's just doing an errand for the bank and decide I no longer need to follow her. I make my way back to the grey brick wall I had been kicking in frustration just ten minutes ago. I'll wait there until Vincent leaves. I had thought about going for a stroll around Merrion Square earlier but I turned around when Darragh rang me. I don't want to miss the look on Vincent's face when he walks out with those two cases.

Becoming a father changed me dramatically. I would stay awake at night just to watch Frank breathing in his cot. I was overcome with emotion. Karyn spoke to her father on my behalf, asking him to only use me for jobs when it was necessary. He agreed, but I was still required to carry out the odd protection run with my brothers-in-law at least once a week. Harry's sons were called Leo and Craig. They were both okay to me, but they could be nasty fuckers to other people. My splitting from the group wasn't solely down to the fact that I had a young son – I genuinely didn't want to be involved in crime. I was working forty hours a week at the print factory as it was. Harry was happy for me to have an honest job, but it took him a while to get used to it. The Ritchies didn't do honest labour. Harry was fine with me most of the time. I think he was delighted that his daughter had fallen for a regular guy. I was different to the sort of men she would have grown up with.

As the years went by Harry used me sparingly, as promised, but he would fume at me once or twice after being informed I wasn't as forceful as I could have been on the job. There were a couple of scary moments but we always seemed to get by. Harry didn't tell me too much but I'm pretty sure he had some cops on his payroll. He kept insisting we didn't have to be fearful in that regard. But I was always more fearful that rival gangs would begin some sort of turf war with us. The thought of Frank growing up without a father was just not an option as far as I was concerned. Frank's youngest years seemed to go by so fast. I'd fill with pride watching him walk off to school. It nearly killed me when, at seven years old, he turned around to me one day and insisted I didn't walk him to the school gates. Leaving him to his own devices scared me but it was all part of him growing up. It was only a six-minute walk to school anyway, but it was a body blow to me. It's the simple things that break your heart as a parent.

It sounds conceited but Frank, Karyn and I were as happy as any family I've ever known. There are plenty of days that stand out for me during my son's childhood, but certainly none more than the day he was set to make his football debut for the school team. He wasn't as tall as I had been at nine years of age but he was still taller than the rest of his year. The coach had stopped him in the school corridor two months earlier and asked him to trial as a goalkeeper. He impressed the coach so much that not only was he asked to be the team's number one, but he was also given the captain's armband. He had Karyn's personality traits to thank for that. He was as loud and as forthright as his mother. A doctor's appointment meant Karyn couldn't attend the game but I brought the family camcorder with me to record the action. I remember following the game up and down the touchline with perfectly steady hands. I felt guilty about wishing the other team to play well for the fact that it would involve Frank more in the game. He didn't do anything wrong, nor did he do anything outstanding that I could catch on tape to bring home to his mother. The highlight of the footage was the smile he beamed at me before kick-off when he noticed where I was standing. I was out of his mind as soon as the game started though. He was immersed in what was going on in front of him. The game seemed to be petering out to a nil-all draw when an opposition player broke free from the defence and raced towards my son. Frank's teammate desperately tried to get back at the attacker but when he slid to deny him the ball, he missed and brought the player crashing down instead. The referee pointed to the penalty spot to roars of disappointment from parents beside me. I closed my eyes in a deep squint of disappointment before I realised this could be Frank's big moment. I managed to creep around to behind Frank's goal to get myself a good shot of the penalty kick. When we watched that footage back I could be heard whispering, 'Save it, save it, save it!' And he did. Frank dived to his right, guessing where the penalty taker would kick the ball, and stuck out his hand to tip it around the post. His teammates reacted by bear-hugging him. The referee blew the final whistle there and then. He had literally saved his team from a loss in the dying moment. I knew he was looking over at me while he was being smothered in celebration, but I couldn't look back at him. I was in tears. The pride I felt that day has never been matched. By the time Frank had dressed and joined me in the car for the trip home I had composed myself. We must have spoken about the penalty save for the full duration of our drive, stopping twice to view the footage on the camcorder. Karyn smiled solemnly at us as we both chanted Frank's name on returning to the house.

'You have to see this, you have to see this,' I said to her, turning the camcorder back on. The three of us sat around our kitchen table and replayed the save at least a dozen times. Tears welled up in Karyn's eyes but I was able to hold mine in in front of Frank.

'I'm so proud of you,' she told him before asking him to go and take a shower. 'You stink of sweat and effort.'

I watched his tiny ass make his way upstairs before turning to my wife. Tears continued to roll down her face.

'I'm dying, Jack,' she said, staring into my eyes. 'Cancer. It's gone right through me.'

09:15

Ryan

I THOUGHT HE'D LAUGH AT SUCH A REQUEST SO I'M SURPRISED when he reaches towards the two legs of my chair to spin me around to face the TV. If I look sharply right I can still make out the clock on the microwave. He then hands me the remote control and tells me to watch what I want. He must be very grateful for that cocaine. I know I should have a lot going through my mind right now but I still want to watch that Champions League match. That's why I giggled at his shit joke earlier. This guy's a sucker.

'You like football?' I ask, hoping to spark up some conversation with him now that I don't have the tape wrapped around my mouth. Let's see how gullible he really is. Suddenly I'm teaching him about the sport he says he used to like when he was a kid. This exchange makes me wonder whether I should aim for his heart or for his mind in my attempts to get free. I could get personal with him and bring him to a level where he sees me as a human being and not as a pawn in his game. Maybe I could pull on his heartstrings to get out of this mess. Or maybe I should start playing mind games with him. I could just tell him out straight that he's already fucked. That the cum he tried to wipe from the TV screen earlier this morning hasn't really covered his tracks. I should inform him that cleaning the TV and the carpet beneath it a hundred times still wouldn't ensure that his DNA was not left behind. If I tell him all this and get him to realise he's so fucking dumb that he's already tripped himself up, he might decide to abandon the operation. But I decide playing to his heart is probably my best option. For now, anyway. If I confront him over the cum he may react aggressively. And he's so stupid I'm not sure what actions he would take. The TV screen is smudged slightly but it's not interfering with my watching of the game.

We only bought that TV about five months ago. I say we; I mean Vincent. He owns practically everything in here. I used to love this apartment so much. It was great to leave it in the mornings to earn a crust because coming home was always a fulfilling experience. To take the elevator up this building and to walk through the front door of the penthouse used to be a thrill. But waking up in this place and remaining here until I go back to bed at night has dimmed my fascination with it. Sometimes it feels a bit like a prison. It certainly does today. Vincent and I have fucked in every corner of this place.

We were both on such a high when we first moved in and the high didn't seem to waver for the first four years or so. I think I started to feel down once I got my promotion at work. The thrill of PR seemed to end for me once I gained a decent bit of responsibility. It also didn't help that I hated most of the guys I had to deal with on a daily basis now that I was a senior member of the team. The higher up in PR you go, the more wankers you have to endure. I found a soul mate in Ruairi though. He seemed to share my opinions on the egos of our fellow employees. He noticed it as soon as he walked in the door, despite being just a kid. He was an intern the company signed up for a year. I liked him. We used to bitch about the place on a regular basis and became good pals because of it. Bitching is such a great way to bond with somebody. Ruairi was content with his job but he didn't feel married to PR. He thought bigger and brighter things were out there waiting for him. Despite the fact he was thirteen years younger than me, he was the only person in the office I felt comfortable around. He was a likeable chap and no doubt always in great form because he was engaged to a girl who, I have to admit, was the most perfect-looking bird I have ever seen – and that includes celebrities. Her skin was flawless. Ruairi was happy that his position at Wow was bringing in a steady, albeit tiny, income for the two of them.

A junior account manager is the best position to be in. You get the perks that come along with the job without much of the responsibility and pressure. I used to stare at Ruairi at work with envy. He and I would sneak to the toilets at least twice a day to shoot a line of coke up our noses. I'm guilty of getting him hooked. But like me, he was disciplined with it, despite the fact he was only twenty-one. Neither of us got so high that we couldn't function through our working day. We saw it as a recreational drug and it helped us get through the monotony of rehashing shite press releases some famous sports star had their personal assistant type up. Sports stars are so fucking drab due to the media training they endure these days. They are afraid to say anything that doesn't toe the professional line.

If it hadn't been for Ruairi's friendship I would have given up my job at Wow sooner. In the end, he was the reason I left. One night, when he was staying back to wait for some golf tournament to finish before getting a quote for a press release, I decided to hang back with him. We could watch the end of the tournament in the company of a few lines of coke. It was unusual that we'd get this high in the office.

Everybody else was long gone and we knew Ruairi only had one small paragraph of text to waffle through. I'm not a huge golf fan and can't even remember how the play unfolded but it was a memorable evening for me for a very different reason. As I sat perched on Ruairi's desk, laughing at something he tried to say that came out wrong, he leapt up and kissed me. Never in a billion years did I see that coming. I wasn't even sure if Ruairi knew that I was gay. We took advantage of the deserted office and fooled around all night on his desk, only stopping so that he could write up the last bit of copy and email it on to some newspaper editors. We didn't fuck, but we did everything else we could think of. Ruairi was a seriously handsome young man. Any guilt I felt was overridden by the excitement of it all. Whenever Vincent popped into my mind I would dive down to the desk and sniff another line of coke.

I've already done two lines, but I must keep a level head if I'm to somehow talk my way out of this situation.

'So how come you like Manchester United then if you're not a big footie fan?' I ask, looking at him.

'Me da was a fan, back in the day,' he replies.

'Are you from Kerry originally? There's a lot of United fans down in the Kingdom.'

'I'm not from fuckin' Kerry,' he replies like only a Cork man would. 'Stop fuckin' askin' me questions about meself or I'll tape your gob back up, do ye hear me?'

I nod as a reply and stare back at the TV. I thought he'd be dumb enough to give me more details about himself.

Out of the corner of my eye, I can tell he's glued to the football. Because I'm adjacent to him, he would have to twist his neck to see what I am doing with my right hand. While still maintaining a posture that suggests I'm watching the match I can reach down to pick at the tape around my right ankle. For fear of making a noise while trying to release some of the tape, I increase the volume on the television. It doesn't raise any suspicion.

'Great atmosphere at Old Trafford,' I say, looking at him. When he turns to me I can tell his eyes are glazed over from the coke. He just glares at my face before turning his attention back to the screen. His high is helping him to get engrossed in the game. I'm glad I'm such a lazy bastard that I don't cut my fingernails regularly enough. My scratching at the tape is certainly working. I feel my ankle release somewhat and an adrenaline rush hits me. I take a moment to reassess. His gun is on the glass table in front of him. If I could free this leg before turning my attention to my left side, I'm certain I could get to it before him. I take another peek at my captor before slowly reaching back down. I'm gonna be the hero for once in my life.

09:15

Vincent

CHELLE'S OFFICE WOULD BE QUITE ROOMY IF IT WASN'T FOR the enormous oak desk she placed in the middle of it. I drum my fingers against it in anticipation of Janice returning with the ink. Chelle doesn't know what to do with herself. She's fuming. I'm not sure if it's the noise I am making with my fingers or the fact that I haven't said a word to her for five whole minutes that's niggling her mind the most. I've rarely been upset with her. I've never really had a professional reason to be upset with her. She's such a great employee. The printer's run out of ink and she doesn't have any spare in the supply room – big deal. It happens. It's not even Chelle's fault. If she was worried about the ink gauges on her printers then I'd be worried about her priorities.

I stare at the family portrait on her desk as I continue to tap my fingers. The photograph must have been taken about four years ago. Her twin sons are only babies in it. Jake looks as handsome as ever; Chelle's husband is an estate agent and possesses both the charm and the smile required for such a cheesy career. They met travelling through Europe. Chelle and I actually share a mutual fascination with Rome. That's where she met Jake. Aesthetically, it's such a stunning city, but only a small part of the magic of that city lies in its architecture. The pace of life is totally different there. There's a deep understanding away from the tourist traps that life is about contentment. The Romans don't get too high, and as a result, they don't get too low either. Their mentality towards life is in total contrast to the rest of Europe. Probably the rest of the world. Both Chelle and Jake were actually married to other people when they first met. Intrigued by the coincidence of hearing a fellow Irish accent on a tiny rooftop bar in a different country, Chelle couldn't help flirting with the handsome man sipping on a whisky cocktail. Before the end of the trip, they had shared a kiss and were plotting to meet up when they arrived home. I christened him Jake the Snake and giggled when Chelle filled me in on the story for the first time. Having got to know him well since then, I'd have to admit that he's no snake. He is a genuinely charming man. His jokes are a bit shit, but he's easy to like. Ryan and I would often go on double dates with them but we haven't hung out in a couple of years. Ryan and Jake used to obsess about sports over dinner while Chelle and I would roll our eyes at each other. There are a few reasons why the four of us don't socialise as much these days. Part of it is to do with the fact that Ryan seemed to get himself into a state of depression having left Wow PR and rarely has the inclination to go out anymore. And part of it has to do with me getting pissed off with Chelle's fascination with my sexuality. We all remain on good terms, but we just don't see each other as often as we used to.

I pick up the framed photograph and finally remove Chelle from her discomfort. 'How's Jake?' I ask.

'He's doing well, thanks,' she replies with a smile. 'He's away on business today. Up in Belfast at a big consultancy conference.'

'And the kids?' I ask.

'Good. Oliver is gearing up to start school this September and George is just happy once we put a football at his feet. He did really well in his first school exams.'

I wink at her to relieve the tension. I actually don't care about her kids that much. I don't really care for any kids. Like everybody else, I find bold kids repulsive but I'm not a fan of good kids either. I just happen to be one of those people who can't stand children. Unlike Ryan.

I see Janice before Chelle does. It's only twenty past nine. She must have run to Frederick Street and back.

'Hi, Michelle, hi, Mr Butler,' she says breathlessly as she enters the office. 'I've got the ink.'

'Well go put it into the printer,' Chelle says firmly, passing my original annoyance back on to her personal assistant. 'And get me those papers in the next three minutes.'

Filling out paperwork for such a task seems old school considering the evolution in digital technology. However, every transfer from branch to branch needs to be accounted for in both hard copy and in our complicated computer system. It's a lengthier process than is actually required but I can understand the board's strategy in this regard. It works. It's very rare for any money to get mixed up between the banks. Every new and used note is accounted for in both of our systems. It's used notes I'll be taking from the banks today. Ryan's captor told me what he wanted. Used notes can't be traced outside our branches. Once they leave our banks they can be used anywhere. The dizziness seems to enter my head once again as the thought of the robbery takes over my mind. I've got to get my feelings under control. I'll have to go through some simple paperwork with Chelle here in her office before we take a little trip to the vault. There, we will have to count out the amount of cash between us. We have to do that four times before updating the computer system. I should be out of here in about twenty-five minutes' time, I reckon.

'Two mill is a hell of a sum,' Chelle mentions once again while we await the paperwork. 'Are you sure you're okay transferring it yourself?'

'Ah, it's fine,' I say. 'John is at the doorstep waiting on me. Plus, someone's gonna have to chop my hands off, aren't they?' I say, wiggling the two handcuffs chained to the cases.

'I'd cut your hands off for two mill in used notes.' Chelle laughs.

'Yeah, fuck it, so would I.' I giggle back before noticing Janice is standing in the doorway to the office. I normally act super professional around all employees. I'm not sure whether she heard me swear, but she certainly doesn't let on that she did.

'Here you go, Michelle, Mr Butler,' she says, placing the paperwork in front of us. She then picks up a pen from Chelle's desk and hands it to me. I take a deep breath. Here we go.

09:25

Darragh

THE FOOTBALL IS MAKING ME REFLECT ON THE TIME I FIRST moved up to Dublin. I really missed home for a month or two. I've only ever driven through Cork since I've been in the capital, I've never actually gone back. Us Galligans don't do holidays. The fact that I'm watching Man United is quite ironic. Me old man used to make me watch them in the early days, but I guess I didn't show enough interest. I'm enjoyin' this though. But that's probably all down to the coke. I noticed that I was smiling ear to ear just a few moments ago and had to check meself before squinting towards Ryan, making sure he didn't catch me in the moment. He was talking me through the game earlier but he seems to have gone quiet now. I'd love to know who he buys his coke from.

After about four months of selling on the streets of North Dublin, part of the profit seemed to be winging its way into me pockets. The Boss would only ask for about ninety per cent of what I'd taken and would wink at me as he handed back some of the notes.

'You're doing well, Darragh,' he said to me one day. It was

unusual to get a compliment from him. 'We might get you involved in some of the fun stuff, huh?'

'I'd love that,' I said. 'I want to get involved as deep as I can, like.'

The fact that I passed the mock arrest test with flying colours seemed to get me closer to the lads. I got the sense that The Boss was hesitant in involving me any further but the rest of the gang seemed to put in a good word for me. Pretty soon afterwards I was being called into their meetings to discuss shipments. They knew they could trust me. I began transferrin' large quantities of the drug to Belfast. It was a long three-hour drive to Clifton, but I was happy to do it alone. At times I'd have up to twelve kilos of coke in the boot of a rented car, which would have resulted in me spending around fifteen years behind bars had I been caught. But I felt invincible. I didn't even go to any great lengths to hide my merch. I would just pack the trunk of the car with the bags of coke and throw a blanket over them. I wasn't being paid well, but the few quid I did pocket was enough for me. The Boss also didn't mind me skimming the odd bit of coke from the packages for myself as long as I didn't go overboard. The rental on the car was legitimate but The Boss had sorted me out with a very convincing fake driving licence. I didn't need to produce it at any stage of my dozen or so trips over the border. But for some reason, I ended up doing a run to Limerick one Wednesday morning and ended up almost shittin' me cacks.

The Boss asked me to drive to an estate to deliver ten kilos of coke to a new connection of his. I had a fear that something would go wrong from the outset. I never felt comfortable. I had to try to convince meself that I was just out on a drive. What could possibly go wrong? A broken fucking tail light! I was literally ten miles from the estate when I heard a siren blare behind me. In a split second me mind flipped between stepping on the accelerator and stepping on the brake. The fact that the siren only sounded for a second and so asking me, rather than telling me, to pull over made me mind up. I figured that the cop must have just noticed me committing a minor road offence I didn't even know I'd committed.

'Licence,' said the grumpy-lookin' fuck after he'd strolled slowly up to my rolled-down window.

'Here ya are, Garda,' I responded politely. 'Did I do something wrong?'

He squinted looking at me licence. 'That a Kerry accent, Mr Chomsky?'

I was about to reply with a polite 'no', when I realised that was exactly where Grant Chomsky was from.

'Eh, yes,' I say with a smile. 'Dingle.'

'Ah, my wife's from Tralee,' he replied. 'You know your driver's side tail light is out, Chomsky?'

I felt such a relief with his words. I had stayed composed but I could still feel beads of sweat forming on my forehead as he held that licence.

'I'm just heading to Limerick city for a bit of a work errand,' I said. 'I'll stop at the first mechanic I find on me route and make sure I get the bulb sorted. I promise.'

'Wouldn't get it fixed in Limerick city, if you know what I mean,' he replied. I think he was joking. So I laughed. Maybe I laughed too loudly. It made him look up at me for the first time.

'You got bad dandruff or is that cocaine on your shirt?' he asked, poking his head closer to me.

Shit! I'd been doing a couple of lines on the drive.

'Get out of the car.'

I managed to brush some of the powder from me chest as I got out, but I knew he was going to search me. I had a tiny bit of powder in me jeans pocket. It was nothing compared to what was in the boot. After asking me to rest my hands on the top of the car he searched my pockets. He held the small plastic bag up in front of me face. I focused to look at it and gritted me teeth. There was literally enough for two decent-sized lines left in it.

'Just to get me through Limerick city,' I said, smiling. My joke didn't work.

He opened my car door and knelt inside to have a look around. He didn't find anything but sweet wrappers and an empty water bottle. I was delighted to see him crawl his heavy ass back out without having reached for the boot popper. But then he asked me to turn around and face him.

'Open your boot for me,' he said as he walked to the back of the car.

Bollocks.

'Sure,' I said kneeling back into the car. I stared at him in the rear-view mirror before I swung me legs into position in the driver's seat and lashed on the ignition. I clicked the gear stick into reverse and heard the bumper crash against his kneecaps before I sped off. At no time did I feel afraid. I was lovin' it. The thrill of a car chase is insane. I watched in the rear-view mirror as he called for assistance on his walkie-talkie while hobbling to his car. I easily had a quarter of a mile head start on him. His sirens were in full flow but he didn't make any ground on me. I wasn't sure whether he'd recorded me licence plate. I had to assume he did, so I knew I needed to get out of the car as quickly as I could. I made a sharp left off the motorway towards Clyduff and sped into a kip of an industrial estate. There were dozens of cars parked in and around the warehouses. As quickly as I could, I parked my car up, broke into another and switched the coke over. I was out of there in two minutes. The Boss had taught me how to do that. I delivered the merch as expected and even made it back to Dublin in a different stolen car. The gang were fuckin delighted. I'd been in touch with The Boss the whole ride through, keeping him updated after I'd nearly got done. He was filling me in and helping me get back safely by recommending different routes and opportunities to change cars. He hugged me like I was his brother when I returned. These gangland guys really don't respect you until you nearly get caught. It's incredible. You have to be bad enough to almost get arrested before they will realise you're good enough.

'You're a fuckin superstar, Darragh Galligan,' The Boss said, kissing me on the forehead. 'Let's have a celebration. You got any plans tonight?'

'Nah, nothin',' I said, high as a kite.

'Well you do now. We're taking you out, kid.'

I'm certain it's not my fondness for Manchester United that has my heart racing. I'm enjoying the match but I know I've probably taken too much of this shit. If I was lying about at home I wouldn't be panicking about being high but I need to keep a level head today. I fuckin swore to meself I wouldn't overdo it this morning. I look at Ryan. He hasn't budged an inch. He's just sitting there enjoying the game. I puff out me cheeks before getting up off the couch. I need to splash some water on me face. The last thing I need to do right now is have a full-on fuckin panic attack.

09:25

Ryan

I CAN SEE THE GREASY LITTLE SHIT OUT OF THE CORNER OF MY eye. He's grinning to himself as wide as I've ever seen anybody grin. He's super high. You can snort coke every day of your life and still not be immune to a new batch. It's the same with most drugs. Some new formula that you haven't tried before can really fuck you up. Unfortunately, he's only taken two lines of the stuff so far. That's not enough to tip him over the edge. But I don't think he's going to have any more. He can't be that stupid. Either way, I need to somehow release my right ankle before turning my attention to my left side. The coke is probably giving me the focus I need to get this tape off my wrist and ankles, but it may also be responsible for me eventually getting caught. I can't get too erratic with my approach. It's important I stay calm. I'm trying to figure out in my head whether I can reach the gun if I just release my right ankle. I'd have a clunky kitchen chair holding my left side down and I wouldn't be able to put one foot in front of the other to walk. But if I could leap forward and somehow grab the gun, I'd hold all the aces. My gut feeling tells me I would make the leap towards the gun and end up falling flat on my face against the corner of the glass table while this prick laughs at me. The table is about three large strides away from where I'm sitting now. It's just too far to leap in one go. I need to release both sides from the chair. After ten minutes of picking away I'm making good progress on my right ankle, but this could take a while. I peek at the clock on the microwave again. 9:26. Two and a half hours left. Reaching my right hand back down I try to tug at the tape instead of scraping at it. But it's just not doing me any good. The tape is just too strong. I need to pick away at each layer of it with my nails, and work my way through it that way. There must be at least ten layers. This'll take a while.

To my surprise, the fantasy night with Ruairi didn't make things awkward between us the following day. I texted him in the morning with a feeling of dread, thinking he wouldn't get back to me. But in a matter of seconds he replied telling me he enjoyed the night. When we met in the office later that evening he winked at me. Butterflies filled my stomach. I felt just as excited as I did when I first fell in love with Vincent. Ruairi and I ended up going for drinks on a regular basis. It normally ended in us fooling around, but we never had full-on sex, despite my pleas. We were both enjoying our new relationship, even though Ruairi would often piss me off with his 'I'm not gay' insistence. The guy fuckin' loved cock. About one month into our affair I began to dream of a life with him. It wasn't fair on Vincent at all. Vincent had turned me from a nobody into a somebody and I owed him all the joy I had in life. Besides, I was living in one of the hottest and trendiest places in the whole of Dublin. There was never any guarantee that Ruairi would leave his girlfriend for me, but it didn't stop me thinking about the possibilities. My relationship with Vincent wasn't in dire straits. We weren't arguing or even that sick of each other. Our bond just seemed to plateau after a few years. We weren't keeping things fresh enough. Fooling around with Ruairi gave my life the spark it needed. That was why, when he came to me to say he no longer wanted to see me outside the office, I spiralled into depression.

'Listen, I've enjoyed it and had some fun, but it was just experimental on my part,' he said, staring into my eyes while at our favourite pub one evening. 'I'm in love with my girlfriend. I can't do this anymore.'

I stayed silent initially. I had a million ways to approach this with him but I couldn't figure out which one to choose. In the end I opted for defensive and arrogant.

'Your girlfriend will find out you're a fuckin' cock lover eventually, you piece of shit,' I shouted at him as I stood up to leave. Everybody in the pub turned to face us. I was too hurt to care.

My anger soon turned to bitterness before genuine heartache set in. It was only a swift affair but I got caught up in the emotion of it all. What made it even worse was having to work with him. Although he worked shifts, I'd still have to see his face and hear his voice in the office at least three times a week. I made excuses to not turn up in the early days of the heartache but soon after I had to face up to the torture. The worst part about getting your heart broken from an affair is the fact that you can't actually confide in anybody. I couldn't talk to any colleagues about the fling nor could I tell any of my friends. All my friends were Vincent's friends anyway. I tried to immerse myself in my computer screen when I was at work, but at home I'd just curl up into a ball on either the bed or the couch and cry myself to sleep. I'd wake up each morning and convince myself that today was the day I would finally get over Ruairi but I knew deep down I was kidding myself. To numb the pain, I promoted cocaine from a social drug to a daily habit. I contacted an old student friend of mine who made the greatest coke ever, to get so wasted I would forget Ruairi's handsome face. Vincent could tell I wasn't myself but he believed me when I told him I was just dejected with my career. That was partly true. I had, after all, fallen out of love with PR way before I'd fallen in love with Ruairi.

I'm getting a bit paranoid that my captor will notice my right hand missing any time he looks up at me. I have to reach lower now, right to the bottom of my ankle, to finish the job. If he looks over at me he'll notice I'm slightly hunched, but I suppose my posture isn't anything out of the ordinary. My face is still towards the screen, watching the match as I pick away at the tape. The high definition big screen and the sound the fans are creating in the stadium seems to be distracting him. It's imperative I get this tape loosened as soon as I can. I freeze, though, when I notice him sit more upright. After rubbing his eyes, he stares over at me before standing up slowly. He takes a walk behind the couch and heads towards our main bathroom. He's left the gun on the glass table right beside his phone. This guy is a full-on fucking moron. When I hear the tap turn on in the bathroom I think about making the leap towards the gun. I won't reach it in one go, but with him at least fifteen feet away from me, I'll have a few seconds to crawl my way towards it. I need to do this now. I force the balls of my feet deep into our carpeted floor and begin to count myself down.

09:25

Jack

MY ASS IS GROWING NUMB PERCHED ON THIS WALL. I'VE STOOD up to stretch my back so many times that I'm starting to get paranoid somebody has noticed I'm up to no good.

I check my watch again. I've estimated that Vincent should be coming out of the bank at around nine-thirty; that's only five minutes from now. I'm afraid to go for a walk, in case I miss his exit. I just need to know he's doing okay. His collapse is continuing to worry me despite Darragh confirming everything is back on track. I know Vincent's next port of call is Camden Street. That's another twenty to twenty-five-minute walk for me. He'll arrive there with his driver, John, before I do. In an ideal world I'll observe Vincent entering and exiting each bank, but I can't physically stay on his tail too much. I'm wary of getting public transport because there are cameras on buses, and taxi drivers will be asked about their fares as part of the investigation into this robbery. I'd made a decision early on in this process that I would walk to each of the branches and I must continue to follow through with that. It's a long walk and a lot of effort, but the pay-off will be oh so worth it.

Sticking to the plan is paramount. I'm absolutely sure there is no way I can get caught. I've covered each and every possibility. Another look at my watch causes me to blow out my cheeks. Only seconds have gone by.

Some people say, spending time with a loved one when you know they have limited time left to live is rewarding. I think that's bullshit. I loved Karyn dearly, but the pain it caused my heart to leave the hospital every night feeling that I'd said my final goodbye was monstrous. The doctors told me one afternoon in late June 2005 that my wife would only last another three months. She shocked them by staying alive for another half a year. But from that day up until the night she passed away, just two days into 2006, was torturous for me. I felt really selfish for feeling such pain when it was Karyn who was dying, but I couldn't help it. I hate saying goodbye. I must have said at least a hundred goodbyes to Karyn. A part of me wished that she had died in a car crash and I just had to receive a terrible phone call. It would be shocking and painful in other respects, but losing my wife in that way wouldn't have been as mentally challenging and exhausting for me. The whole process was very hard on poor Frank who really didn't understand what was going on. I didn't fill him in on every detail but he knew his mother was close to death. He wasn't stupid. She looked like she was close to death. Karyn decided to take a large course of chemotherapy in the hope that a miracle would occur, which made her face appear gaunt in her final months. I remember being angry that she chose to have the treatment. It prolonged her passing. Selfishly, I just wanted her to die so Frank and I could move on with our lives. Her family were very supportive. They really are a super-tight bunch. Harry and his third wife, Yvonne, visited the hospital almost as often as I did. I used to hear them praying in the ward. That always amused me. These guys had no problem ordering people to be murdered, yet they somehow still believed there was a God up there who would answer their prayers. On the day Karyn finally passed, Harry sat me down and told me he considered me as part of the family still, and he would look after me in any way I sought. I thanked him but insisted I'd stay away from organised crime for Frank's sake.

'You made my daughter very happy for nearly twenty years. So I will make you happy in any way you want. If you ever need me, you just call, okay?' he said before hugging me and walking away. But I knew that wasn't the end of the conversation.

I'm finding myself clicking through this old phone. I miss my iPhone. I left it at home for a very valid reason. Mobile phones can be easily traced. It amazes me the amount of times I read about idiots being found guilty of certain crimes because their phone was traced to the scene. How stupid can you be? There is nothing on this cheap phone except today's call history and a game called Snake. It's a boring little graphic but it beats staring at the doors of ACB across the street. I finish a couple levels of the game before staring at the time on the top of the phone again. It's nine thirty-one and there has been no movement out of the bank. I know I'm impatient, but I feel like I have to ring Darragh to get some information.

'Have you not got your phone right beside you?' I ask when he finally answers. He has annoyed me again by taking his time picking up. 'Any word from Vincent?'

He hasn't heard a thing. I'm not surprised. It's literally one minute past the time we thought Vincent would exit. But that doesn't stop me from acting the hard man.

'Listen, I'm worried about him. Give him a call for me, will ya? Tell him he shouldn't be messing about or you'll kill that little darling of his, alright?'

09:30

Ryan

As I lean slightly forward, allowing my toes to take most of the weight, the two hind legs of the chair lift up. I play the jump forward in my head. I figure I will make one giant leap that will leave me about four feet from the gun. From there, I should be able to pull myself up on the edge of the glass table and grab it with my right hand. I puff out my cheeks three times fast and count myself down in my head. *Three ... two ...* The noise of his phone rattling off the glass table scares the shit out of me. The legs of the chair immediately fall back down to the carpet and I look backwards to see if my captor is coming from the bathroom to answer the phone. I shake my head in amazement at the timing of the call.

'That my phone?' he shouts out as I hear him turn the tap off.

I sigh. 'Yeah.'

Why the fuck am I helping him?

He sprints out of the bathroom and scoops the phone up as quickly as he can.

'Hello? Yes, I have the phone here beside me all the time,'

he says after a pause. Seems like his partner in crime is ranting at him again. They're like fuckin' Laurel and Hardy. 'No, he hasn't been onto me yet. It's just gone half nine now, he shouldn't be too long.

'Okay, I'll give him a ring now,' he says, sounding exhausted after another pause.

They're getting worried. But it should be me who's most worried. It's my life at stake, after all. I notice my captor fumbling at the phone to make an outside call. He's obviously trying to get onto Vincent, but he doesn't seem to be able to get an answer. Vincent is at the bank with colleagues. Why would he answer that cheap-ass phone you gave him in front of them? Idiots! Vincent would hate to be seen with such a cheap mobile phone. He's a bit of a snob in those respects.

The pain of seeing Ruairi almost every time I went into the office proved too much for me in the end. Vincent could see the depression etched on my face. I had to tell him that I hated being in PR and I hated the people I worked with. He bought it. The fact that I'd been bitching to him about my colleagues over the years paid off. He had insisted for a long time that I should write a novel. I always have ideas for stories, but I totally lack the discipline to be that kind of writer. Even before I handed in my notice at Wow I knew all too well that I wouldn't get up in the mornings and motivate myself to write a few chapters of a book. Vincent set out a plan that meant I would have to wake up with him when his alarm went off at seven o'clock every morning. And after he headed to his office, I would open the new MacBook Air he bought for me to work on my novel. A few ideas that I had in my head for years made it onto a Word document in the early days of my working from home, but that was literally it. Ideas. I had one story concept in my mind about a celebrity paparazzo, which had a chilling twist, and another one about a stunning blonde bombshell who was also an amazing slutty private investigator. She would sleep with all the men she was investigating to get the details she was looking for over pillow talk. I wasn't bad for ideas, but I was pathetic when it came to work ethic. PR doesn't help you become a good writer. In fact, it does the opposite. It teaches you how to write shit formulaic copy as quickly as you can. The creative promise I had before I joined Wow was wiped out within a couple of months of working there.

It's just over nineteen months since I left media to write a book. I have added little to those two story concepts on that Word document since. That's pathetic in its own right, but it's not as pathetic as the reasons for which I now use that MacBook Air. I have zero career ambition. I feel like my old twenty-year-old self again. A no-hoper. Only this time I'm lacking hope in the more comfortable surroundings of a glorious penthouse as opposed to a tiny, untidy bedsit.

He looks a little frustrated that he can't reach Vincent on the phone, but he also seems a bit lost. He's scrunching his nose up again, a habit all coke users have after snorting a line.

'Where was I?' he asks himself before spinning around. He looks over at me before picking up his gun and placing it in the band of his jeans. He then makes his way back towards the bathroom. I hear the tap turn on again and curse to myself.

How the fuck did that other cunt happen to ring at the exact moment I was about to leap for the gun?

Staring over at the television, I continue to watch the match before remembering what I had been up to. With my captor out of the room, I can work on my right ankle with more vigour. I reach down and begin to tug really hard at the tape. It's loosening its grip of my ankle to the leg of the chair but I still can't remove my foot fully. I pick away at the tape with my nails as quickly as I can. Doing this without fear of making any noise is much more effective. I seem to be making huge progress when I hear the tap turn off. The bathroom door closes and I feel the presence of my captor back in the room. He lets out a satisfied yelp before throwing himself back on the couch, placing both the phone and the gun down on the glass coffee table in almost the exact same positions they occupied a minute ago. I stare at him but he hasn't even noticed me. He's now watching Paul Pogba running one-on-one with Bayern Munich goalkeeper Manuel Neuer and smacking a ten-yard effort off the inside of the post.

'Ouch,' he says while still staring at the screen. 'I would have scored that.'

The atmosphere in the Old Trafford stadium rises in volume and, as it does, I allow myself a strong tug at the remaining thin sliver of tape until finally I feel it snap. Relief fills my whole body as my foot releases. My whole right side is now free. I'm halfway to getting myself and Vincent out of this mess.

09:35

Vincent

NEITHER CHELLE NOR I WANT TO READ THROUGH THE paperwork, but it's a legal requirement. We've read through this jargon thousands of times over the years. But Chelle knows that I would demand she follows protocol at all times. So rushing her through it today would look suspicious. The fact that I'm taking out two million euros is suspicious enough. We flick over page after page as Chelle mumbles through the contents and then we each sign on the dotted lines at the bottom. There are eleven pages in all and each of them must be signed by both of us. To be fair to Chelle, she is getting through it as quickly as she can. She's still cringing about the ink.

'… to extract two million euros,' she reads with emphasis while raising an eyebrow at me. She keeps mentioning this, but then again, she should. This is a hell of a lot of money to be transferring from one branch to another.

As she twirls the paperwork towards me for another signature I feel the cheap phone vibrate in my suit pocket. There's no way I can answer it. Chelle would piss herself laughing if I took out an old Nokia phone to take a call.

Besides, if I did answer it, what sort of conversation could we have in Chelle's company? I'll have to excuse myself later and pretend to go to the bathroom or something and call this prick back. I try to calm down after the vibrating stops but it doesn't last long. The gobshite tries to ring me back straight away. He really is one thick fuck.

Although my professional life had taken off, my personal life had taken a bit of a step backwards. I had frequented the gay bars around the city for a full six years but I had to force myself to stop going out after I'd become manager of the Drumcondra branch. It wasn't just the responsibility of the new job that made my mind up for me. I genuinely couldn't cope with the hangovers anymore. Something chemical happens in your body after you get into your late twenties when it comes to alcohol. Suddenly hangovers, which used to last a morning, start to stay with you for two or three full days. But that didn't stop me getting back on the party bus after I met Ryan. We were both just high on life in those days. I'd had two semi-serious boyfriends in my twenties. I dated Seamus Gaughran for all of a year before I found out he was fucking as many blokes behind my back as he possibly could. Then there was Simon O'Dea. I met him on a trip to Sligo. We stayed close for a couple of years but it got tiring for the two of us. The west of Ireland is a great place to travel to, but it's a pain in the ass to drive there. That trip on a regular basis is so monotonous. After Simon, I was celibate for almost three years, bar four guilt-riddled one-night stands. I'm not sure why I felt so guilty about having sex with strangers. I was free and single. But one-night stands – which I had been fond of fifteen years prior – just seemed so juvenile to me. I knew I'd be a great catch for somebody but I couldn't seem to find any man I'd like to live with. I was earning over €250,000 a year and was just about to complete the purchase of one of the trendiest penthouses in the whole of Dublin, yet I had nobody to share all that with. There was one guy who interested me, but I was afraid to ask him out. He'd been in and out of my bank on a few occasions to discuss a possible loan. I could see an awful lot of potential in his look, despite the fact that he had the appearance of an early nineties boy band member. His curtains-style haircut was so wrong in 2002. But under his hanging fringe beamed a really cute smile. He had dimples that sunk into his cheeks when he smiled, but smiling seemed like an irregular occurrence for him. He had heavy eyes. I felt straight away that he came across as if he wasn't enjoying his life. That part of it was actually a turn-on for me. The opportunity to kick-start this guy's life really was quite fascinating. I started to become a little infatuated with him. There's little more exciting in life than really fancying somebody. I knew by his manner that he was gay. You wouldn't place Ryan in the 'camp' category but you wouldn't have to possess the greatest gaydar on the planet to recognise his sexuality.

'Would you be interested in discussing this over dinner some evening?' I asked him while checking over my shoulder one Wednesday afternoon. I knew I was taking a risk. It was a totally unprofessional thing to do, especially for somebody like me. He looked at me as if I had two heads. He'd later tell me that he didn't realise I was asking him out on a date. He genuinely thought it was a service I was offering as a bank manager.

'… and last one,' Chelle says, spinning the paperwork back over to me. I sign it with extra emphasis on the cross of my 't' before grinning at her. She tidies the paperwork with a quick bounce of the sheets off her desk before standing up. She then leads me out of her office towards the back of the building.

'You got your key, Vincent?' she asks as we stand either side of the vault door. I answer her by waving my card at her.

'Three, two, one,' she counts down, just before we swipe at the double lock entrance.

As the vault door opens I take another look at my watch. It's twenty to ten. I can feel my phone buzzing again. I think about dismissing myself to ring that asshole back but I've gone too far now. He'll have to wait. Chelle and I came straight to the vault after completing the paperwork so I think it would look rather odd if I headed off to the toilets now. I'll only be in here for another ten minutes or so. The prick will be happy enough when I ring him back. I'll have the first two million with me in the car. The first vault door brings us into a small corridor that holds a lot of the bank's paperwork. There are six shelves on each side filled with heavy files of stuff nobody will ever read. There's a small steel door at the other end of this corridor that will lead us to the cash. Chelle keys in a five-digit code that allows the door to click open. You can smell the banknotes as soon as she pushes through. It's a scent I've never become immune to. There are all sorts of bonds and notes neatly packaged in eight large vaults but it's the vault at the front right corner of this heavy-lit room that I need to make my withdrawal from today. This vault houses the cash that the bank uses on a daily basis. Used notes.

'You wanna do the first count?' Chelle asks as she turns to a computer screen on the right side of the small room.

'Sure,' I say. 'Will that take long?' I'm asking about the computer system. I know it only takes a few minutes but I'm really suggesting she works quicker than normal. She gets the gist.

'I'll be as quick as I can,' she answers.

You would think counting out two million euros would take a fair bit of time, but when the notes are neatly packed into ten-thousand-euro piles already it's quite a straightforward task. I just need to pull two hundred of these packs out of the vault and place them on the countertop beside me. I'm done counting the money before Michelle has updated the database.

'Jaysus, two mill doesn't look that much when it's laid out like that,' she says turning to me, laughing. 'Now, let's see. There should be two hundred packs, right?'

'Yep,' I answer with a sigh.

I know we have to do this two times each as part of the protocol. On Chelle's second go, we count the notes into my cases. On each of the four counts we manage to make up the two million without any errors. You'd want to be fucking stupid not to be able to count to two hundred, after all.

'It's all there,' she says as I pack up the second case before tightening the handcuff around my wrist.

'Chelle, it's been an adventure,' I say sarcastically.

'I'm so sorry about the ink,' she says. 'I feel awful about—'

'Don't worry about it,' I interrupt, then kiss her on both cheeks. 'I really need to get going to Jonathan. I'll call you later, okay?'

I don't hear her answering. I'm too busy rushing out of the vault and through the large steel doors before pacing onto the bank floor. A couple of employees wish me goodbye. I only offer a fake smile in return. As I stand in the glass hallway between the two exit doors I can see John reading his newspaper in the driver's seat of the car. I let out another big sigh before murmuring to myself, 'What the fuck are you doing, Vincent?'

Adrenaline pumps through my veins as the second door beeps open. When I push through I feel the heat of the morning sun hit me straight in the face.

What a fucking day this is.

09:35

Darragh

I'M JUST ABOUT TO FILL THE CUP ME HANDS ARE FORMING WITH cold water when I'm sure I hear me phone ringing.

'That my phone?' I call out after turning off the tap.

'Yeah,' he answers. Fuckin idiot.

I race out to answer it with me hands still wringing wet.

'Have you not got your phone right beside you?' JR shouts down the line at me.

'Yes, I have the phone here beside me all the time,' I lie. This is the second time I've left the phone behind while I'm out of the room. I need to get me fuckin act together. This is not how proper gangsters do it.

'Have you heard from Vincent?'

'No, he hasn't been onto me yet. It's just gone nine-thirty, like, he shouldn't be too long.'

'Listen, I'm worried about him. Give him a call for me now. Tell him he shouldn't be fuckin about or you'll kill that little darling of his, alright?'

'Okay, I'll give him a call now,' I say before hanging up.

It's literally five minutes past the estimated time Vincent should be coming out of the bank. And even at that, nine-thirty was just a rough guess. JR is certainly lacking patience. When we were planning all this, JR said Vincent will be thirty to forty minutes in each bank. He's given him thirty-five minutes in the first one and I already have to get in touch. Maybe he's freaking out because Vincent collapsed earlier. I'd almost forgotten about that. Bleedin' coke.

JR has the number for the phone we gave Vincent stored in as number two on the speed dial, but I can't seem to get my head together to dial it. I wipe my wet hands on my T-shirt. After a fumble, I manage to dial his phone, but it's ringing out. I kick the floor in frustration and try him again. He's still not picking up. He must be in the vaults filling his cases with notes. He fuckin better be. I'll leave it for a few minutes before I try him again. I'm about to put the phone back down on the coffee table to return to the bathroom when I realise I really should be bringing it with me. I pick the gun up too and force it into the waistband of me jeans. I need to be more careful. Ryan wouldn't be able to get to the gun, but I know I must get me head together and stop flutin' about. I stare into the mirror over the sink in their huge bathroom and shake my head. My eyes are fuckin purple. I need to chill. I twist at the cold tap again and let out a big sigh that clouds up the mirror. I gotta splash me face.

The Boss insisted I didn't put my hand in my pocket throughout the celebration night. He must have thrown his arm around me at least a hundred times. I felt like the young Henry Hill at the start of *Goodfellas* when De Niro greets him on the steps of the courthouse.

'You took your first pinch like a man and you learned the two greatest lessons in life – you never rat on your friends and you always keep your mouth shut.'

I'd performed even better than the young Henry Hill. I didn't even get pinched. I don't like champagne but the whole gang kept popping bottle after bottle in celebration. It wasn't just my heroics that we were celebrating. The Boss now had a major player from Limerick involved in his circle, which was likely to bring in another half a mill or so every year. The lines of coke were being shared among us as often as the bubbly was being poured out. If I remember correctly, there were twelve of us out celebrating that night. Every one of us was wasted. The Boss may have been talking drunk bullshit into me ear most of the time, but what he was saying was really getting' me excited. He wanted to start getting' me involved in a big money laundering scam he was starting up. He said it would bring me in a rake of dough every couple of months. It was the compliments more than the cash that got me pumped. I could finally sense that The Boss liked me. I think that was the first time I ever felt accepted. I remember the air hitting me when meself and two other lads left the club that night. The champagne went to me head instantly. One of me new mates, who we called Smack, started to take the piss out of a group of slutty-looking bitches because that's what Smack did for fun. He had a way with words. I don't think I've ever known anyone funnier than Smack, not even a professional comedian. I don't know why I ever thought I could outdo him. But I did try that night as we walked further down the Tallaght Road and came across a couple sucking the faces off each other outside one of those run-down gaffs.

'She must be easy, snoggin' an ugly fuck like you,' I shouted out to the laughter of me two mates. They were egging me on, especially after the fella stopped kissing his bird to stare back at me.

'What you lookin' at, you ugly piece of shit?' I barked over to him.

Then his girlfriend turned around.

'Ah, I see now,' I continued, laughing. 'She's ugly as fuck too.'

Me mates didn't really laugh at that one. I got the feeling even Smack felt I'd crossed the line. I felt so uncomfortable that I couldn't leave it there. The bloke wrapped his arm around the bird to walk away from me and for some reason I jogged towards them in a rage. I watched the girl fall to her knees as she began to run. The thought of picking her up crossed my mind for a split second before I noticed a fist coming at me. I just managed to dodge it with a quick turn of my head before responding with an upper cut of me own. I'd never caught anyone sweeter. I heard his jaw shatter. He fell backwards, smacking his head off the bottom step of a doorway. I can still hear the two noises today: the smack of my fist off his jaw and the smack of his head off the step. I remember every beat of that whole ordeal because I replayed it over and over in me head for months afterwards. Smack and Greggo grabbed me away from the scene as quickly as they could. I knew that bloke was dead there and then.

I seem to be able to focus a bit better now that I've splashed water on me eyes. This match is getting really interesting. United are desperately chasing a goal to advance to the next round and they seem to be getting closer each time they attack. They hit the post two minutes ago. I lean forward to check the time on my phone. 9:45. I seem to have got lost in this match. JR will be wondering what's going on. It's been nearly a quarter of an hour since I told him I'd get onto Vincent. As I lift the phone to my ear after dialling JR, I hear a strange beep piercing through the speaker. I take at a look at the screen to see if I can make out what's causing the noise.

Incoming call from 2

That's Vincent calling me. Perfect timing! I tap on the green button to answer it, hanging up from JR. He won't mind waiting. Not if it's good news.

'What up, fag?'

09:45

Vincent

I wink at John as I approach the car. I don't know why I feel excited. Adrenaline is a bipolar hormone. It doesn't always relate to what the mind is thinking. John raises both his eyebrows at me before getting out of the car. He pops the boot just as I reach him and assists me in unlocking the two cases from my wrists.

'I got 'em,' he says as he grabs both before shoving them towards the back of the boot. 'Some day, huh?' he adds, gripping both of my shoulders.

'Sure is,' I reply. I realise the smile is still etched on my face as I say it.

'Now … it's Camden Street you want to go to next, right?'

I hesitate. 'Yeah, Camden Street.'

John opens the back door and I immediately feel the cold waft from inside the vehicle hit me. John had left the air conditioning on while he waited on me. He was probably freezing. But I'm delighted. It's a welcome relief from the heat.

'Ye look a lot better,' he says, readjusting his rear-view mirror after climbing into the driver's seat.

146

'I feel it, John, thank you.'

The drive from here can take less than ten minutes, but the traffic around Stephen's Green is unpredictable. I check the time and realise I have less than two hours and fifteen minutes to complete the whole mission. That wipes the smile from my face. I take a peek at my reflection in the car window and stare into my own eyes. I let out a small sigh as I register with myself. Time to make a call. I hit speed dial one as instructed and squint my eyes as the tone rings through my ear. I haven't thought through what I'm going to say.

'What up, fag?' snarls the greasy little prick in my ear.

'It's all done,' I say quietly.

'Two mill?' he asks.

'Two mill,' I reply. 'I'm on my way to Camden Street now, should be there around ten. How is Ryan?'

'Ryan will be fine up until midday,' he snaps back at me. 'Call me once you're out of Camden Street with two more million, huh?'

I glare at the small screen of the phone after Ryan's captor hangs up. But that doesn't stop me from noticing John staring back at me through the rear-view mirror. He never questions anything I do and I know for certain that he won't ask anything today. But maybe my suspicious mood swings are playing on his mind. He's probably worried about me. To quell this feeling in both of us I offer a wide smile into the rear-view mirror just for him.

'I need a little pick me up, John boy,' I follow up with. 'You got some classical in the CD player?'

'You betcha,' he replies, reaching over to one of the many buttons on his dashboard. Ah … Tchaikovsky. He's no Beyoncé, but he'll do. Classical music can take the mind places.

Our first date went perfectly well. I've often told him that I fell in love with him at our very first dinner, but that's a bit of a lie. If I recall correctly, I was thinking he wasn't as cute as I initially thought he was when he dressed up in a shirt and tie to see me at the bank. He wore a T-shirt – that didn't fit – on our first date. The round neck was out of shape and one sleeve seemed longer than the other. It made me question whether I fancied him or not. I guess I used to be shallow. I went on our second date feeling it was make or break, and he somehow won me over by opening up. My instinctive observation of a sadness behind his eyes turned out to be true. His father sounded like a right stubborn prick while his mother, though dear to him, seemed weak. I felt this kid could do with a father figure and I knew the perfect man for the job. Me! I probably spilled the beans on my wealth a little too hastily, looking back. I couldn't help it. It made me realise I had an ego. People used to tell me I was vain but I never thought I was. I guess I figured telling him about the plans for my new penthouse and alluding to how much I got paid would help him fall in love with me. I didn't want to lose him. Especially not after I'd restyled him – finally getting rid of that stupid haircut. The new and improved Ryan looked absolutely delicious and I was only too delighted to show him off. He told me he didn't fall in love with me until I sorted out his career about four months later. After I'd gone to the trouble of finding him a journalism placement at DCU and filling out his application forms, he grew really close to me. I think I was the first person he really trusted. I would have been happy for Ryan to stay at home, but he felt he needed his own path. I wasn't surprised when he told me he wanted to be a writer, but I've never considered him very talented. I've never told him that, of course. I genuinely sensed from the outset that PR was the wrong profession for him. I felt he'd get eaten up and spat back out by the sharks in that game. I guess that's what happened in the end. Out of all the gobshites who worked in media that I met through Ryan I don't recall meeting anyone I liked. People who work in that industry tend to be cunts. For some reason, they have massive egos that don't equate to their status in society. They are literally middlemen. That's what media means: medium. Why the fuck would being a middleman afford you an ego? I could never understand that.

I think this one is from *Swan Lake*, though I'm only guessing. I like to listen to classical music but I'm no expert. John would be able to tell me which Tchaikovsky composition this is. He listens to this stuff whenever he can and is responsible for my recent fondness for it too. He keeps looking at me through the rear-view mirror. Perhaps he does this every day and I'm only noticing today due to paranoia. I can see his lips hum along to the strings of the violins. Inspired by the music, I stare out of the car window feeling like I'm in a movie. I've had a habit of doing this ever since I was a young boy. We're stuck in traffic at the back end of the Green. I watch people walking by almost in slow motion with Tchaikovsky's mid-tempo concerto as a backdrop. It helps me calm down.

I've got this.

Jonathan Reilly will be quick and professional. I should be in and out of the Camden Street branch in no time. I allow myself a peek at John's dashboard to read the time again. 9:51. I've definitely fallen behind but I can make it up in this next branch. It won't be long now until I have four million euros in the trunk of this car. That'll have me halfway there.

09:50

Jack

I'M WALKING TOO QUICKLY FOR THIS HEAT. BUT I CAN'T HELP it. I'm agitated. It's 9:50 and I still haven't heard from Darragh, despite watching Vincent leave the first bank what must have been about ten minutes ago. It's just over a twenty-minute walk to the Camden Street branch from here, right through the Green. I should arrive there around about ten past ten. Hopefully Vincent will be well in the branch at that point. Just as I turn onto Kildare Street the phone finally buzzes in my hand, but when I answer it there's nobody on the other end of the line.

What the hell is Darragh up to?

We went through this whole plan countless times in meticulous detail. He can do the difficult tasks no problem, but he seems hopeless at being able to make or take phone calls. I hope Ryan isn't getting inside his head and changing his mind. Nobody knows more than I do just how gullible Darragh is.

Frank missed his mother for about two weeks before getting back to normal. Karyn hadn't been herself for months so he slowly got used to her not being in our home.

She was mostly in hospital for her final half a year. I was relieved that I didn't have to go through much of the grieving process with him. I felt relief initially after Karyn passed but it soon turned to heartache about a month in. I just missed her presence so much. It hurt my heart. But I don't believe in looking backwards. It genuinely is a complete waste of time. I tried to be positive. I saw a bright future for Frank and me. I wanted us to be the best dad and son combination ever and to go out and take on the world. Unfortunately, taking on the world meant me having to take a job at a paint factory out in Blanchardstown. It was fine. It was a half-an-hour drive from where we were living but it was an okay way to make some honest money. They offered me a manager's position and it paid better than any normal job I'd had before.

The Ritchies were practically throwing money into my pockets for months after Karyn died. They went out of their way on a regular basis to make sure Frank was okay. I never minded them calling by to see him and I felt obliged to take their money offerings early on – for his sake, of course. Frank adored his grandparents and uncles. When I told Harry I wanted to go straight, he held his hands up and said it was understandable. I think he genuinely respects me. And I respect him. The Ritchies' generosity gave my bank balance a good cushion. It meant Frank and I never had to go without the necessities in life and things never got too tight. I was able to sit on the savings and felt positive we would have a bright future. Frank needed minding during the day while I worked. That was how Margarite came into our lives. She really was adorable. She was the very first person I interviewed for the position of minding Frank and I loved her straight away. She was mad about my son, and he her, from the very first moment they met. Margarite was one year older than me and possessed the kindest smile I think I've ever seen. She had Norwegian heritage, but that was from two generations back. I'm certain she used to be really pretty but by the time I met her, she had let herself go. I loved her, but I never fancied her. I'm sure people used to think we were an item but we never were. Margarite fancied me though. She never hid that fact even though she never actually said it out loud. I sometimes tried to will myself to be interested in her that way. It never worked. It would have made so much sense for us to be a couple. We were both otherwise free and single but for our dual responsibility of taking care of my son. I was happy being a single dad and assumed I'd stay that way forever. I was living a contented life, despite the tragedy that had struck me. After a while, the Ritchies started to phone us rather than knock, which made things more ideal for me. Harry was trying to stay low-key after the Criminal Assets Bureau kicked into gear in Ireland. He was afraid he'd lose all his money. He and Yvonne moved to London. It still didn't remove the niggle I had in my head that they would, one day when he was older, expect Frank to get involved with the family business. I always felt Harry's 'low-key' move to London was temporary. The last thing I wanted was for Frank to get involved in any sort of trouble. I lived every day to keep us out of it.

As I'm trying to call Darragh back for the fourth time, the phone starts to buzz in my hand again.

'Sorry, JR,' pants Darragh. 'Vincent rang me just as soon as I was about to ring you back, so I thought I'd take his call first.'

I pointlessly nod with approval while saying nothing, allowing Darragh to fill the silence.

'Well, he had no problem in Nassau Street apart from the delay. He has two mill in the car and should be arriving at Camden Street in the next few minutes.'

'Great stuff, Darragh. How are you getting on over there? Don't let Ryan get into your head.'

'Course I won't!' he grunts back. 'The little fag is helpless. He's just watching some poncey football match now, tied up in his chair. He knows there's nothing he can do but wait.'

Waves flow through my stomach as I watch the sunshine beat down on strange faces in the Green after I hang up. Dubliners of all ages are taking strolls around the pond. Wow. We already have two million euros. The morning has gone perfectly so far. I'm aware we're literally only one-quarter of the way through this process, but the fact that Darragh seems to have Ryan under control fills me with so much confidence. We're gonna pull this off! I whistle along to the tune of 'Let's Go for a Little Walk' yet again as I pass over the tiny O'Connell Bridge. I'm only about ten minutes away from the next bank. Vincent's driver should be pulling up outside there any second now.

09:50

Ryan

HE'S HAD THE PHONE UP AND DOWN TO HIS EAR FOR THE PAST couple of minutes. After hanging up on Vincent a few seconds ago he's now onto his partner in crime. Vincent has robbed one bank of two million euros. That's insane. The reality of the whole ordeal has been trying to take over my mind, but I won't let it. I have to stay focused on this one task – getting free. The tape is so fucking hard to rip off in a discreet manner, but I'll get through it before this dumb fuck notices.

'The little fag is helpless,' I hear him say as he stares straight at me with a straight face. 'He's just watching some poncey football match now. He knows there's nothing he can do but wait.'

He grins at me while he's hanging up.

'Pogba miss another chance there, yeah?' he asks, straight as a die.

What a dumb-ass prick! He didn't even have the decency to laugh after saying that. Was he trying to be funny or is he just that fucking stupid that he didn't realise he just called the game 'poncey' ten seconds ago? This guy is a fruit loop. But

I'm confident I'll get the better of him once I'm free. I take a peek at the microwave clock. 9:51. There's just over two hours left. The maths isn't looking that great for Vincent to get to three more banks and back before midday. I wonder how he's feeling right now. I bet he's still playing it cool. So many things could go wrong his end. I need to get myself out of this situation. I need to be the hero. At least I've got something to do today.

It's amazing how doing nothing breeds into more doing nothing. You would think that the less you have to do, the more inclined you would be to do something. That's not true at all. The less you do, the less you want to do. It's staggering how addictive doing nothing can become. I have three pairs of what I call apartment pants. They're not apartment pants at all. They're just pyjama bottoms but I don't want to call them that. Pyjamas sounds a little bit more pathetic than apartment pants. I wear at least one pair of them every day sitting on that big-ass L-shaped couch. For some reason the TV's always on – I don't know why. I barely watch anything on it. I spend a bizarre number of hours each week clicking through each of the hundred odd channels we have. It's the same mid-morning bullshit on every bloody channel. Well, in fact there are two kinds of programmes on TV during the first hours of the day. There's either a live show being presented by a couple of dicks like Piers Morgan and Susanna Reid beaming their fake smiles into our living rooms. Or else there are straight news channels. And news channels only offer up bad news. They thrive on bad news. War and worry is big business for the media. So, there's an option of either sickening positivity or dour negativity on our screens every morning and afternoon. I can never decide which one I want to watch. That's why I keep changing the channels. I guess it reflects real life in some way. Life is either rosy or it's downright shit. I've only ever been really high or really low in life. I'm not sure a happy medium exists. Same as TV – there's just nowhere else to turn to. I guess that's why I spend so much time on my laptop. And that's what has me depressed the most.

I have a routine for surfing the web that's rather sad. It even saddens me. As soon as I open the lid of my laptop I search for sports news. It's an old habit I can't kill off. Why would I? Just because I'm no longer in sports PR doesn't mean I can't be a fan. But searching news updates doesn't take that long and I inevitably end up using the Internet for the same reason most people do – porn. The amount of porn, and different types of porn, I see on the Internet continues to astound me. People really are into all kinds of sick shit. From dwarfs fisting each other's assholes, to men shitting in women's mouths, you really can search for anything you want, whenever you want. Imagine that. Somebody invented a window to the world where we could access any information and entertainment we could possibly ever think of. And what do we do? We watch porn more than anything. I'd only ever been interested in regular intercourse. I'd watch videos of handsome men fucking for hours until I felt the need to orgasm myself. Everyone has their own fantasies. I always loved rugged, handsome faces. That's all. If a porn video included a really good-looking guy, that would do for me. I like dark hair and cute faces. John Stamos would be my ideal man. Vincent thinks my celebrity crush is Piers Morgan. I've no idea where he got that from. I think I said Piers looked well once. Vincent took it as a compliment, because he thinks he looks like him. There is a resemblance. They're both blotchy and bloaty. Vincent has never really been my 'type' but I love him so much. I used to type 'Italian men' into the search menu on porn sites. That's just genuinely what I was into. But it's easy to get dragged into the murkier world of porn online. There are so many hidden links that drag you down trapdoors. I wonder what sort of sick shit this spotty prick is into.

He's sat still staring at the game. I can see him glance towards the coke every now and then. He's dying for another line. I don't blame him. I know how he feels. One line should always be enough but it never is. I'm glad I know this match goes into extra time because it's keeping his attention away from me. Getting my free hand across to my left leg is a bit more difficult, but I'm pretty certain I'm being discreet. The arm of the couch is blocking his view to me somewhat, so I continue to scratch away at the tape. I try to play out the eventual scenario in my head but it all depends on where his gun is placed once I peel myself free. It's currently back on the glass coffee table but it's been in and out of the waistband of his pants on quite a few occasions. I guess that's down to his anxiousness. If the gun is on the table when I'm free from the tape, I'll get to it first.

A plucking technique, rather than the scratching I was using earlier, seems to work better. Tiny fragments of the tape are peeling off into my fingernails. I look at the time again. 9:58. I give myself a time frame. I want to have this left ankle free by half ten before I begin to work on my left wrist. All going according to plan, I should be shoving the gun into that dumb ass's face before eleven.

09:55

Darragh

'POGBA MISS ANOTHER CHANCE THERE, YEAH?' I ASK THE FAG after I hang up the phone.

He sniffs an answer – almost as if he's laughing at me. Little cunt! I thought we were getting on just fine, too. He seems to be getting a little too quiet for my liking. But he can't get up to anything. He's just sitting there helpless. A rush fills my mind as I take in the fact that Vincent now has two mill in the boot of his car. Half of that is mine. That's unreal. I never thought I'd have that much money in me life. I'm literally a millionaire right now. My money just happens to be sitting in the trunk of a chauffeur-driven car rather than sittin' in my own bank account. But it's all fuckin mine. I think of that brilliant scene in *Goodfellas* where Ray Liotta opens his wardrobe to a fuck-load of designer suits, I guess that's what a millionaire gangster's life looks like. I think I'll buy one of those huge wardrobes and fill it with suits meself. I don't wear suits, but that doesn't matter. Maybe I'll start wearing 'em. I'll be a multi-millionaire, after all. I'll have to wait a while though. JR has told me I shouldn't flash the cash so soon after getting' me hands on it. He said we should both wait it out for around six months before spending. He knows his stuff. He has figured out every tiny piece of this jigsaw. He has both the brains and the brawn to be a perfect mob boss. I wish I was more like him. I hope he continues to teach me. By the time I'm his age, I'll be a fuckin mastermind in the criminal underworld. I wonder how old JR actually is. It's hard to put a number on him.

The Guards released a photofit of what the newspapers labelled the 'One-Punch Killer'. It looked nothing like me. I'm not sure if witnesses sent cops in the wrong direction in fear of The Boss; but surely the girl who was at the scene of the crime must have had a say in the image the police were putting out there. Perhaps it was too dark for her to remember what I looked like. The man in the photofit had the same colour hair as me but that was about it. I was so fuckin relieved to find out the cops had nothing to go on in their investigation. The Boss told me they were chasing shadows. He had a few contacts on the inside. He wasn't happy with me at all though. He didn't mind that I'd broken me duck but he was disappointed in how I did it. He kept saying I was really immature. And that accusation annoys me. It would annoy anyone. I kept apologising to him, but I wasn't even sure he was ever listening to me. I think the adrenaline I drowned in after the murder flicked a switch in me. I began to envisage killings almost every day. As I watch people, I can imagine I'm battering them to death. Not everybody I see, just when the moment takes me. It's normally men I imagine killing. Mostly smug men. But I never planned another murder for real until I met JR. The Boss told me to stay out of trouble for a while, so I kept meself to meself for a bit. My fascination with Netflix helped. I watched all five seasons of *Breaking Bad* in less than a week. I think there's over sixty episodes in that show. It was fuckin deadly. Aaron Paul's character is the bomb. I've never tried meth. It was never offered to me. I guess I probably would have tried it if someone did have some. All the boys I was hanging around with drank beer and snorted coke. That's all I've been introduced to over the years. It's fine by me. I love coke.

I'd fuckin love another line of Ryan's shit right now. But there's no need for me to do any more. I've done enough. I'll celebrate later. Ryan probably thinks I haven't noticed, but I can see him looking over to the clock on the microwave every few minutes. I don't mind. It's probably making him panic even more. I envisage blowin' his brains out yet again. Even if I was to do it now and walk away, I'd be a million euros richer. But there's more of that to come. Besides, I have no intention of swerving off course from JR's plan. I wonder what he's up to now. He never really told me exactly where he'd be for each bank robbery. I wonder how close to Vincent he's actually getting. I'm sure he's all okay. He knows how to swerve all the CCTV cameras. He even has an alibi. He sorted one out for me too. It's brilliant. I've left me mobile phone in me bedsit and my laptop programmed to log in to certain websites at certain times of the morning. JR is some genius. If we are ever caught for this in any way, shape or form then I can easily show proof I was at home all morning. The alibis are just a backup to the backup of a backup. They won't be needed at all. JR and me have this totally under control.

I take a look at the microwave clock meself. 10:03. I need to get this straight in me head. Vincent has three hours to rob four banks, yet one hour has passed and only one bank has been hit. That doesn't sound right. I wonder why JR hasn't mentioned this yet or why he hasn't been getting on at me about it. Surely Vincent is getting close to Camden Street now. The next I'll hear from him will be when he exits there. He'd want to hurry the fuck up. Time is ticking. I turn my eyes to look at Ryan sittin' in his chair like a pussy. Bang! I imagine his brains splat all over the window behind him again. This is really gonna happen. I can feel it. It'll be my third murder. I guess that'll make me a serial killer.

10:05

Vincent

I TURN THE AIR CONDITIONING BACK UP TO FULL AGAIN JUST AS John turns into Camden Street. I don't fell as panicky anymore, but I just fancy one last blast of cold air before meeting Jonathan. I look calm in the reflection of the car window. I can see the ugliness of Camden Street behind my reflection. Camden Street is a typical example of tradition meeting contemporary to create ugliness. That mess of architecture is ripe around Dublin city. Some people love it. I don't. I love old-school Dublin. The city used to be full of character, but these modern buildings take some of that character away. I mean, it's fine around Sir John Rogerson's Quay where I live because it's full of modern buildings, but here, on Camden Street, they look out of place. The ACB branch on Lower Camden Street is almost directly across from Cassidy's pub, right next to Concern Charity's headquarters. The board of directors for some reason leased half of that new building and then replaced the clear windows with blacked-out glass. Their reasoning behind it was so people couldn't see inside from the outside. But you also can't see the outside from the inside because the windows they ordered were too dark. Fuckin' idiots! That was the decision of these young board members who earn a combined annual salary of almost a billion dollars. I genuinely think most of the multi-millionaires I've met through my life, and there's been a few, have all been a bit thick. Maybe they're good at playing thick and that's why they're so successful or maybe, as I suspect, they've just been fuckin' lucky.

The board of directors used to be perfect at ACB. They ran all the banks like clockwork and they had a real eagerness to agree on decisions. That was their best asset. But the current board take an age to make any decision at all. And they keep me at a huge distance. I used to be more involved with the important decisions made over in the States, but not anymore. There's one little spoilt prick on the board, Clyde Sneyd, who is only twenty-eight years old. I used to be close with his old man, Bernard. But Bernard's offspring has no respect for me whatsoever; I'm not sure he even has respect for himself. It seems he lives a very eccentric life in New York that I'm not sure even he's happy with. He brings that depressive attitude to his work. Sometimes it has taken the board over a week to even get him by phone. It's not just him, though. None of 'em seem to give a flying fuck. They think they're all heroes for taking the bank through the economic crash. It's a bit sad, really. Everyone else knows I'm the reason ACB pulled through in Ireland. They're a mismatch of spoilt personalities. It's such a shame. I genuinely couldn't give a shit anymore.

John doesn't always get a parking spot right outside the Camden Street branch but there's one available today. It allows me to take in the sorry building as we come to a stop. I often chuckle to myself looking at the blacked-out glass with the ACB logo flying proud above it. How the fuck can they be proud of this shit hole? Jonathan won't have known

I've pulled up. He can't see out of the building! I need to head in as quickly as I can. My palms aren't even sweaty about this one. Tchaikovsky's been a big help. I've barely thought about reality on the way over here.

Ryan said he fell in love with me when I sorted out his career path, but I'm pretty sure the fact that I moved him into my brand-new penthouse helped too. We were both high on love and cocaine for the first two years we were together. I bought the penthouse from the building plans but not on a whim. I've never regretted it. ACB's mortgage expert, Dave Cauley, put me on to it. He said the area it was being built in was an up-and-coming trendy neighbourhood. His estimation then was that the penthouse would be worth almost two million in ten years' time. That was a bit inaccurate. The value of the penthouse was €1,100,000 a decade on. It's worth €1,200,000 now. It's still a great investment. I bought it for €650,000 and now only owe the bank a little over two hundred thousand. Nice. I guess that makes me a millionaire, in bricks and mortar at least. But nobody's told my bank account. I earn a quarter of a million a year, but you wouldn't think it because my money somehow seems to drift in and then quickly out of my bank account every month. All I've really got from all my years of hard work is the penthouse. I allowed Ryan to have a tiny bit of input into the finishing touches, but it is, and always has been, my design. I've got better taste than Ryan. He's not really into that sort of thing anyway. As long as he has a large TV screen, he's happy. I don't know why he insisted on a massive TV, though. He spends most of his time looking into his twenty-one-inch laptop screen. We used to host mammoth parties when we first moved in. I probably got carried away with the socialising aspect of life back then. Maybe I was a bit too old for it. But I wouldn't swap those days for anything. I'm sure there were lots of people who turned up for sessions at our place that neither I nor Ryan knew. The penthouse would be crammed some Saturday nights. Ryan often rounded up dozens of students from DCU and I'd invite some of the bank staff over on the odd occasion. The students used to bring the greatest cocaine anybody could ever have snorted. Not even Colombia could manufacture a purer dose. Three of them had set up a lab in their cheap student accommodation and were cashing in big time. They had their student loans paid for within two months of creating and selling their own coke. It was great while it lasted. But after a couple of years I started to feel a little down. It wasn't depression or anything but I knew I had to give up the partying lifestyle. I'm proud that I made a quick decision to cut down on the drugs and alcohol cold turkey. Ryan didn't seem to mind too much either. I think it was getting on top of us both. He had just got a job at Wow PR and wanted to take his career seriously. I was very proud of him, if a little fearful. We were finally two grown-ups in a serious relationship. Our lives became less fun, but boring can be rewarding in its own way.

I can see my own reflection in the bank's dark windows as soon as John lets me out of the car. I stare at myself walking towards the entrance, the two briefcases hanging from my arms. Somebody's just cut the grass on the small lawn in front of the building. That smell's eternal. The scent of freshly cut grass takes everybody back to their childhood. I let out a small sigh of warm air as I wait to be buzzed through the first door. The glass in the small entryway is clear, so I can finally see the staff at work. They're certainly not hard at it though because there are currently six members of staff and only two customers inside. I stare down towards the back offices to see if I can spot the seventh member of this team. Somebody must have told him I'm coming through the second door because Jonathan wheels out of his office on his chair to offer me a big smile.

'Hi, Mr Butler,' calls out one of the junior members of staff as I enter. I can't think of her name, despite sanctioning her employment about a month ago. I offer her a nod in return.

'Vincent!' Jonathan calls out a little bit louder than normal.

'Hey, Jonathan,' I say offering him my handcuffed hand as we make our way towards each other.

'Everything in order?' I ask before the small talk can begin.

'Yeah, yeah. You mean for the collection?'

'Of course I mean for the collection, Jonathan. I told you I needed it all as soon as poss—'

'Yeah, yeah,' he interrupts me. 'I have all the paperwork ready.'

He wraps one of his palms over the top of my left shoulder and practically escorts me into his office.

'Everythin' alrigh'?' he whispers to my annoyance.

I don't show that in my answer though. But I am pissed off that he's asking questions. This was supposed to be an easy branch.

'Of course, I'm just in a hurry. I can't believe Michelle's got so low. I could do without this today, to be honest,' I say, justifying why I'm coming across agitated.

'Ah … it happens,' he says. 'Not to the tune of two mill often. But it happens.'

'You've got a tan,' I say, changing the subject. It wasn't exactly seamless.

'Ah, the golf course does wonders for a tan,' he replies.

I didn't say out loud what I was thinking, but I would love to see Jonathan's reaction if he knew I was aware he uses sunbeds. Belinda told me. Jonathan is a nice guy, but he is definitely the sort that thinks he's a little more successful than he really is. There's plenty of these guys around Dublin. They're harmless. He likes to talk the talk. I don't really mind that to be honest. I think he's good at what he does. Just not as good as he thinks he is.

'Here ya go,' he says, handing me a pen. The paperwork is all ready on his desk. Perfect!

'Thanks, Jonathan,' I reply, offering him a wink. I could be out of here in the next twenty minutes.

10:15

Jack

I'M ABSOLUTELY SWEATIN'. I'VE PACED HERE WAY TOO BRISKLY for this kinda heat. I hope my walk didn't look suspicious. If anything, it looked nothing like my normal walk, so that's good, I suppose. Nobody would have been able to recognise me. I keep thinking people are suspicious, but it's just a pinch of paranoia. It's understandable I'd be slightly paranoid this morning, even though I'm one hundred per cent confident my plan will go perfectly. No one has any damn clue that this robbery is taking place. Two million is already gone and not one person in this city is any the wiser. My heart rate slows the more I think about how soundproof the whole plan is. I don't walk directly onto Camden Street. I walk up Harcourt Street and turn at the corner of the Bleeding Horse pub so I can stare down at the ACB branch. It's an odd-looking building. The first two floors are surrounded with black glass while the top floor has clear windows. It looks like a stubby pint of Guinness. I place myself at the entrance of a large apartment building with the phone to my ear. I don't look suspicious here at all. It's a massive apartment complex built over four buildings. There are so many people living in this place that nobody knows who their neighbours are. I could easily be one of them. I'm out of sight of the CCTV and I'm blending in with the passers-by. I planned this position months ago. I can see Vincent's car parked outside. I wonder what time he arrived at. It couldn't have been much before ten o'clock.

'Hey,' calls out a woman from inside the apartment building.

'Hi,' I reply, turning around. Holy shit! It's Antoinette. I'm staring at Karyn's cousin as she struggles to open her mailbox in the hallway.

'All good with you?' she asks. She can't possibly know it's me. Can she?

Harry and Yvonne cut their visits down to roughly one a month. The intimidation Harry used to invoke in me receded dramatically after Karyn's passing. He never mentioned business to me, but would often ask how I was getting on at the factory. If I hadn't flat-out refused more money from him years ago, he'd still be offering it to me now, I'm sure. I think Harry's a bit embarrassed to offer me money now. He totally understood that I wanted to fend for Frank on my own terms. Myself, Harry and Yvonne would sit and talk about golf for hours while Frank played around our feet. Yvonne's a bigger golfer than Harry, and probably me if I'm being honest. She'd be able to call Rory McIlroy's swing changes before I could. She had a real eye for the strategy of the sport and would often amaze me with her insights. Yvonne was a very interesting woman. She loved being a gangster's moll. She thrived on it. But I'd mostly describe her as having a decent heart. She loved Frank as if he were her own grandchild. She either really liked me or felt sorry for me. I could never quite figure out which it was. I think we got on well. Yvonne's only eight years older than I am. Harry has a good sixteen years on her. I'm pretty sure Yvonne's Dublin accent grew stronger the more she spent time with Harry. It was like she grew into her role as a gangster's wife. It was the only irritating thing about her, but Karyn and I used to laugh about it. A lot of men would probably find Yvonne attractive. I never did. She's not natural looking at all. But she's Harry's type and that's all that matters. Their marriage is still going strong after all these years and that doesn't surprise me one bit. I was impressed that Harry didn't mind Margarite being around Frank so much. He did ask me if we were an item at one stage, suggesting it in a jokey manner, but I answered him honestly. I also re-emphasised the point to Yvonne the next time they called over just so they knew for sure that I hadn't replaced Karyn. I used to get odd pangs of paranoia about Harry, but on many occasions, he let it be known that he appreciated what I was doing with my life. He said being in his line of business wasn't obligatory. When I asked one day if it would be obligatory for his grandson, he looked disappointed in me.

'He's your son,' he said. 'You raise him how you want. He's my grandson and I will love him whatever he does with his life.'

I felt instant relief when he said that to me. It was all I'd ever worried about. But days later the words 'whatever he does' started to reignite my paranoia. Did he mean Frank would be offered a choice?

I grunt a reply at Antoinette which was meant to sound like a polite way of saying 'I'm not interested in talking'. But she is still behind me going through her mail. She's changed somewhat. You would know she's middle-aged but she's still pretty. She has deep lines either side of her eyes but the eyes themselves haven't lost their sparkle. They're not unlike Karyn's. I had no idea she lived here. My heart is now racing quicker than at any moment it had done this morning. I keep playing what she said to me over and over in my head. *Hey.*

And *All good with you?* Does she know it's me? She can't. Can she? My whole face is covered. And she barely even saw my face. She greeted me from behind. Shit! Perhaps that's where I'm recognisable. From behind. I didn't do anything to disguise myself from the back. Is my back even recognisable? Maybe I'm going mad. What if she does know it's me? The whole plan is fucked. Too many questions are spinning around my head. I feel like I need to talk to her, to find out for sure she doesn't know who I am. I check my watch. 10:21. I doubt Vincent's exit is imminent. Surely he'll be another ten minutes at least. I think I'll have to talk to Antoinette. I can't let her go not knowing for sure whether she recognised me or not. I take a bite of my bottom lip. I have seconds to make up my mind, then I find myself spinning towards her.

'Is your name Lisa?' I say, changing the pitch in my voice. Antoinette stares back at me.

'Sorry?' she asks. Shit! I've to repeat that.

'Is your name Lisa?' I reply. I think the pitch sounded the same.

'Oh.' She giggles. 'Sorry, I didn't hear you the first time. No, my name's not Lisa. Are you looking for somebody in particular?'

I feel relieved. She has no idea she's talking to me.

'Oh no. My neighbour upstairs is called Lisa and I have yet to meet her. I thought you were her. Sorry.' Brilliant. I have nothing to worry about. And I nailed the pitch in my voice again.

I hope she doesn't want to keep talking. I stare out of the apartment archway looking down the street as if I'm waiting on somebody to come and pick me up. Antoinette hasn't said anything in reply. She just offered a smile before turning her attention back to the envelopes in her hands. I can still hear her ruffling paperwork in the background. She must get a huge amount of mail. Or maybe she's just back from holidays and is getting her mail for the first time in a week or two. She looks glowing, she might have been away in the sun. To relieve myself of the discomfort, I pretend to make a call, surprising myself with my improvisational skills.

'Hey, sweetheart,' I say. Pause. 'Can't wait to see you.' Pause. 'I know it is going to be a long time. But just think how much it's going to be worth it.' I pause for ages this time, taking a glance to see if Antoinette has left the building. Shit. Maybe I'm pausing way too long now. But who am I pausing for? I look around and see nobody in earshot. It doesn't stop me from finishing my charade. 'Okay, I love you. Ciao.' I even pretend to hang up with a fake press of a button. My finger misses the phone by about two whole inches. It's unusual I make myself laugh. But I did this time. I'm still smiling when I finally look back at the apartment entrance and see Antoinette heading straight towards me with a smile of her own. Bollocks!

10:15

Vincent

JONATHAN SEEMS AS EAGER AS I AM TO READ THROUGH THE paperwork. I'm supposed to be following along as he mumbles the jargon, but I can't help but look around his office. He thinks highly of himself. But it doesn't show on the walls of his workplace. It's a very muted office, painted what I could only call magnolia. It's probably some other bland shade of cream with a fancy name like pertwee off white or something or other. But I know it as magnolia. The only piece of artwork hanging on his wall is in contrast to the wall itself. He told me before who painted it, but I can't recall the name. I like the painting. It's like a 3D mix-match of colours that seems to form an eyeball, I think. I like how the blue evolves into purple down the bottom before it meets with red. But that's about as far as my art knowledge goes. I like colours, that's about it. The only photograph in the room sits on his desk. I can only see the back of the frame from here, but I know the photo. I've seen it before. It's a family portrait of Jonathan and his wife Sabrina with their two sons.

'Two million is a huge amount, Vincent,' he inevitably

says to me as he gets down to the finer details of the paperwork.

'You're telling me?' I reply, rolling my eyes before taking a look at my watch. He knows too well that I just want to get a move on. We've both signed two pages so far.

'Don't worry,' he gurns. 'I'll get you into the vault soon.'

I like Jonathan. He doesn't run his branch as effectively as Chelle because he's too concerned with being liked rather than being successful. But he still runs a steady ship here at Camden Street. The only thing that's ever really pissed me off about him is his fascination with Belinda. I wonder what she's up to now as I take a genuine glance at my watch. This time I actually want to know what it reads. 10:17. I wonder if Belinda's finished sorting my paperwork into alphabetical order. Perhaps she hasn't even started. Even if Jonathan gets me in and out of his vault in the next twenty minutes, I'd still be behind time. But I'm catching up. As Jonathan continues to murmur through the paperwork, I reach for the frame on his desk and turn it my way. I don't ask him how Sabrina, Kai and Taylor are, I just assume they're okay. I've often wondered if Sabrina really is okay. I think she's besotted with her two sons, but I wonder if she knows her husband isn't totally devoted to her. Jonathan and Sabrina have been together since they were both twenty-one. They met in their final year at UCD. I think couples tend to stay in the same mentality they are in when they first meet. Jonathan is a mature, professional man and Sabrina is very bright and articulate. But they seem to rub each other up the wrong way like twenty-one-year-olds do when they're together. They're still petty to each other. I've often heard Jonathan being short with Sabrina on the phone and have observed them at office get-togethers in a huff with each other. I'm sure Jonathan was very much in love with Sabrina once upon a time. Maybe he still is, but he doesn't show it – not to her. I'm not sure how she feels. I know Jonathan has cheated on her in the past. I watched him leave clubs with strange girls many years ago and he once hooked up with Ryan's cousin at one of the parties at our penthouse. Given a chance, I'm sure he'd fuck Belinda without a second's thought. But I do wonder if he'd ever leave his wife and kids for her. That's played on my mind often.

'They're keeping well,' he says to me.

'I didn't ask,' I joke back. 'You nearly done?'

'Jeez, you really are in a hurry. You okay?'

'I'll be happy when this morning's over with.'

'Ah, one of those days, huh?' Jonathan replies. 'You, eh … you just want me to sign this?'

'Jonathan,' I say really slowly, allowing myself time to think. 'Read through the bloody paperwork for me, let's sign all the pages and then get me out of here. Please.'

I'd love to skip all the obligatory reading and for us to get into the vault, but I have to toe the professional line. He knows I'm a little more tense than usual and I've let him know I'm in a hurry. I can't risk evoking any further suspicion in him.

'I'll be five more minutes,' he says, flicking through the rest of the papers. As I stand up to impatiently pace around Jonathan's office, I feel the cheap mobile phone buzz in my pocket. I immediately dismiss any notion of answering it, and then decide I can't take any more of Jonathan's murmurings.

'Sorry, Jon,' I say. 'Need to take this. Keep on reading. Finish it off.'

I walk outside his office and hit the green button on the phone.

'Gimme one second,' I say before palming the phone and pacing through the bank floor towards the exit. I don't want anyone to see this old thing. I wait until I'm buzzed through the first door before putting it back to my ear.

'I'm just in the Camden Street branch, what's up?'

'Don't "what's up" me, fag,' says Ryan's captor. 'What the fuck's going on? It's coming towards half past ten – you've gone beyond time.'

A rage fills up inside me.

'What the fu …' I say, and stop myself. 'Listen … I can't do anything more than I am. I can't make this process quicker. This is just how—'

'They're your fuckin' banks. Get the eight mill back here by midday or I'll splatter Ryan's brains all over this place.'

'I'll get back with the eight mill,' I reply, trying to catch my breath as I'm finally buzzed out of the second door. 'Forget about the time. I'll get it back once the whole process is done. Let me—'

'Midday,' he snaps down the phone at me. 'Get it back by midday or that's fucking it, boy.'

'I'm doing the best I can. Just … just … please, extend the time by another half an hour and I'll definitely be back,' I plead.

'Mid-fuckin'-day!'

I stare at the phone after he's hung up. This guy sounds like a lunatic. Fear engulfs me for the first time since I left Chelle. I'm not sure why I've been so relaxed over the last half an hour. I pace slowly back to the bank's entrance taking in my reflection once again. The reality of the whole situation flows through my mind as I stare into my own eyes for what seems like an age, until the mobile phone buzzing in my hand snaps me out of it.

'I'll ring you back in two minutes with an answer to your request,' he raps in his mongrel accent. Then he hangs up again.

I've no idea what to do. Do I go back inside to Jonathan

or do I wait out here? I take a look towards my car but John isn't paying any attention to me. All I can do is stare past my reflection into this horrible black glass. If anyone could see out, they'd see a confused man. I remove my glasses and wipe my face to try to defuse my current state of mind. I wish I was throwing handfuls of cold water on my face. I need to chill out. I breathe slowly to stave off any signs of panic.

Think, Vincent, think.

I try to focus on the positive, but my stomach is starting to turn. So much for this being the easy branch to take money from. Jonathan was eager to get me in and out as quickly as possible and everything was going smoothly. Now I must look a little panicked and out of sorts. Jonathan will be wondering why I left at the tail end of a contract read-through. Especially after I'd just insisted we must follow protocol. I'm wondering why I left too. I wonder if he's finished reading through the paperwork. My phone doesn't seem to be ringing back. I'm not sure staring at it will help. The longer I stay out here, the more suspicious I look. Rather than think it, I say it to my reflection: 'What the fuck am I doing?' I can't stay out here much longer. I decide to stroll back into the bank, get the money out of the vault and then deal with any deadline discussions when I finally exit. I refocus my stare to look at myself one final time before heading for the door. I can see Jonathan eyeballing me after I get through the first entrance. He must have been on his way out to me. As I stand trapped inside the two doorways I don't know where to look.

What must Jonathan be thinking right now?

I would never leave a withdrawal read-through before it's finished. I can't bring myself to look at him. Then I hear the second door buzz me through.

'Let's go, boss,' he says, winking at me. 'Paperwork's done. Let's get you that money.'

10:25

Darragh

NEITHER OF US SEEMS TO BE TALKIN'. THAT'S FINE BY ME. I'M happy to just watch the match as my high wears off. It's looking like it will go into extra time. Both legs have finished one all. I only learned what 'legs' meant in football a half an hour ago. It's when a knockout is played over two different games, one in each team's home ground. Still don't get why they call it 'legs', like. But that's all the chatter me and Ryan have had over the past while. Small talk about football. I think the sport is winning me over again. I'm willing United to score. As the referee blows for another foul, I take the mobile phone from the table to make sure it hasn't been ringing while I was transfixed on the game. I would have heard it surely, but I am high, I guess. I don't want to miss another JR call. He'd go fuckin nuts. There's been no activity on the phone. I decide to palm it rather than place it back on the glass table just in case there is a call. I'll be able to feel it vibrate. I look at the clock on the microwave again. 10:26. I expect Vincent will be another fifteen minutes at least in the Camden Street branch. A distant ringtone makes me raise my eyebrow. I look to Ryan to see if he heard anything. Then at the TV. Maybe it was a noise from the football supporters? Then I realise the phone in my hand is dialling out. Shit! I lift it up to see that I am dialling two. That's a relief. I'm ringing Vincent, not JR. I don't want JR to think I'm losing it. I've no idea what I am going to say. Hanging up crosses me mind but that would look suspicious. He probably won't answer anyway.

'Gimme one second,' says Vincent abruptly down the line as I hear him walking.

What's going on?

'I'm just in the Camden Street branch, what's up?' he finally says.

'Don't "what's up" me, fag,' I bark back at him. Cheeky cunt. 'What the fuck's going on? It's coming towards half past ten – you've gone beyond time.'

He almost swears at me. He must be stressin' out big time.

'Listen ... I can't do anything more than I am. I can't make this process quicker. This is just how ... how—' he says, stuttering.

'They're your fuckin banks. Get the eight mill back here by midday or else I'll splatter Ryan's brains all over this place,' I reply cool as ice. I really am cut out for this kinda shit. I'm a natural gangster.

'I'll get back with the eight mill,' Vincent whines. 'Forget about the time. I'll get it back once the whole process is done. Let me—'

'Midday,' I snap. 'Get it back by midday or that's fuckin it.'

He stutters some other whiney bollocks before I repeat meself with a firmer tone.

'Mid-fuckin-day!' Then I hang up.

It might have sounded cool. Or maybe it was a little too dramatic. I'm not sure. I take notice of Ryan out of the corner of me eye, but he's not showing any reaction to the call at all. I swing my head at the microwave again. 10:29. There's no way Vincent can get in and out of all three remaining banks in the next hour and a half. I call him back immediately.

'I'll ring ya in two minutes with an answer to your request,' I say much more coolly before hanging up again.

Then I let out a sigh. JR will probably want to kill me if I bother him with requests from Vincent. But I think this is somethin' we need to talk about. If we want all eight million, we may have to give Vincent an extra half an hour. JR doesn't take long answering. Like me, he must have his phone in his hand waiting for it to ring.

'He's not out already, right?' he asks.

I decide to put my case forward straight away. 'No. Listen. Take your time to think about this. He's doing a good job but he needs more time.'

JR tries to stop my flow but I'm determined to make sure we give ourselves the best shot at getting all the money. Nobody knows more than I do just how much JR will want to stick to his plan.

'Think about it, JR. He's only in bank number two and it's almost ten-thirty. We can get all eight mill if we just give him a bit more time.'

'I'll think about it,' he says.

Great! JR has listened to me. He hangs up, leaving me grinning and almost skipping around the kitchen table thingy. We're a proper partnership, JR and me. He kinda needs to hurry up thinkin' bout it though. Vincent is waiting on me to call back.

I'd exhausted all the decent Netflix shows within a couple of months. It got boring. I wasn't sure how long The Boss wanted me to chill out but I was certain the cops were nowhere near finding the One-Punch Killer. All this lay-low bullshit was beginning to bug me. I'd call Smack every day pleading with him to speak to The Boss on my behalf, to tell him I was bored and eager to get back to work. But I'd rarely hear anythin' back. And after a while Smack's phone had a habit of dialling all the way through to his voicemail. I was starting to lose the will to live. I knew The Boss wouldn't be happy if I turned up at his club unannounced. I'd been told to stay away until he contacted me, but I couldn't sit around doing nothin' for the rest of me life. As soon as I walked into his club, though, I knew I was doing the wrong thing. I knew exactly where he'd be sitting, up in the back booth where he always is. I could feel, not see, the faces in the club staring at me. Before I got to his table, Smack raced towards me.

'What the fuck you doin' here?' he asked.

'I need to see him, Smack. I haven't heard a thing back from you and—'

'He'll fuckin kill you, Darragh. He told you to stay away. Trust me, for your own good, turn around and walk back out that door.'

I should've listened to him. I knew he was right but for some reason I tried to plead with Smack to let me talk to The Boss. But just as I was being pushed towards the exit, The Boss noticed me. He called on Smack to bring me towards him. Within a split second of me getting to the booth, I was thrown sideways by The Boss and pinned to the red leather couch. He had both his hands wrapped firmly around my neck.

'I told you never to come here, didn't I?'

I couldn't answer.

'You little fuck. Don't bring your shit near me. You hear?'

I felt like cryin'. This was heartbreak for me. A break-up. A break-up of the only relationship I ever wanted to have. I think The Boss could see my sadness. After releasing his grip on me, he clipped my face with the palm of his hand.

'Follow me, kid,' he said. I walked slowly behind him until we reached the back porch of the club. With one flick of his head The Boss cleared the porch of the two security men who were guarding the back entrance. He sighed heavily before speaking. I took it as a sign his heart was a little broken too.

'We can't have you involved, Darragh. There was heat on us over that killing. I had to stave it off and in doing so I agreed to distance myself from you. You know you can't bring any heat near me and your fuckin freelance killing, nothing to do with my business, can't come near me. If I order a fuckin hit it's because I know everything is good to go. You can't go around killing people, Darragh. You fucked up.'

I hung my head in shame. He was right. I knew I fucked up.

'Stay here,' I was told. I didn't lift my chin from my chest in all the time I was alone in that porch. I was too saddened to even think about what might happen next. When The Boss burst back through the front door, he headed straight towards me.

'Twenty thousand,' he said shoving a wad of notes into my hands. 'Best of luck, Darragh. I enjoyed working with you.'

'I … I …' I stuttered.

'I enjoyed working with you,' he repeated, before going back inside.

I must have looked like a lost puppy. When I was outside the club moments later in the pouring rain, I thought about throwing the wad of notes back into the porch in anger. I'd never felt such a depression.

I can't pace around this kitchen table thingy any longer. I stare at the phone in my hand again. I need to know if the time is going to be extended. Vincent is waiting to hear back from me.

Ring me, JR, for fuck's sake.

10:30

Jack

'I think Lisa's the woman with the red hair,' says Antoinette, pacing towards me. I can't believe I'm looking into this face again. It's been years. She has no idea this is me. 'Are you on floor four?' she asks, not going away.

Now I have to remember the pitch in my fake voice again.

'No,' I say, missing the pitch by some distance. I hold six fingers up into her face. It's terribly rude. I feel really bad. Nobody should be rude to Antoinette. She's too lovely. But I can't bring myself to talk again.

'Oh, six,' she says offering another smile. This is so awkward. A huge silence fills the two yards between us. 'Okay, have a good day, sir,' she says, trying to defuse the awkwardness before walking off.

I cringe, but I let out a sigh of relief as she paces away. I know from her face that she didn't recognise me at all. I never should have engaged in conversation with her in the first place. But I had to know for sure she wasn't aware of who I was. I watch her walk in the opposite direction down Charlotte Way and stretch my bottom jaw in some sorrow. That's the last time I'll ever see her. I look at the buildings across the street and realise it will be the last time I'll ever see them too. I'll miss Dublin when I'm gone. I've equally loved and hated Dublin for as far back as I can remember. I'll miss the city centre more than anything but I've become a bit bored with it. Dublin used to be the prettiest little town, but it seems to have been swamped with homeless people and meth users over the past six or seven years. I don't know what happened, but overnight the druggies seemed to appear in the streets again. It seemed to coincide with the economic crash. The streets of Dublin are ugly now. I get a little embarrassed thinking of all the tourists from all over the world coming to Dublin only to be approached by a few skangers off their heads, asking their usual question: 'Any change, bud?' I won't miss that. I will miss the new modern architecture in Dublin, even though some of the buildings lack real character. I'll miss the thick Dublin accent. I love it. I'll miss spring here. Dublin's at its prettiest between April and June. I'll miss Pat Murray. He's the only employee from the factory that I've stayed in touch with after I left a few years ago. I'll miss his wise words. But I'm eager to take my life in a totally different direction. The excitement I've been feeling about this move is huge. But today, I'm anxious. My whole life – our whole lives – hang on what happens over the next ninety minutes. I'm still reminiscing about this old city when my phone rings. It's Darragh.

'He's not out already, is he?' I ask, staring back at the bank entrance.

'No. Listen. Take your time to think about this. He is doin' a good job but he needs more time.' Darragh's never spoken to me like this. I'm taken aback.

'Darragh…' I interject. But the kid is determined to keep talking.

I already know I'm not giving Vincent more time. But as Darragh continues to plead with me, I decide to play along, to keep him sweet. I don't want him feeling dejected. He needs to feel like he has some sort of control over this heist too.

'I'll think about it,' I say. Now Darragh sounds like he's the one taken aback. But it's a good tactic from me. It keeps his boredom at bay.

I can't believe I'm going to be a multi-millionaire in the next couple of hours. I don't necessarily want to be super rich. Wearing a Rolex watch or driving a Ferrari doesn't interest me one bit. I just want to see out the rest of my days in the most comfortable manner possible. We're going to have so much fun.

I remember the first time I went to Italy. I pleaded with the factory to allow me to take three weeks off work one summer when Frank just turned thirteen. I figured a trip around Europe would help broaden his mind. My boss at the factory was always good to me. I concocted an itinerary that would see us take in London, Rome and then Paris. We cut our Paris trip short by a few days because we loved Rome so much. It's steeped in history and really helps put life into perspective. Frank wasn't as amazed as I was, but I was very conscious of this precious time in our lives. This was our summer – the boys on tour. I set initial plans in motion for us both to move to Rome on a permanent basis but it just didn't make any sense. Neither of us could speak Italian, and Frank was still years from completing school. We'd have to wait. I don't need to wait much longer. In a couple months' time I'll be sipping expensive wine on a rooftop bar overlooking the ancient city.

Vincent shouldn't be much longer in this branch. John is waiting patiently for him outside. I take a look at the screen on the old phone. 10:36. I should ring Darragh back and give him the bad news, but I'll word it so that he feels as if I've taken his concerns on board and that I view him as a genuine partner in crime.

'Hey, JR,' he says, answering the phone rather quickly.

'Listen, Darragh. I've had a long think about this. I understand where you're coming from and I think you did the right thing talking to me about it. But you and I have planned this for so long and I think the only proper thing to do is to abide by the plans we drew up early on. We cannot go beyond the deadline. Not just today, but in any robbery we make from here on. We need to be strict.'

'I understand,' he replies.

I thought he'd be disappointed, but he's not. He's probably buzzing because I mentioned future robberies. He's often talked to me about the future, about being included over the long term. I think being a gangster is all he's ever wanted to be. He used to be involved with Alan Keating's gang a few years ago, until they let him down. He needs an excuse to be relevant. I'm his excuse right now.

'So, if it comes to midday and I order you to kill Ryan, what are you gonna do?' I ask in a tone similar to how a teacher speaks to a student in secondary school.

'Kill Ryan,' he says.

Correct answer.

'Exactly. Me and you, buddy, we're gonna be the most feared gangsters in the whole of Ireland. But we must stick to our plan, okay?'

'You got it, JR. You got it.'

10:35

Vincent

'Yep, two mill again,' I say, having counted the bundles of notes for the second time.

'Okay, one more time each,' Jonathan replies with a sigh.

He's going through this as quickly as he can. I really need to get a move on. I haven't checked the time in a while but it must be gone half ten by now. I swipe all two hundred bundles of notes towards his side of the counter and let out a sigh of my own.

'One, two, three, four,' he tries to whisper.

'Do it quietly, Jon, will you? My head's a little sensitive today.'

'Sorry, Vincent.'

It's very warm in this vault. It's a larger vault than the one on Nassau Street but this one is cooped up in a basement, and the air conditioning is as useful as a fart. The contrast in my anxiety is confusing me. It's up and down. When I arrived at Nassau Street I was really nervous and then I settled somewhat when I got to the vault. This time around it's been the complete opposite. I was relaxed coming into this branch but now my head is starting to feel faint again. It could be the heat but I've been feeling weak since I was outside fifteen minutes ago. The little fuck hasn't rung me back to extend the deadline. I'll probably be another five minutes in here, at least. It's going to be close to eleven when I reach Church Street. I really am cutting it close.

'Yeah, two hundred there,' Jon says, scooping as many bundles of notes as he can in one go towards me. Time for me to count to two hundred … again. Then we're done.

Our 'grown-up relationship' lasted several years. We were both happy with our lives, even if everything was vastly different to what we got up to when we started dating. Ryan was living the high of being involved in sports media. He'd get to hang out with big-name stars on odd occasions. I'd join him now and then. I'm kinda fascinated with celebrities. Even celebrities I didn't know existed. I'd often stand at the back of the room during press conferences tiddling the Press badge Ryan had signed over to me. The buzz from that lasted a couple of months. It had already dissipated in Ryan. He said he only enjoyed working in media when he was working as a junior account manager. As soon as he started working with the professionals, he realised how pointless his career actually was.

'It doesn't matter one fuckin' jot,' he'd say to me after another boring day at the agency. 'Football. Rugby. Who gives a shit?'

'You do,' I'd respond, trying to cheer him up.

I knew how he was feeling. I was starting to hate my own job but I didn't confide in Ryan. I knew he got bored any time I mentioned work. All the great men I admired at ACB started to resign in the wake of the global recession. I couldn't blame them. They'd had enough. I miss those men so much. They were real men. Not like their offspring. It was a huge compliment to be told I would be kept on and even promoted during the cuts. But I found it difficult to be excited about it. My lack of excitement didn't affect my work ethic though. Motivated to make the most of the four remaining Irish branches, I managed to get my way with all four assistant manager appointments, initially – making sure I was working with people I wanted to work with. There's nothing worse than working with people you detest. That's why Noah Voss's appointment – over my head last year – really pissed me off. I don't want to be working with fuckin' Christians. I was starting to feel content with my life again when the branches began to pull out of trouble. Inch by inch, we helped all four of them improve. But just as I was starting to feel good about myself again, Ryan's depression started to spiral out of control. I knew it was work related and insisted he hand his notice in at Wow, but he wasn't having any of it. Months later, I added two and two together. The little fucker was having an affair on me. I wasn't sure who was banging him, but it certainly wasn't me! Our sex life was dead – or perhaps barely breathing was the more appropriate way to phrase it back then. I'd give Ryan a good blowjob for his birthday. That was practically our sex life. I knew what was going on, but I decided to turn a blind eye. If he left me, he'd lose everything. On his shitty little PR wage, he wouldn't be able to afford an apartment one-eighth the size of ours. I wasn't actually in denial about his affair – I knew he was just having a small fling and it would end with him crying back into my arms. I was right. Of course I was right. I usually am. He told me, with tears rolling down his face one morning, that he couldn't face going into work.

'Fuck it!' I said to him. 'Fuck that place. You're better than that. Hand your notice in. I'm going to buy you a new laptop and you can work from home. All those book ideas you have … let's get one of them written, okay? You are now an author, you hear me?' I said, wiping a tear from his eye.

He smiled and nodded a reply. I knew I'd got my Ryan

back there and then. We could return to being the popular couple everybody envied again. I'd got my way once more. I knew I could keep an eye on Ryan if he was at home all the time. What trouble could he get up to cooped up in our penthouse on his own all day?

'Yep, two hundred,' I say, winking at Jonathan. We pack a briefcase each with one hundred bundles before I wrap my arms around his shoulders.

'Thanks, Jonathan,' I say, surprising him.

'Gee, you alright?' he asks me. I'd never hugged him before in my life.

'Long morning,' I reply. 'Long morning.'

What the fuck was I thinking?

I must be emotional. I handcuff the two cases to my wrists and bid Jonathan farewell. The phone begins to buzz in my pocket just as I'm exiting the vault. I decide I'll ring the fucker back when I'm outside.

'I'll give you a shout this afternoon,' I holler back at Jonathan. 'I'll let you know when I can get this money back to you. Won't be long.'

'No rush,' he shouts after me as I pace across the bank floor. I just about hear him.

A rush hit me when I left Nassau Street with the first two million but I'm not sure how I feel right now. Ringing the kid back is my main priority. I wonder if he's going to extend the deadline.

10:35

Ryan

I PRETEND TO BE NOT BOTHERED BY THE TELEPHONE conversations that have just occurred. But I am. Vincent is clearly looking for more time. I think he might get it, but I can't wait around on the answer coming from this prick's partner in crime. JR, his name is. Yeah right! They've probably made up initials for each other. Perhaps this spotty little fuck is called BJ during this kidnapping. I couldn't even imagine getting a BJ from BJ. His skin is way too fuckin' greasy. He disgusts me. I can't even bring myself to look at him. I'm pretending I'm soaked up in this game, but my main priority is peeling the tape from my left ankle. Tape is flicking its way onto our carpet but it's bit by bit, literally. The game is moments away from going into extra time. That'll keep the prick occupied for an extra half hour. I think he'll be delighted that Manchester United end up winning. He seems to be urging them on.

The apartment is really hot today. The sun is scorching in through the windows. It must be over twenty degrees out there. It certainly feels like it from where I'm sitting. I was hoping to have released this ankle by ten-thirty but I've already missed that deadline. Just as the ninety-minute whistle blows in the game, his mobile phone rings again.

'Hey, JR,' he says.

I'm trying my best to hear what the cunt on the other end of the line is saying, but it's pointless.

'I understand,' replies my captor.

Shit. This isn't good. Maybe they're not going to offer Vincent more time after all.

'Kill Ryan,' he then says, staring over at me. I can see him in my peripherals, but I'm not showing him that I'm shitting it.

Kill Ryan. Holy fuck. Is this really happening or is he just running fear through me every so often on purpose?

I need to get myself out of this mess as soon as possible.

The Internet's corridors are plentiful. There are literally millions of little websites you can access with the click of a button that would almost have your eyes popping out of your head. From being only interested in straightforward pornography, I got lulled to the darkest of X-rated arts within a matter of weeks. It all started when I began posting on forums out of pure boredom. I'd discuss my innermost fantasies with random strangers who had even more random usernames. When I began discussions about my fascination with handsome dark-haired men, other posters thought I was being sarcastic. 'It's such a boring fantasy,' they would tell me. 'Open your mind.' I had no idea how much my mind was about to be opened. Within forty-eight hours of logging on to these forums, I was watching videos of all kinds of crazy shit. I watched one of the most beautiful women I've ever seen suck off a horse. She did her best to swallow the load too, only to gag on it and then throw up. I remember seeing a video, which has since been seen by millions of people around the world, of two Asian chicks puking and shitting into a cup before sharing the contents with each other. None of this weird shit turned me on. Whenever I fancied cracking out an orgasm, I'd return to my usual 'Italian men' search.

I had to be discreet though. Vincent wasn't particularly tech savvy, he knew what the best up-and-coming gadgets were, but he wouldn't know the ins and outs of how they operated. I've been deleting all the porn activity from my laptop anyway. It's easy to lose a browser's history. Besides, I never once saw Vincent opening the lid of the laptop he bought for me. He has his own to play with. I often wondered what he got up to online when left alone, but a sneaky search of his laptop's history provided no evidence of naughtiness. Vincent is only interested in hard news. I'm not sure he is aware of the full delights the Internet has to offer. And I don't just mean pornography. There's a wealth of information online that I know he'd love. But all he seems to log on to is the BBC News website. Oh, and Bill Maher clips on YouTube. He fuckin' loves Bill Maher. He cackles away to his old clips, nodding his head in agreement. Vincent thinks he's as liberal as Maher but the truth is, Vincent is a liberal *because* of Maher. I don't know why he's more interested in British and American politics than he is Irish politics. But I really don't give a shit. I wish my video viewing on the Internet was restricted to YouTube. Even YouPorn is old school for me now. YouPorn is boring. There's not much fun to be had on there anymore. It was YouPorn that attracted me to commenting on videos in the first place though. I got chatting to a few of the fellow contributors to that website and they led me to other forums. It got dark really quickly. I blame the coke. I couldn't give up my daily habit after I'd finished at Wow. I hid it from Vincent. Well, I didn't really hide it, I just never told him I was still snorting lines while he was hard at work. I thought the coke would initially help me with the novel. Instead, it assisted me in digging deeper into the world of pornography. None of it seemed to really turn me on, but I was still fascinated by it. From Kaiju porn through to clown porn and anime to bestiality, I watched it all. Just because I would rather do anything than write. A guy with the username TeenCum069 led me through most of the corridors. He would post the sickest videos on the forums and we'd chat shit about them for hours each day. Then he posted one video that turned my brain upside down. I will never forget the child's face. It was the innocence in his eyes that turned me on.

This prick has been pacing around the kitchen since the full-time whistle blew in the game. I can see him eyeballing the small mound of coke on the glass table again. His tension is creeping over to me. I've been particularly panicky since he got off the phone a few minutes ago. But I'm hiding it well. There's little over an hour and a quarter left until Vincent's deadline. I am hopeful I can get myself free of this tape and outmuscle this fucker. But even if I struggle, I still have the cum to fall back on. I can tell this fruitcake that he left his DNA at the crime scene, that he's fucked either way. That'll stop him in his tracks. It's my plan B.

Just when I think the tape around my left ankle is getting the better of me, I form a small gap in the top of it with the tip of my thumb. It's tight, but if I can force my thumb down the side of it, I should be able to snap the rest of the tape off. The sweat forming on my fingers due to anxiety is helping me. I manage to slide my thumb down the side of some of the tape and begin to tug at it. The prick is still pacing in the kitchen, humming some shit tune to himself. He's been trying to ring Vincent back to give him the bad news, but he's not answering. He must be in the second vault. I wonder how Vincent is feeling right now. He must be sick with worry but I bet he's not showing it.

'Your cock buddy better hurry the fuck up. You don't

have much time left,' the prick shouts over to me. It's the first time he's spoken directly to me in ages.

'I … I …' I stutter before remembering I had been doing well ignoring him up until this point. 'Vincent will be back,' I eventually muster up. I shouldn't have bothered.

He points his finger at me.

'Bang,' he says, cocking his thumb.

My thumb is doing an exercise of its own. I feel it pop through the tape. My leg falls free and I feel my heart rate quicken instantly. Both my legs and my right arm are now free. It won't be long now until I can get to that gun. I remember my yoga breathing techniques again.

In through the nose, out through the mouth.

'Let's see, shall we?' I say in return. Prick!

'Exactly,' he says. 'Me and you, buddy, we're gonna be the most feared gangsters in the whole of Dublin.'

I feel a huge grin stretch across my face. That's all I've ever wanted to hear. JR is such a legend. I'm delighted that he sees a future for the two of us. I recall that sentence over and over in my head as I continue to pace around the kitchen table thingy. Kitchen island, that's it! That fuckin word's been on the tip of me tongue all mornin'. I try to ring Vincent back to give him the bad news but he's not picking up right now. He must be close to leaving the second bank. He better be. I stare over at the coke on the glass table again. I really shouldn't.

'Your cock buddy better hurry the fuck up. You don't have much time left,' I bark over at Ryan.

He looks shocked. I haven't said a word to him in ages. He's still sittin' there like a helpless pussy. Just as he's mumbling some stuttered response to me I point my finger at him and mock shoot him. His face is priceless. Poor fag. I take a peek at the time. 10:42. I can't see how Vincent is going to get to two more banks before midday. But I don't care anymore. Even if we come out of this with six million and one dead body, it'll be all worth it. Me and JR have a future together. I know that for certain now.

I didn't know what to do with the twenty grand The Boss gave me. I've never been good with money. I left it under me mattress. That's probably not very smart, but nobody ever comes into my bedsit but me anyway. And nobody would want to rob my bedsit, that's for sure. I thought about getting a better place to live in, to put a deposit down on a nice apartment, but I was comfortable where I was. I bought meself a new TV and a PlayStation 4 with some of the cash, but I soon got tired of sitting on the same old couch, pressing the same old buttons.

After a few more weeks cooped up in the bedsit all day, I decided to start a new daily routine for meself. I spent a lot of my afternoons in the Deer's Head on Parnell Street. I'd sip cold beers talking shit to either Aisling or Billy. They were the only two bar employees in the place. I didn't really like either of them, but they were the only company I had. I tried to sell weed for a local dealer but I'd only manage to get rid of a couple of twenty-euro bags a day. Seeing as my cut from each bag was only five euros, it really wasn't worth me while. But I wanted to be involved in some sort of underworld crime in any way I could. I missed the big time, but I didn't know who to turn to. I thought about investing the money in something worthwhile but I had no clue what that should be. All I knew was that I wanted a better life. But a better life to me wasn't a nice big gaff or a convertible car. I wanted to be a gangster. That's what a great life to me looks like. Somehow, I'd managed to get involved with the best criminal gang in Dublin and fucked it all up. And I did fuck it up. My unravelling was all my own fault. Moving to a different county crossed my mind regularly. Dublin had fuck all to offer me and I had fuck all to offer Dublin. But I'm glad I didn't move. Billy the barman told me one day that some geezer had been enquiring about buying weed in the area and asked if he could arrange a meeting between the two of us. Billy knew I flogged the odd bit of grass here and there.

'Well, you know I'm here every day from about two-ish,' I replied.

'Perfect, I'll let him know.'

It didn't take long for me to meet this guy. He dropped by the pub the very next day. I feared he was a cop straight away, but he convinced me he wasn't by showin' me his dirty fingernails. He told me he worked in an old paint factory. It's unusual to come across a middle-aged man looking to buy a small bag of weed in some city centre pub, but he seemed very cool to me straight away. Behind his odd haircut and strange beard, JR has kind eyes.

I stop pacing round the kitchen island and sling myself back onto the couch as extra time begins in the game. I have to remind myself constantly not to look at the coke. I take a sly look over at Ryan. I try to figure out if I feel sorry for him in some way. I don't. I don't know why I don't. I just don't. It's not because he's a fag. I don't mind fags as long as they keep their fuckin dicks away from me. Maybe I don't care about him because he's been such a jammy cunt. This guy doesn't even work yet he lives like a king. He's a little bitch, I guess. I like the way coke makes me think. I can dig deeper into my thoughts when I'm high. Me imagination runs wild. I come to the conclusion that this spoilt little asshole has had luck at every corner he's turned. I've been nothin' but unlucky all my life. Well, that changes today. I haven't done anything to scare Ryan since I whipped me cock out earlier this morning. Maybe I'll try somethin' in a while just to fuck with his head again. A few possibilities are skipping through my mind when his boyfriend calls back.

'Hello,' he whispers down the line to me.

'Midday is your deadline and that's it,' I say as straight as an arrow. This is my opportunity to act like a gangster again. But he stumps me.

'Whatever,' he snarls back.

His reply is a surprise. Fuckin fag! I'm about to hang up on him when I realise I need to ask if he's out of the second bank. I guess he is.

'Yep. I'm walking towards the car with another two million now,' he replies, tryna act as if he's not bothered.

'Well, hurry the fuck up,' I say, giving me the perfect opportunity to hang up in style yet again. I'm good at this shit. I toss the phone back onto the glass table, making a point, before realising I need it to ring JR back. I was almost cool then.

10:45

Vincent

BEFORE I'M BUZZED OUT OF THE SECOND DOOR I HAVE THE phone to my ear.

I've barely finished saying 'Hello' before the fucker snaps at me.

'Midday is your deadline and that's it!' Fuck him.

'Whatever,' I say trying to act like I don't care. I think it stuns him. He falls silent for a few seconds before asking me if I'm finished in Camden Street.

'Yep. I'm walking towards the car with another two mill now.'

'Well, hurry the fuck up,' he snarls back before hanging up. I bet he thinks he's cool.

John rushes to the back of the car when he sees me approaching.

'You okay, boss?' he asks, with a touch of concern in his voice.

'I'm a hundred per cent,' I lie. I'm such a good actor.

John unlocks the two briefcases from my wrists and places them in the trunk for me.

'Church Street, John boy,' I say before climbing into the

back of the car. Tchaikovsky's still playing and the air is as cool as it's been all morning.

Church Street then Mayor Street, half an hour in each plus at least twenty minutes of travelling time. That would take me just past midday.

I let out another sigh before winking at John through the rear-view mirror to try to act like I know what I'm doing. He must be wondering what the fuck is going on today but he won't dare ask. And I won't offer up any lie. I never divulge any information to John so it would only add to the oddness of the morning if I did. John doesn't add to any of my worries though. He'll just do as I ask him. It will take us about ten minutes to drive to Church Street. I wonder if Noah Voss has been trying to ring me. I take out my iPhone and turn it on. I dread to think how many voicemails I've received. I have to listen to the nonsense Vodafone robot calling out my own mobile phone number before I get my answer. Five voicemails. My heart races in anticipation of listening to them. I know from the mobile number being called out that the first is from Noah.

'Hello, Mr Butler,' he says. 'Just making sure you will be here at about ten-thirty like you said this morning. I have everything ready, sir. Look forward to seeing you.'

The next voicemail is from Derek Talbot. He's an old employee of mine who has tried to keep in touch with me ever since he left my old job a couple of decades ago. I like him. But I'm not really that interested in hanging on to our relationship. He rings every couple of months for a catch-up. That's okay with me, I guess. I never follow up with his loose plans for us to meet for a drink. He's part of my past.

The next call is from my office. Fuck! Belinda is looking for me.

'Vincent, I've just noticed six missed calls on your phone

here. Do you want me to listen to them? Let me know. Talk soon.'

Bollocks! I hang up from my voicemail and ring her straight back. I wonder if she'll answer. I have asked her to stay away from the phones all morning but if she notices my mobile number ringing, she should pick up.

'Hi, Vincent,' she says.

'Belinda, leave the phone alone. Have you got that paperwork in order for me yet?'

'I'm still doing it, Vincent,' she says. 'It's taking a long time. I don't know how you got them in this mess …'

'I just haven't been keeping on top of paperwork, Be. If you can just concentrate on that for now and leave the phones until I get back, that'd be great.'

'Will do, boss. I did notice that Jonathan had been looking for you. It was his number that rang a few times.'

My blood boils instantly. I surprise even myself with the tone I take.

'Stay away from the phones, Be,' I say more sternly than I've ever said anything to her before.

'Okay, okay. I am, Vincent. I'm just keeping note when they do ring. I … I …'

'I know you are, darling,' I say, relieving the tension. 'I'm sorry. I'm having a crazy morning. I have a conference call with the board members later and I need to have all that paperwork in order. Please.'

'A conference call with the board? I didn't know anything about—'

'They contacted me directly first thing this morning, Be,' I say, making my story up on the spot. 'They're looking for a total update. I just need to have all in order.'

'Is there anything I can do to help?' asks Belinda.

'Yes. The paperwork,' I reply, laughing. 'Get those files in alphabetical order and stay away from the phones.'

She laughs in return.

'Just as you asked me this morning!'

'Exactly. Just as I asked this morning.'

'I'll have them sorted before you get back,' she says.

'Thanks, Be.'

I'm desperate to get back to my mobile phone voicemails. I grunt, having to go through the process of dialling into the system again. It seems to be taking ages.

Bollocks. It's Jonathan.

'Hi, Vincent, just making sure all is okay. You said you were heading over to Michelle straight from here but I noticed your car pull off in a different direction. Everything okay? I can't reach you and I can't reach Belinda by phone. Let me know what's up.'

This is so frustrating. I should have left my phone on through the morning. I was an idiot for turning it off. I need to quench these fires as soon as they come in. The voicemail informed me this call was made at ten-forty. Just eight minutes ago. I decide to listen to the last voicemail before getting back to Jonathan. It's Noah again.

'Mr Butler. It's gone ten-thirty now and I hope everything is okay with you. I am awaiting your visit. Your phone seems to be switched off. Call me back at your convenience to let me know.' Fuck off, Voss!

I liked the fact that Ryan was always home, initially. He used to work most evenings so it was great for the two of us to make the most of dinner dates. He'd search for the best restaurants in Dublin through TripAdvisor and we'd go and pay them a visit. It was great for us to rekindle our romance, but it did get kind of boring after a few months. We didn't have a whole lot to talk about. When we did talk he would spout some shit about wanting to move to Sydney. We'd travelled through Australia back in 2010 and while I certainly enjoyed it, I harboured no ambitions to move there full time. Ryan did, however. Ryan had some bizarre notions. He never really thought things through. On the odd occasion that we would talk about something other than his dream move to Sydney, I'd mention his book. He explained the concept to me a couple of times and I think I understood it. It's about some paparazzo who stalks Hollywood stars. Doesn't sound very original to me. I was never sure Ryan was capable of writing a book but I wanted to support him. I bought him the latest Apple Mac and iPhone as a retirement present when he left Wow. He was so grateful. That shut him up about Sydney for a while.

I roll my eyes as I ring Jonathan back.

'Ah, Vincent, how are you? Is everything okay?' he asks.

'Jonathan. Calm down. What is going on? I just got your voicemail.'

'I just … I just thought I'd check everything was okay? I saw John pull away and—'

'Everything is great, Jonathan. Calm down. John was just getting some petrol in the tank before we headed over to Michelle. Are you okay?'

'I just couldn't reach you … or Belinda. I just thought I should keep trying.'

Ah, he's mostly upset because Belinda hasn't been returning his calls, I bet. I finish the call by telling him I have urgent engagements. I'm pretty certain he'll be okay for an hour or two while I get this completed. I stare out of the car window after I hang up. John has just turned right onto Church Street. I wonder how pissed off Noah is that I'm arriving twenty-five minutes later than I told him I would. I don't give a shit. I need to be bullish in here.

10:45

Jack

I CAN SEE HIM HOLDING THE PHONE TO HIS EAR AS HE EXITS. He must be ringing Darragh to let him now he has a further two mill in tow. A packed briefcase is hanging from each of his wrists. Vincent looks to be in control. It's a cocky approach, but I like it. John seems to be taking everything in his stride too. He greets Vincent at the trunk of the car and helps him place the cases inside. As they both climb back into the car, I take a look at my watch. They should be arriving at Church Street a little before eleven a.m. He's not really that far behind his deadline now. I won't be at Church Street. It's the only branch I'm not going to witness being robbed today. I have another appointment. And it's very important that I attend. As soon as I spin on my heels towards the South Circular Road, where my first car is parked, the phone buzzes in my hand.

'All looks good,' I say in an upbeat tone.

'Yeah, he has the other two mill,' bellows Darragh. 'And I told him the deadline is the deadline. He seems to be quickening up.'

'You're doing a great job, Darragh. In just over an hour

we'll both be millionaires. Call me when Church Street is done.'

'Will do, chief.'

The giggle I allow myself after hanging up isn't supposed to be loud, but it is. It startles the old woman walking towards me. The car's a four-minute swift stroll from here. I've made this walk three times in the build-up to today. It'll take me ten minutes to drive to Dinah's from the South Circular Road.

I reminisce about my time travelling with Frank while I walk. We both suffered a little post-vacation depression when we finally arrived home from our first European trip. But it didn't take us long to get back into the swing of things. I don't think Frank loved golf as much as I did, but he never turned down the opportunity to have a round with his old man. I think he felt it was his obligation as a son. I'm not sure I would have minded if he told me he didn't love golf all that much. Or maybe I would. I'm not sure. Sometimes I felt he opened up more to Margarite than he did to me, but I never minded that either. In fact, I encouraged it. Margarite was a proper mother figure to him. I still stay in touch with her, though it's a rarity these days. She moved to Edinburgh about six years ago with her husband. She met Marcus two years prior. I liked Marcus. He was a good man. I'm sure he still is. Some people thought I was jealous that Margarite had met somebody else, but I genuinely wasn't. There were times when I felt I should be jealous but I couldn't bring myself to be. I was worried Frank would be heartbroken once Margarite moved on, but he proved to be of strong mind again. He was nearly sixteen when she left.

I get to the car twenty seconds shy of four minutes. I made a short appointment with Dinah, telling her I'd call by around eleven-ish. I wanted to leave the timing vague. I knew Vincent would be heading to Church Street any time between ten-thirty and eleven o'clock, and that would be my cue to head towards Dinah's. She's been amazing to me. She's really sorted my head out.

Frank may have been a cocky teenager but that's a much better trait in a child than that of lacking in confidence. He was a handsome young man and had a natural charm. He definitely got his gift of the gab from the Ritchies. I was never that charming. I told him once about my attempt at winning over his mother and he had to stop laughing just to breathe. We had our moments. Frank always felt like he knew it all, which was hard to deal with. But apart from the occasional spat, we were an ideal father and son combo. I've heard from other fathers that a father and son relationship is a lot tougher to control than a father and daughter. Daughters tend to adore their dads while mothers and sons have a preferable bond. It sounds about right. I would say on a scale of one to ten in father–son relationships mine and Frank's would rank at about an eight or nine. I was proud of my decisions in parenthood and watching Frank grow into a fine, albeit overly confident, young man filled me with joy. I'm always surprised by how quickly time flashes by when I'm thinking of my son.

I made sure not to go over the speed limit on the way to Drimnagh, but I must have got lucky with the traffic lights across the canal. I make it to Dinah's a full minute quicker than any time during my trial runs. I was quick getting my wig and beard off. It's four minutes past eleven now. I imagine Vincent is inside the Church Street branch by this stage, dealing with Noah Voss.

Community centres always look bleak from the outside. Yet inside this building everything is freshly decorated. I don't know why none of the budget goes on the exterior of these buildings. They always look uninviting, which is totally against the point of them. Dinah's room is the first on the left past the small reception. A dark-haired man I've never seen before greets me as I make my way towards her.

'How-a-ya?'

'Hello. Is … eh … is Dinah here?' I ask.

'She is,' replies the man. 'I've just finished a session with her. She works wonders.'

'She does, doesn't she?' I reply with a soft smile.

'Sorry. My name is Trevor. Trevor Kirwan. I … I lost my wife five months ago.'

'Oh, I'm sorry to hear that. Jack,' I reply, shaking the hand he held out to me. I don't offer any more until I notice him arch his eyebrows, willing me to open up. Fuck it. Why not? We're both in a bereavement help centre.

'I lost my wife too,' I say solemnly. 'And my son.'

10:50

Ryan

DAVID DE GEA'S LONG THROW TOWARDS MARCUS RASHFORD on the halfway line lets me know the winning goal is imminent. As I'm attempting to peel away at the tape wrapped tightly around my left wrist, I watch Rashford skip by two defenders before bearing down on Manuel Neuer in the Bayern Munich goal. The German's mistimed dive brings the United attacker tumbling to the ground. It's an obvious penalty kick. I've watched it a dozen times since it happened. The referee had no choice. But of course, the media made a meal of it, because it was a decision that went in favour of Manchester United. It takes a few moments for this prick to realise what's just happened before he leaps to his feet.

'Penalty kick, penalty kick,' he roars.

He really is into this. I haven't been able to tell him this match was played out two weeks ago. I figured it best to let him believe it's live. It has assisted in his infatuation with it, meaning he hasn't been paying me much attention. I know Paul Pogba will take the penalty kick and blast it straight down the middle of the goal while Neuer dives towards his left post. That's how Manchester United made it to the final of this year's Champions League to face Real Madrid. That game takes place in a couple weeks. I hope I'm fuckin' alive to see it. The prick roars with delight upon seeing Pogba almost break the net with the penalty. He barely glances at me as he celebrates. I think he asks me a question but I don't answer it.

'That's it, that's game over isn't it?' he says.

It is, yes. But he can figure that all out by himself. Bayern would have needed two goals in the final few minutes of extra time and they barely even registered two shots. I don't have to stretch as much to get my hand across to the remaining tape but it is a more difficult task. My arms are more visible to the prick than my legs are. But I can sit back in a relaxed state while I delicately peel at the tape. The gun is still sitting on the glass table next to his mobile phone. I hope it's still there when I free myself. Shouldn't be long now. I'm thinking through my plan of action once again when I notice him grab at the chair he had Vincent perched on this morning. He spins it around until it mirrors my chair, and then he plonks himself on it. His nose must be only two feet from mine. I can smell his breath. It smells like baked beans. I immediately curl my ankles around the front legs of my chair, hoping with all my might that he doesn't notice they are now free.

'Game over!' he says with a grin. 'Who will they play in the final?'

I think about not answering before deciding that's not the best route to take right now.

'Real Madrid play Juventus in the other semi-final tomorrow,' I offer up. 'Do you want to call by to watch that with me too?' He finds my retort funny.

'I'll be out spending my millions tomorrow, fag boy,' he responds. It's so juvenile to call anyone a fag. I'm glad he's immature. I can take this fucker down once I'm free. I'm certain of it. 'Who'll win that?'

'Real Madrid,' I answer with absolute positivity. I know. The game was actually played last week.

'Really? You think so?'

'I know so. They won the first leg one–nil and they'll see out a nil-all draw tomorrow to go through.'

He screws his nose up trying to take in what I say. I know the two legs thing still has him baffled despite me explaining it to him when he first settled down to watch the game. His silence is welcome. I'm wondering if he's going to leave it at that. I can see he's thinking about what to do. The palms of my hands are clammy with sweat. If he notices my ankles are no longer taped then all my morning's work will be undone. I glance at the microwave clock, ignoring his gaze. Anything to get away from the stench of his beans. 10:58.

Holy shit. Do I really have just an hour to live?

After a while the only videos that TeenCum069 was sharing with me involved kids. It was very strange watching them, but I found it quite addictive viewing. I was half turned on, half feeling sick with guilt. I remember feeling the same way when I watched "regular" porn for the very first time. I had the nerve when I was just fourteen years old to ask the local video rental guy if he had any porn movies. He didn't hesitate in ducking down behind his counter to show me what he had to offer. I'd heard of pornography then, but I'd never watched any of it. I pretended to school friends that I knew what sex was all about but I hadn't got a clue. I remember waiting on my mother to go to work that evening before placing the VHS in our dated video recorder. The film opened with a beautiful blonde girl stranded on the side of the road after her car broke down. Fast forward to three minutes later when the hero who stopped to help her began to unzip his jeans. I watched stunned as she took his hard dick to the back of her throat.

What the fuck's going on?

My stomach flipped upside down. I felt like throwing up. But so too did my dick. It stood on end. That mixed feeling between a sour stomach and horniness thrashes through my body every time I watch kiddie porn. TeenCum069 introduced me to other like-minded Internet scum. It wasn't long until they were teaching me how to contact kids online. I still can't believe how easy it is for us to interact with teens. Why the fuck do their parents allow them this sort of access online? I guess they can't help it. Every kid wants to have their own social media accounts and that is where they're most vulnerable. All it takes is for people like me to set up a fake account, using images of a hot young girl, and boys will do or say anything you ask them to. I'm pretty sure I wouldn't have been this gullible when I was ten or twelve years of age. Kids these days are more stupid than ever. Despite me contacting quite a few cute kids when I first set up my fake account, it was a ten-year-old named Brady Donovan who fell for my bullshit first. He was fascinated with Nicole Blake, my alter ego. It didn't take long for him to agree to meet me. But I kept putting it off. Every time we arranged a date, I would freeze. So many permutations crossed my mind. The guys in the forum tried to help me fight those fears. They'd all been through this countless times before. They knew how to deal with the fact that the boy was looking to meet a cute schoolgirl only to be met by a middle-aged man. They gave me all the lines, all the subtleties required. It was like being handed ammunition. I remember the date well because it etched itself on my mind. I arranged to meet Brady in the car park of the Travelodge in Derry on the sixth of December. That was about a year and a half ago now. I had a room booked in the hotel under the names of

Charles and Brady Donovan – a father and son. When I first bumped into him in the car park, I figured straight away that the guys' hints and tips would work almost effortlessly.

'She can't make it,' I told Brady's disappointed face. 'I'm her uncle. She asked me to come and meet you just to make sure you can be a good enough boyfriend for her. If you come with me, she asked me to show you some things. She wants to know if you're ready. Ready to meet her. To really love her.'

'Okay,' he said, shrugging his shoulders.

'Cool,' I reply. 'I have a room booked up here in the Travelodge hotel. I have some videos for you that Nicole would like you to watch.'

'Let's do a fuckin' line, dude,' the prick finally offers up after a long silence.

He'd been staring at me all that time. I sigh. I don't want another line. I just want to get the fuck out of this mess. The prick grabs at the magazine lying on the glass table with the mound of coke and the old five-euro note sitting on top of it.

'Me first this time,' he says while rolling the note back together.

I don't have time for this.

10:55

Vincent

THE CHURCH STREET BUILDING IS SIMILAR TO THE ONE ON Camden. It's a modern slice of Dublin architecture, right next to St Michan's Church. But it's nicer. It's fully clear glass. No dimmed black pointless windows here. I don't visit this branch that often, at least not anymore. The further I stay away from Noah, the better for everybody involved. Nobody notices as I come through the first door. By the time I'm buzzed through the second, Kelly at the first Customer Service desk is smiling at me. She waves out from behind her glass-protected window. I mouth the name 'Noah' to her in return and she points me towards his office. I rattle on the door before letting myself in.

'Noah,' I say, fake grinning as he reaches for his mouse to click a button.

What the fuck is he hiding?

'Ah, Mr Butler,' he says, flashing both his gums and his teeth.

Are some people just not aware that they do that? Nobody wants to see anybody's fuckin' gums. I really hate this prick.

'I thought you were coming at ten-thirty, sir?'

'No – I said ten-thirty*ish*, Noah and I've been held up. So if you don't mind I'd like to collect the funds as quickly as possible.'

'Yes, Mr Butler, of course, sir,' he says before walking towards me, holding my stare.

He's an awful-looking asshole. I initially thought he was coming to hug me, but he rests his left arm on my shoulder and shouts past me.

'Gary!' he calls out.

His spotty junior member of staff screeches back, 'Yeah, Noah?'

'The paperwork for Mr Butler, please.'

'Yeah, I got it.'

'Okay then, will you bring it to me, please?'

'Yeah, in a minute, Noah.'

This is why I don't like Voss. Nobody has any respect for him.

'Excuse me, Gary!' I shout so loudly that everybody in the branch takes notice, including the queue of customers. Gary must have leapt to the sound of my voice. He sprints towards Noah's office, his stupid haircut flopping on top of his head.

'Gary, do you think it's okay to talk to your boss the way you just have?' I ask, flippantly.

'What way, Mr Butler?' he answers, looking puzzled. I don't have the energy for this shit. Not this morning. I swipe the paperwork out of his hands while offering him an evil stare.

'That is Mr Voss, do you hear me?' I say, pointing the paperwork in Noah's direction.

'But eh … but … He told us not to call him Mr Voss, Mr Butler. He … he said it's too formal.'

I breathe heavily in the direction of Gary, thinking about

what to say next. I then look at Noah who offers no support, just that ugly gummy smile of his.

'Well I'm telling you formal is what we do round here. He's Mr Voss, got it?'

'Yes, Mr Voss, Mr Butler, sorry,' Gary replies as his head sinks lower into his shoulders. What a mess of a branch this is.

'I'm sorry, Mr Butler,' Noah says as Gary makes his way back to his desk. 'I just thought I would change things up a little. It's no problem keeping it formal. I understand your decision on that, sir.'

I don't respond. Instead I try to think what lurks behind Noah's fake politeness. This fucker is dark. I need to know what he's hiding.

Noah told the interview panel that he rose from bank clerk at Barclays in London to eventually managing his own branch within three years.

'They really liked me and rated me. I got promoted seven times in my first two years,' he boasted, flashing his gums at everyone.

My nose pinched itself as I recoiled in my seat, but I was the only one. Each of the other three board members who bothered to turn up for the interview were grinning back at him, nodding in approval. They'd clearly hired him in their heads already. I was devastated. I didn't want to be working with this prick. On his first day in the job he told me God was looking down on him that day in the interview and that he has since prayed for each of us that were in that room. My mouth opened and closed in a swift second as a response. I was about to screech something in return but managed to stop myself.

Don't you fuckin' dare pray for me!

I wish I had followed through and said it. I should have nipped this religion bullshit in the bud, right from the start.

He hasn't told me he's prayed for me since, but if he does today he's getting a fuckin' reality check. I really shouldn't allow myself to get wound up by him. I need to get in and out of here as quickly as I possibly can. It's hard for the blood not to boil in here though. There's a pathetic looking figurine on his desk of baby Jesus being swaddled by his whore of a mother. There's a framed picture of an older Jesus with a halo above his head eyeballing me on the wall behind Noah. It's creepy as fuck. I saw Noah hang that on his first day in the office – the day he told me he had prayed for me.

'I looked at the specifications of the withdrawal procedure,' Noah says, flipping over the paperwork on his desk. 'You know it doesn't specify an amount you can personally withdraw, Mr Butler. I think two million euros is a lot of money—'

'Of course it's a lot of fuckin' money, Voss,' I shoot back. It stuns him. I've never sworn in his company before.

'I … I'm sorry, Mr Butler. Yes, of course it is a lot of money,' he stutters with his African accent weighing more than his put-on posh English tone for a change.

'Listen, Noah. I don't have time for this box-ticking nonsense today. I'm under stress from the board members to take two mill from here this morning and deliver it to Mayor Street, okay? That's what I've been ordered to do and it's what I am ordering you to do, so can we just please get to it? I've a hundred and one other matters, more urgent than this, to get to today and I really need this out of the way.'

'The board asked you to do this?' he asks, looking up at me.

'Yes.'

'It's just I mentioned it to Mr Sneyd this morning and he didn't know anything of it.'

I feel my face flush with rage. If I was to touch it, I'm sure I would burn my fingers.

'Clyde Sneyd?' I ask in a firm tone.

'Yes. But it's okay, Mr Butler.' Noah is panicking. 'He said you're the boss. He said he doesn't know anything about bank transfers and that you know what you're doing, so all is … all is …' he stutters again.

'Listen you, Voss,' I say as I rise to my feet. 'You ever fuckin' go behind my back again and I'll—' I don't get to finish.

Noah stands up, matching me for height. 'Sir, sir, please, please. I'm sorry. I'm sorry.' He keeps repeating himself. He knows he fucked up. 'Please sit down, sit down. Relax, Mr Butler.'

I tug at my tie, loosening it from the collar and perch back slowly onto the chair, keeping eye contact with Noah.

'I am sorry, Mr Butler,' he offers once more. 'I just wanted to know the amount allowed to be taken in one lump. That's all. I couldn't reach you by phone, so I contacted Mr Sneyd.'

I allow a silence to wash over us both as I take all this information in. It's a good job he contacted Sneyd and not any of the others on the board. Sneyd is the least interested. I bet he's forgotten all about Noah's call by now anyway. It would have been too much trouble for him having to field such an enquiry. I'm surprised he even answered, to be honest. It must have been midnight in New York when Noah called him. He doesn't answer any of my calls when I ring him at a reasonable hour. He never has.

'Let's just get this done, Noah, shall we?' I suggest, trying to defuse any tension between us.

'Yes, Mr Butler,' he agrees, picking up a pen from his desk. Even his fuckin' pen has a picture of Jesus's face on it.

10:55

Darragh

I MAY HAVE GONE OVER THE TOP JUMPING FOR JOY WHEN PAUL Pogba scored that penalty kick. I don't mind. Only this fag saw me anyway. I take a moment to think this through. United are now two–one up in this game but three–two up in total over the two legs. Even if Bayern Munich score a goal here, they won't go through due to the away goals rule. It's complicated but cock breath here explained it to me earlier and I think I've got it right. Bayern need two goals in the remaining five minutes and they're not gonna get them. Game over. I fist pump the air and make a silent vow to follow United's fortunes from now on. They remind me of home, even though home isn't Manchester. The fag is staying pretty silent. He's obviously not a United fan. I grab at the kitchen chair close by and drag it right in front of him. He shits himself, I'm sure of it, as I sit down on it and eyeball him from close range. Our kneecaps are almost touching. I decide to play nice cop to start off with, but only because I still haven't figured out what to do yet. We talk football again. He thinks Real Madrid will make it to the final to play United, but I think Juventus will do it. I've seen them play before, years ago. They're an Italian team and very good as far as I remember. This little fag doesn't know what he's talking about. Fags really don't have a clue when it comes to sport. He doesn't seem to be in the mood for talkin'. He's just shitting himself, not knowing what I'm gonna do next. I guess neither of us do. I pause to take a look around the room. I'm looking for inspiration.

'Let's do another fuckin line,' I say, grabbing the sports magazine from the glass table.

I don't need him to test this shit for me anymore, so I'm going first this time. I use my library card to separate enough for two decent lines before rolling up the five-euro note. This coke burns the edges of the nose before it's even in the system. I love this stuff. The little fag cunt ain't getting his bag of coke back. It's coming with me.

'Here ya go,' I say, handing him the note. I haven't forgot that his right arm is free. I'm not stupid. He sucks up his line in less than a second before staring up at me with his eyes watering.

'That's some fuckin shit, dude,' I say, laughing into his face. He doesn't respond. Fine by me. I just wanna have some fun. I am a gangster after all.

JR's kind eyes reflect his personality. They kinda sparkle a bit. That was the first thing that struck me about him. It's probably because his eyes are the only feature you can actually see on his face. He told me his work at the paint factory was a front for his real job. He used to work for one the hottest gangs in Dublin but had given up on a life of crime years ago to go straight. But after losing his family he turned back to crime. He thought life was too short for pussyfooting around with a regular nine-to-five job. He needed that adrenaline buzz again. He told me he was on the lookout for an apprentice who could handle the sort of shit he wanted to get involved in. It was like music to my ears. He knew I'd been involved with The Boss before and had been told I was very trustworthy. He had a lot of information on me. JR is a perfectionist. It's why I love working with him.

'I'm not interested in any drama,' he would say to me repeatedly. 'I just want a guy who can get the job done.'

'No better man than me, JR,' I would tell him over and over again.

He liked the fact that I had a clean record and decided to take me on after meeting me a couple of times. I couldn't believe my luck. I still can't. I've gone from earning ten euros a day for selling two bags of weed to, today, earning four million for five hours' work. From day one, JR has been open and honest with me. He told me how he made his way up the ranks of the criminal underworld in Dublin, from being a junior member of a protection racket right through to aiming to become the number one bank thief in the whole of Ireland. We would meet up in the Deer's Head and he would amaze me with stories of his past. He told me from the outset that if we were going into business together he would only consider it fair that we split everything down the middle. He said that's how his boss operated with him when he first started. I insisted it wasn't about the money. For me it was about the work. I think that's what ultimately won him over. He liked me right from the start and I adored him. I owe him so much. He's my knight in shining armour, really.

I'm not sure what real-life gangsters do in these situations. I flick through the movie library in my head for inspiration. *Reservoir Dogs* springs to the forefront of my brain for some reason. Probably because Ryan is tied to a chair. Yes, of course! The fuckin ear cut-off scene. Brilliant! I leap for the TV remote and push at buttons to find the music channels. How many fuckin channels do these fags have?

'What number's the MTVs?' I have to ask.

'They start on 701.'

I continue switching through the music channels until I see something I like. Eminem. I notice the title of a show currently on called *Eminem's Top 10.* Fuck yeah! The channel's on a commercial break at the moment. I look over at Ryan. He has no idea what's coming. Poor fag. While the ads play I head towards the bathroom mirror. I noticed a razor in there earlier. I clip the head off to give me access to the blades. The final ad is playing on the TV when I return. I know it's the final one because it's for the channel itself. They always advertise themselves each side of a programme. You get to know this kind of shit when all you do is watch TV all day. Then I hear the beat kick in. 'Cleaning Out my Closet'. Probably me favourite Eminem track. Well it's in my top three anyway. I hold up a pretend mic to my mouth and dance towards Ryan.

'Have you ever been hated or dis-sumtin-ated against?
I have, I've been protested and demonstrated against
Spicky signs for my rhyme-y rhymes, look at the times
Sick as the mind of the motherfuckin' skin skanny skind
Dosy ocean techosim um dip oceans explodin'
Tempers flaring from parents just blow ee owe ee o-opin ...'

I know this spit so well. I nailed the lyrics years ago. Well, I know most of them. If you don't know a particular line in a rap song, then it's easy to just flow over it. Just make similar sounds to the rapper. Everyone does it, it's simple. I sway in front of Ryan, moving my arms to the beat of the track, spitting out the lyrics. It's such a good fuckin tune. I try to think what the dance is like in the *Reservoir Dogs* scene. I think I know it. It doesn't really suit this beat, but I make up my own version. I pace my moves to and from Ryan, just to freak him the fuck out. That's the way the guy does it in the movie. I feel sinister cool right now. This is the feeling I've been chasing all me life. I palm the blade in my right hand. I bet Ryan is shitting himself. He must think I'm a fuckin psycho.

11:00

Ryan

My nose is still stinging from that line of coke. I really didn't want it. At least he's left me alone now. He's too busy changing channels on the TV. He wants to know where the music channels are. He eventually settles for a channel with adverts on and then walks out of the room. He's unpredictable, I'll give him that. His departure gives me time to really tug away at the tape around my left wrist. It's tough to get a good grip on it to free myself. I have to give up when I hear him strolling back into the room. He appears in front of me, his arms flapping.

What the fuck is he doing?

He begins mouthing away to the Eminem song that's started playing on the TV. *Holy shit, he's seriously rapping this shit to me.* He doesn't even know the words. I feel like laughing but for the absurdity of it all.

Is he dancing? Is that supposed to be dancing? This guy's a fuckin' psycho! He swings his hips trusting towards me and then back to the TV. *Seriously. Is that dancing? What is going on?*

It's 'Sick as the mind of a motherfuckin' kid that's behind' not 'Sick as the mind of the motherfuckin' skin skanny skind' for fuck's sake. I'm beginning to think I'm on a hidden camera TV show right now. I actually look up into the two corners of the room facing me to see if there are cameras bearing down on us. That's how long it takes me to take that delusion away from the realm of possibilities. I'm snapping right back to reality when the prick sits on my lap facing me, still rapping made-up lyrics. This is getting so much fuckin' weirder with every passing second. I'm not sure if he's grinding on me or whether he's continuing the dance that led him here. I feel frozen. Stunned. Then he produces a razor blade in his hand and holds it right in front of my stare. A ton of thoughts float through my mind, but at the forefront is the dreaded feeling that this guy is going to cut my fucking balls off. His grinding continues as he lifts the blade with one hand while grabbing at my left ear with the other.

Holy fuck. This kid thinks he's in Reservoir Dogs. *He can't be for real. Can he?* I react like any man would, even though it will give my game away. I jab my knee right up into his bollocks. It goes deep, as hard as I can muster. He squeals like a cat, and slumps to the floor. The squealing lasts long enough, but the silence that follows is going on way too long. He remains curled up in front of me. I think about making a jump for the gun but pause just as he stirs. I'm an idiot. I wasted valuable seconds there when I should have jumped. Even with the chair tied to my left arm I would have had a big advantage over him. I didn't think his pain was going to take that long to recede. He finally manages to shift himself into a sitting position on the floor, pinning the top of his back up against the edge of the glass table.

'I was only fuckin' messin' with ya, fag. I wasn't going to cut your ear off. Who do you think I am?' he snaps back at me.

'A murderer, a kidnapper. Isn't that what you told me you

were?' I reply like a hero. But I need to shut the fuck up. I need to get him back focused on something else, anything but me. I'm almost free. How has he not noticed that my legs are no longer taped? How does he think I managed to knee him so hard in the balls?

'Listen, dude,' I say, cringing. I hate the word 'dude' but he said it earlier on and it's stuck at the forefront of my mind. 'There's an hour left till the deadline. Can we both just wait it out? Go back to watching TV or somethin'?'

'I'm in charge here, fag,' he replies, lifting himself slowly to a standing position. 'I'll decide what we'll do. You ever knee me in the bollocks like that again and I *will* cut your fuckin' ear off, boy, d'ye hear me?'

'Understood,' I say, nodding my head while he waves the razor blade in my face.

'Right,' he says, limping back to the couch. 'What's normally on this time of the day? Do you watch *Jeopardy?*'

Brady won my heart in the short elevator ride we took to the sixth floor of the Travelodge. He was adorable. He kept asking how Nicole was and if I thought they could ever be husband and wife one day. Guilt welled up inside me. I could feel it as I stared down at him. He chatted away without removing the smile from his face. I bet his parents were really proud of him. He was super cute. He bounced up on the bed like any ten-year-old would when we entered the room. He was still asking questions about Nicole. It would break his heart if I told him I was really Nicole and that I'd been the person Facebook messaging him for the past eight weeks. But I couldn't tell him. It was all part of the act. I needed to persuade him that Nicole had insisted he was sexually active before she met him. I'd been told that once I was in this situation, showing him the porn movies and telling him what the girl wanted from him, I'd be able to close the deal one hundred per cent of the time. I practically had little Brady by the balls.

'What videos does Nicole want me to watch?' he spat out. It was about the hundredth question he'd asked, but it was one I took time to answer. I rubbed my face in frustration.

'She … eh … she – you know what?' I said, kneeling down to touch his face as he sat on the edge of the bed. 'I forgot the tapes.'

'Oh no,' he said, appearing really disappointed in me. 'How could you?'

'I … I'll tell you what. Next time I'll bring Nicole with me, huh? And you two can watch the tapes together. I just need to tell her if I think you are a good guy.'

'And do you?'

'Do I what?' I asked.

'Think I'm a good guy?'

'I think you're adorable,' I said, kissing him on the forehead.

He beamed a wide grin at me as an awkward silence filled the room. I took the time to think, rubbing at my face again.

'Go on. Go. I'll tell Nicole you'd be the perfect boyfriend. I promise.'

11:10

Jack

DINAH HAS THE AIR CONDITIONING TURNED ON. I FIND HER office perfectly cool. It helps me breathe. I am certain I'm coming across as normal to her. I'll miss Dinah. She knows our meetings are coming to an end anyway. It's been a couple of months since I last met with her. Before that, I hadn't seen her since before Christmas. We used to meet every week, at the same time of the same day – nine a.m. Thursdays. We'd sit and talk for over an hour about my grieving. Well, that's not strictly true. We would talk about anything. Sports, politics, Dublin, my family, her family – or lack of it – and anything else that popped up. We talked like friends talk but I always knew that the conversation would eventually swing around to how I had been handling my losses. Dinah didn't have to assist with my feelings of guilt. That's a bullshit feeling to have after somebody's died. It's supposed to be a natural part of the grieving process but I leapfrogged it. It's a waste of time. You can never go back, so stewing on feelings such as guilt is a hundred per cent pointless. I began to really understand that soon after Karyn passed. Denial and bargaining are two further features of the grieving process that I didn't need counselling for. Again, they're a total waste of time. Of course, you should accept what's happened to you. It's happened. Deal with it. But I needed Dinah to help me with the anger I felt – not with Karyn's passing, but with Frank's.

It's been eighteen months since I first met with her. I feel slightly sad that I'm going to give her my usual goodbye hug in about five minutes' time, never to see her again. She doesn't know for certain that I'll never visit, but she's aware that I feel I no longer need her. I'm one of her best clients. I guess it helps when you can be open-minded enough to skip most of the processes she has to help you get through. I smile and nod at her as she tells me about the holiday she's just returned from. She and her husband have just been to Oslo. She'd always wanted to go but couldn't afford it. Bereavement counsellors mustn't be paid an awful lot. They should be. I'm not sure what her husband Tom does but I know this is the first time they've holidayed together outside Ireland since they met. She's not suffering from post-vacation blues. She's still smiling from the delights of the Norwegian capital.

'You need to visit,' she insists, staring at me over the top of her retro-style glasses frames.

'I will, I promise,' I say, lying to her. It's such a shame to lie to Dinah.

'So you just wanted to drop by to let me know everything is okay?'

'That's all. I figured I hadn't seen you in too long, so wanted to say hi,' I lie again.

'You look great.'

'I hope I look half as good as you,' I return. 'I guess I need ten days in Oslo, huh?'

Dinah tries to bring up Frank but I bat it away politely. She probably noticed, but she won't be surprised. I don't mind talking about Frank. I'd talk about Frank to anybody. But I don't want to talk about the whys or the hows; why Frank died, how Frank died. I just don't. My mind has to move forward.

I stayed with the Ritchies for eight long days after we lost Frank. I had nowhere else to turn. I think I was depressed, but I mostly remember feeling shocked. Or stunned. It was certainly surreal. I felt like I was walking around in another world. Harry was devastated. He cried for seven of those eight days. As soon as he started talking about revenge I decided to go back to my own place. That was tough. Walking into Frank's bedroom for the first time since I lost him was heart-breaking. I fell onto his bed and allowed it to swallow me up as I forced out some tears. I only cried because I felt I should. I'm not sure it did me any good. His room didn't feel right. The cops had been in days ago, searching through all his belongings and, although they did their best to restore everything, it didn't look the same to me.

The sight of a cop standing at the front of your house, pursing their lips in sorrow, is something that tattoos the brain. I'll always remember Declan O'Reilly's face even though I have tried my best to forget it. He was only a young Garda, maybe in his late twenties. I've often wondered if I was the first person he ever had to bring such heart-breaking news to. His pale face told me Frank was dead. I didn't even have to listen to his words. I stumbled back into the hallway before flopping myself on the bottom step of our staircase. I was always conscious, always aware of what was happening, always aware of what I'd just been told. The surreality kicked in two days later, when I was being smothered by the entire Ritchie clan. They did help in some ways, I guess. I needed people around me. I distinctly remember the pain of Frank's death as being physical. My bones and my muscles genuinely throbbed with pain. And I never thought that pain would ease. I believed I was destined for a lifetime of hurt. Bizarrely I'm fulfilled now; happier than I've ever been. My life is exciting, more exciting than I ever thought possible.

'You know I'd still like to see you on a regular basis,' Dinah says.

She mentions this every time I see her. She's proud of how I've recovered, but I'm pretty sure deep down she feels I got over my losses way too quickly. She thinks I will wake up one morning and a grief explosion will go off inside my stomach. She sees contentment in me, but she has no idea that I'm actually filled with joy. That my life without Frank has actually been largely exciting. I came up with this plan a couple of months after I lost my son and I'm buzzing with anticipation. My new life is going to be perfect. Our new life is going to be perfect.

'I'll come a-calling any time I feel like I need a Dinah hug,' I reply.

'I know you will, Jack. You'll always be my favourite.' She says this every time too. She doesn't precede it with 'I really shouldn't say this, but ...' anymore.

When I stand up to embrace her I know I've nailed it. This meeting went as swift and as normal as any of our last few meetings. A drop by. A catch-up. I've been the exact same person I have always been when I'm in this little office. Dinah would have no idea that I am masterminding the greatest bank robbery Ireland has ever seen at this very moment. If – and it's a big if – I ever need an alibi for this morning, I've just perfected one. I haven't looked at the time since getting to the help centre. I didn't want to look at a clock any time I was there, consciously. Dinah couldn't say I was preoccupied in our short meeting. She could genuinely just say I was focused on her. But I guess it must be around eleven-fifteen now. Maybe eleven-twenty. I pace towards my car trying not to get noticed by Trevor. He's still sitting in his own car, about ten or fifteen minutes after meeting with Dinah. Poor fella. He winds his window down as I pass by.

'That was quick,' he calls over to me.

Ah, shit, he's getting out of the car. He purses his lips at me again. This guy is desperate for consolation. I have nothing to say to him. I could rant on and on about him having to deal with the hand that he's been dealt, that his story is his story and he needs to just continue it, that his wife's passing was just a big blemish in the narrative of his life. But I don't have the time for that. I also don't have the personality for it either. I'm too nice a guy to be that blunt to a stranger.

'I … I just see Dinah every now and then for a quick catch-up. She's been very good to me,' I reply.

'Me too.' He smiles. 'She's a huge help.'

I think about patting him on the shoulder and walking away in the immediate silence that follows, but his mouth beats me to it.

'Liver cancer, it was,' he says, looking at his feet.

Jesus, do we really need to do this?

'I'm … I'm really sorry, Trevor. You know … keep seeing Dinah. Tell her everything. She will get you through this. I promise.'

'She's already helping,' he says, trying to sound upbeat. But he's failing. This guy is miserable. 'And you … your wife?' he asks, looking back up at me.

'Skin cancer. Thirteen years ago now. She was gone within six months of diagnosis. Went right through her.'

He looks a little puzzled. 'Same as your son? Was it cancer too?'

'No. No,' I say almost laughing. I don't know why I almost laugh. I think it's the manner in which he seems obsessed with cancer. 'He was killed. Got into a fight one night … y'know.' I shrug. 'One punch and … he was gone.'

11:10

Vincent

'And the last one, Mr Butler,' Noah says, sliding the paperwork towards me.

I'm eyeballing him, not the paperwork. Why has he been so quick reading this? He basically skim-read through the pages, far from as thorough as Chelle or Jonathan were. I should have stopped him, insisted he read every word clearly for me. But I really need to get the fuck out of here. I feel a little disappointed with myself because I let Noah get away with something. I suck my teeth signing the last page. Noah must think I'm still upset with him over his staff not calling him 'Mister'. Then again, perhaps he thinks I'm always upset with him over something. I've never been nice to Noah. I've never been polite to him. It's odd. I'm a really nice person. I'm certain I'm not the only one who thinks that. All my colleagues would consider me fair. Stern, but fair. I wouldn't say people would have reasons to dislike me. Noah would, though. He's probably the only one. Which is why it annoys me that he's always really nice and polite to me. He's got to be fake. He's got to be a fraud.

'Ready, Mr Butler? Three, two—'

I interrupt. 'Hold on, Noah. I'll do the countdown. Okay? Three, two and one.'

We both swipe our keys to enter the first door of the vault. *Fuck you, Voss*, I think, before realising that really was a petty little victory. I shouldn't let this fucker get to me. I need to stay in character. Stay in control. I need to get this job done. Ryan's dimples flash through my mind. He's still kinda cute.

We started to clash when he was home all the time. I didn't have my respite after work. I just wanted an hour to myself to tune out. I always had that when he was working evenings at Wow. But I started to miss that luxury from my day. It irritated me. Ryan didn't irritate me, the circumstance did. But I still took it out on him. I'd casually ask about his novel in the first couple of months, not really caring about the answer. His response was always vague. I just thought I should ask. We began to fuck a lot more then. I think he was bored all day and sex crossed his mind more often. Besides, he wasn't fucking anybody else behind my back for the first time in a while. All his erections were for me. I understood he was most likely living out another fantasy in his head when we were fucking, but I actually appreciated and enjoyed the sex. It was a workout. Besides, most people imagine anybody but the person they're fucking when they're having sex, don't they? I do.

Our relationship was in the 'okay' status, I would have thought. I loved him and hated him in about equal measure and I think he felt the same way about me at that stage. I guess being in an 'okay' relationship is about the average for any couple. But what really bothered me most was that my professional life had sunk to 'okay' status too. I was always a high-flyer. I was always somebody. I felt like somebody when I walked around Dublin. I had control over important matters in this city. But I felt I was starting to become less significant. I could feel it. My walk even changed. There was less of a bounce to it. I knew I was lucky after the redundancies were handed down in early 2009. The board told me they wanted me to stay on as overseer of the four remaining banks. It was a huge responsibility. But there are some days when I think I was actually the unlucky one. Soon after the restructure of the branches, the elderly board members started to wilt away. Slightly earlier-than-they-thought retirement decisions were made and I was left with a naïve board who didn't involve me in any decision-making. It's such a shame. If I had been operating in this position under the previous board I think we'd be back to a similar situation to the one we were in before the recession. As it stands now, we're making slow progress. The progress because of me, the slow because of them. I didn't have a midlife crisis, I had a midlife settlement with myself. I remember sitting down one evening while watching a Bill Maher clip on YouTube and realising I was okay with 'okay'. I was too lazy for anything other than 'okay'. I was beginning to distance myself from social occasions and even reduced Chelle to just a colleague. I was content getting up for work at seven o'clock every morning and arriving home at six-thirty in the evening to crash on the couch with Ryan. I couldn't claim to be the happiest man in the world, but given that the experts were saying one in three people will suffer with depression at some point in their lives and I happened to steer clear of it all my life, being 'okay' was okay by me.

I stand parallel to Noah, intently glaring at his face out of the corner of my eyes. I don't even blink. I really don't understand this guy.

Why did he race through the paperwork? Why does he seem in as much of a rush as I am?

Maybe it's just that I'm such a great boss that when I suggest I'm in a hurry, you are too. It's not even Noah's rushing that's bothering me about him. It's just his face, his bullshit-believing face. I hate it. Even the breaths he's breathing in between each count of ten bundles are annoying me.

'Stop fuckin' breathing,' I spit out of my mouth as if I've got Tourette's. I said what I was thinking. He looks up at me in disbelief. A silence fills the vault and I know it's totally my responsibility to put an end to it.

'Eh ... so loudly. Sorry. It's echoing in here and I can't concentrate on counting along with you.' He's still staring at me, his mouth slightly ajar. So he should. What a ridiculous thing to say to somebody. *Stop breathing.* Fuckin' hell!

'I'm sorry, I'm sorry. That was a really rude thing to say, Noah,' I continue, filling the second silence.

I touch him on the shoulder. I'm sure a vision has flashed past his eyes where he saw himself punching my lights out. I wonder if Noah has a really dark side. I'm sure he does. Most of these Jesus freaks are fronting for a secret life of darkness.

'That's okay, Mr Butler,' he finally says, flashing me his bright pink gums again. They're revolting.

'No, no. I am sorry. Please forget I said that. Please. I'm just under a lot of stress.'

I cringe when he takes his eyes off me. I can feel the embarrassment shudder through my insides. I have never been that rude to anybody in my entire life. I'm just feeling so stressed. I look at my watch. It's almost twenty past eleven. Fuck me. I've forty minutes left.

'Come on, Noah. Let's finish counting these notes, pal.'

11:20

Jack

I find it difficult to get Trevor's sad face out of my head. But I need to refocus. His puppy-dog eyes made me want to hug him and then slap him across the face. 'Move. The. Hell. On.' I felt like screaming at him. Poor sod. My heart went out to him, but I had to make an excuse to get away. I'm glad I bumped into him, though. He gifted me another witness, just in case. After I get to the car and put my wig and beard back on, I hit the standby button on my cheap mobile phone and when the light finally flashes on, I call Darragh. I'm not sure whether I should make my way to Church Street to catch Vincent coming out, or whether I should go straight to the IFSC to watch him enter the fourth and final bank. Either way, I know where I'm driving to now.

'Hey,' Darragh says, answering quickly. He mustn't be letting that phone out of his sight.

'No word from Vincent about Church Street?'

'Not yet. Probably be another ten minutes, I reckon. Time is really tight, JR. Are you sure you don't—'

'Darragh!' I snap down the line at him. 'Me and you, buddy. This is our plan.'

'You're right,' he says. 'I'll call you as soon as he's out of Church Street. Shouldn't be long.'

'How's Ryan?' I ask. It's for a reason. I want to make sure he hasn't been getting into Darragh's head. It's always been imperative that Darragh keeps Ryan under control.

'Grand,' he replies. I don't know what the hell Cork people mean when they say 'grand'. They use it all the time.

'What d'ye mean, grand? He's keeping quiet, yeah? You still have him taped up, around his mouth?

'Yes, JR,' he almost moans back at me. He hates being told anything twice. The problem is, he needs to be told things multiple times. I drilled every aspect of this morning into his head every day for months.

'Good man,' I say before tapping the red button on the phone and starting the car's ignition again.

I'm off to Parnell Street. That's where this car's being left. It'll probably be discovered as having not moved in about a week's time, but it won't link back to me. None of the three cars I'm driving today will. I learned from the best. A walk to Church Street to see Vincent come out of there or to Mayor Street to watch him enter is about eight to ten minutes either way. That's why I chose Parnell Street as the place to leave the first car. Just in case I was caught in this decision. I've thought of everything.

I pleaded with Harry to allow me to handle the hunt for Frank's killer. Even before we'd buried my son, Harry and the lads had been doing their own investigation. Revenge is their reaction to anything, let alone murder. They were ahead of the cops from day one. Sinead, the girl Frankie had picked up in a bar that night, somehow led the police in the wrong direction. She was certain the three lads who encroached on them had come from the opposite side of Tallaght to the one they actually had. That tiny bit of misinformation, innocent to the core, set the cops off on the wrong track. From there, Harry was steps ahead and, within a week or two, the cops allowed him to take control. They continued on their phony investigation, knowing Harry was steering them in the wrong direction. They were happy to do this. The cops in Ireland are like that. They're happy for gangland feuds to play themselves out without having to get in the middle of them. The closer Harry got to finding out who killed Frankie, the more anxious I was getting. I didn't want Frank's death to begin another gangland feud. So I stepped in. I almost got down on my hands and knees to beg Harry to let me take control. I had, unbeknown to him, been led to believe that the killer was part of the Alan Keating gang. If Harry had ever found that out, and he wasn't far off learning it, it would have begun a turf war in the city. I wanted no part in that. Dublin had had enough of that shit for way too long. Frank wasn't involved in that sort of nonsense when he was alive and he certainly wasn't going to be part of it in his death.

'I trust you to do the right thing, Jack,' Harry said, staring into my eyes.

I could see it was paining him to not be directly involved in the revenge on Frank's killer. But he understood my need to see this through for myself.

'I promise I will, Harry. For Frank, for Karyn. I'll make this right.' I had no idea what I was going to do. But I knew if I was the only person who knew who Frank's killer was, then I could buy myself some time to think it all through. Harry had given me great experience on how to investigate without leaving a trace. I'd seen it all before when I used to work for him. His expertise as a gangster really lies in keeping his hands clean. After about a month of chopping my own way through the maze Harry had set me out on, I finally found out who killed Frank.

I feel the phone buzz just as I'm parking up in Parnell Street.

'He's out,' Darragh says.

'That was quick,' I reply, looking at my watch. It's just shy of eleven-thirty.

'He said he got in and out of Church Street within twenty minutes because the manager there is a good friend of his.'

That doesn't sound right to me. Noah Voss is manager of Church Street. Odd.

'And he's all good? He has all two mill?'

'Yeah. It went great. He's made back some time. Just over half an hour to go to the IFSC and out. He's gonna do this, JR. He's gonna do it!'

I can sense the excitement in Darragh's voice. This is not about the money for him. I genuinely believe that. He is excited because of the thrill of the robbery alone. All he's ever wanted to be is a gangster.

'Okay, calm it down, Darragh. Keep cool in front of Ryan. Maybe you're right. We could have all eight mill pretty soon. As I've always said, stick to the plan. You're doing a great job, buddy.' Then I hang up.

Vincent's swiftness in Church Street makes me pause for thought but I really shouldn't let it stop me in my tracks. I need to get out of this car. I shouldn't be noticed in it. The phone call has made my next decision for me. I didn't get to see Vincent walk out of Church Street so I've got to head to Mayor Street at the IFSC. I might get there before him.

11:25

Vincent

EVEN WALKING OUT OF THE CHURCH STREET BRANCH WITH the two cases cuffed to me, I'm trying to figure Noah out. I guess I never will. I got in and out of there within twenty minutes. And I thought that would be the difficult branch. I can't get the 'stop breathing' line out of my head. I'm laughing about it while I pace towards the car. Imagine telling somebody to stop breathing? For fuck's sake. I look up to see John smiling back at me. I shouldn't be seen smiling today, surely. Reality hits. Ryan has only about a half an hour left to live.

'Quick as you can, John,' I say, holding the briefcases up. As I uncuff them, John throws them on top of the others in the back of the boot. That's odd. He's normally so careful. I really am a good boss. If I'm in a hurry, so are you.

'Mayor Street, John boy,' I say, hopping back into the cool air. 'As quick as you can.'

I immediately call Ryan's captor.

'All done in Church Street,' I tell him and hang up.

Fuck him. He'll probably ring back. I allow myself to come out of character listening to Tchaikovsky while I wait.

At least I think it's still Tchaikovsky playing. I imagine what the outcome of this robbery will mean for ACB. The board will hardly bat an eyelid, I bet. I wonder if this could cause one of the branches to close. I hope they choose Church Street if they have to choose any of them. But the reality is, it might not mean a whole lot for the company. Eight million euros is really a drop in the ocean and it will be covered by our insurance companies. It'll be a complicated mess, but it should be swept over in time. ACB branches have been robbed on six occasions in the time I've worked for them. Only once has a bank ever been robbed that I've been in. It was in my early days as a junior employee at ACB, when I was trying to work my way up through the ranks. Two guys entered in masks and held one of my colleagues at gunpoint while insisting the cash tills were emptied into a black plastic bag. I watched on with my fear diminishing into nothingness within seconds. The notes kept falling out of the black plastic bag and the two thieves were forced to scramble around the floor picking them up. We all eyeballed each other awkwardly. They managed to get out of the bank within seven minutes with €110,000, never to be caught. It's not that easy to rob a bank these days. The double door buzz system has killed any attempts at a quick in-and-out cash-till theft. I've always been at the forefront of any advances in security. I think that's why the branches I've worked at since becoming a manager have never been robbed. ACB was one of the first banks in the whole of Ireland to use the double door buzz system and I was the one who pushed for it. The unique thing about this theft is that nobody knows this is happening, so no lives are at risk in the branches. Nobody has a gun pointed at them. Except Ryan, of course. Poor Ryan. I sneak a look over John's shoulder to check the time. 11:28. Half an hour left. I need to get back into character. I need to look like this is an ordinary day. Ken Lockhart won't be much of a problem. He may be over-thorough with the paperwork, but I'll be able to hurry him up.

Ken joined ACB a couple of years after me. He wasn't as good as me initially, but he's learned from the best by now. He's a mini-me. In work mode, not looks. Ken is short and fat; I'm just a little podgy. Ken has round chubby cheeks and a constantly smiling face that makes him endearing to people. But I know the Ken behind that smile. He has a dark side. Not too dark. He's just moody. I think he tries so hard to be nice in public that when he crashes down from that, he crashes hard. As it turned out, most of Ken's crashes coincided with him drinking alcohol. It didn't matter what it was: beer, whisky, spirits, wine. Ken would turn into a totally different person when he had a drink. He threw a punch at me one night. He blamed me for bitching behind his back, but what Ken came to finally realise was he harboured bizarre paranoia traits when he drank. He would just make stuff up off the top of his head and believe it to be true. It sounds so strange, yet it's so common. Everybody knows somebody with this affliction. I've been told it goes undiagnosed in up to ninety per cent of people. But Ken was one of the lucky ones. Thanks to me, he visited a psychiatrist who detailed exactly what was happening to him. He stopped drinking about seven years ago, but he still has mood swings every now and then. He's capable of turning from the happiest man on the planet to depressed in a split second. He manages to keep it under control in work. That saddens me. I know Ken is all smiles all day in the bank and then goes home to feel depressed. And he has nobody to go home to. He owns a beautiful terraced home in Donnybrook but it's wasted on him. He tells me he has good neighbours and a circle of friends that he hangs out with at the weekends. I have to believe him. I spend a lot of my thinking time hoping it's true. I just felt like I couldn't do any more for him. I led him to the psychiatrist and I ensured he got one of the assistant manager positions when the bank restructured. That's surely enough. He runs a decent branch too. He's always done as I suggested, which was why I wanted him as one of the assistant managers. He better do as I suggest today. And quickly.

As John turns onto the quay, I look at my watch. It's just gone half past. This is going to be so tight. We're a couple of minutes from the branch. I need to get in and out of there in less than twenty-five minutes. It's doable.

Stay in character. Don't be anything other than regular Vincent. Stern but fair. One more branch and I am done.

Ryan's dimples flash through my mind again. I'm trying not to think of him. I reach for my iPhone and decide to turn it on again. It takes ages to load up. I notice John turn into the IFSC as my voicemail robot tells me I have two new messages. I sure as hell hope Jonathan isn't one of them.

'Hello, Mr Butler, this is Gareth calling from Vodafone, we'd just like to ask how you are …' I hang up. Fuck off, Vodafone. There's a longer pause than normal before the next message. At least it seems that way. I'd like to listen to it before John pulls over. Shit! It's Jonathan again. Fuckin' meddling asshole.

'Vincent …' he stumbles. 'What's going on? I'm here with Belinda, she says … I've, eh … I've also been onto Michelle.'

Shit!

'She says you've taken two million from her branch this morning as well. I'm sure you know what you're … doing, and it's for good cause, but can you … Tell you what, gimme a call back when you're ready.'

I hit five to listen to the message again. I want to find out what time it was left at. Eleven twenty-six. About seven minutes ago. This is fucked up. The car has pulled over on Mayor Street right outside the branch and John is making his way around to me to open the door. I didn't even notice us stop. I take these seconds to think about what to do. I have to ring Jonathan back. I have to quench that fire. The little cunt is in my office, drooling over Belinda's tits, I bet. I'm about to dial when Ken pops his fat head into the car, scooting John out of his way.

'What's going on, Vincent?' he asks. 'Jonathan's just been onto me.'

11:30

Darragh

ME GUT IS JUST SETTLING AFTER THAT KNEE TO THE BOLLIX.
I've never felt pain like that in me life. I wanted to get up and
shoot the cunt in the head there and then. But while I was
flaked out in pain, I kept hearin' JR's voice.

Stick to the plan.

I shouldn't even be tryna fuck with this fag's head
anyway. I just need to wait it out until I'm instructed to leave
or shoot. There's not long to go now. I stare at the phone in
my hand.

Should I just ring that fucker back?

'All done in Church Street.' Cheeky cunt.

'What is the capital city of Poland?' I shout out.

I'm good at *Jeopardy*. Ah shit. I'm wrong. I'm having a bad
game today. I thought Ascunsion was in Poland. Paraguay?
At least it begins with P. I was on the right track. The fag
hasn't answered one question yet. Dope. I love a bit of
Jeopardy. I love the cheesy ass American TV game shows ye
get on during the day. I look at the phone again. Fuck
Vincent. If he's done, he's done. We've six million guaranteed
now. I'll just get onto JR to give him the good news.

JR and me started out lightly. He used to order me to rob some shops of their tills just to test me nerves, I think. He didn't need convincing for long. He put his trust in me early. He proved it by sticking to his word and splittin' everything down the middle. We weren't makin' much money but he told me that would come with time. He let me in on his big plan and said it could involve a murder and wondered if I'd be okay to follow through if it came down to that. I told him about the murder I'd committed before. If I couldn't trust JR, who could I trust? He's the closest friend I've ever had. I told him that first murder was just an accident but I let him know it gave me the appetite to kill again. JR knows what I mean by appetite to kill. He's been there, done it all, even before I was born. His master plan sounded fuckin deadly the moment he first told me it. He kept the fine details away from me at first, but I knew the big picture. I knew it involved a bank heist and a possible murder. That fuckin excited me. I couldn't wait. We'd meet once or twice a week in the Deer's Head, talkin' shit. JR wasn't just interested in my future, he was keen on my past too. I'd open up to him about how me family left me oul fella behind in Cork to fuck off to Dublin. I even told him how I fell out with me sisters after me ma died and that I was left with nothing until The Boss took me on. I'd never told anyone that before. I don't know if I should look at JR as, like, a da or a brother. I guess he's just me best mate. He's always had me best interests at heart. I didn't need to tell him much about The Boss. He knew him well. It's a small old world, the underworld. JR was aware of what level I'd been able to get to with The Boss. He also knew I was hungry for more. When he sat me down and told me the story of how his former boss had tracked down some scum rapist just outside of Mayo, he got me excited. He wanted me to rob him, then kill him. He used to spike women's drinks before dragging them into his car and rapin' 'em. I couldn't wait to kill the fucker. Throughout the entire four-hour drive to Mayo, I imagined blowing his brains out. Killing somebody is every bit as powerful as you would think it would be. Ever since I knocked that poor fucker's head off the step, I've wanted to kill again. But this time for real. To mean it. I can still hear the rapist cunt denying what I was saying to him.

It wasn't me, you have the wrong man.

'Any last requests?' Bang! Fuck you.

Remembering the high of that killing makes me itch to do it again. I allow meself a little look at Ryan. He's still glued to the TV. He still hasn't answered a question on *Jeopardy* yet. It's mad to think I could be blowin' his brains out in less than half an hour.

'Who is, eh … who is – what's 'is name?' I rush out of my mouth after turning me attention back to the telly.

'Richard Hawkins,' says Ryan.

'Yeah … yeah … yeah, Richard Hawkins,' I shout at the TV.

Correct! That's four I've got right today, now. Maybe it's not been such a bad game for me. I have a *Jeopardy* app on my phone; I'm good at it. But I don't have me phone with me, of course. It's at home. I'll have a game of it when I get back. I need to head straight home after this. I have to follow through on the alibi JR made for me. Me laptop's been pinging all morning. I can't believe the next time I'll have a game of *Jeopardy* on me phone, I'll be a multi-fuckin-millionaire. Holy shit! A wave of adrenaline runs up me stomach, just where the pain was a few minutes ago. I breathe deeply and try to refocus on *Jeopardy* when I notice Ryan leap out of his chair.

11:35

Vincent

COMING CLEAN IS CROSSING MY MIND. I'M ALWAYS HONEST TO Ken. I think about telling him the truth: telling him Ryan is being held hostage in our apartment until I return with eight million euros. Tell him to keep fucking quiet about it though until I'm finished. That it will save my boyfriend's life. But my gut's fighting coming clean.

'I'm taking two mill from each branch,' I say to Ken as I wrap my arm around him and head towards the bank's entrance. I'm bluffing. I have no idea where I'm going with this.

'It's a test,' I continue slowly. I'm trying to buy myself time. Time to think. 'The ... the board have asked me to test security at each bank. They want me to ... to see if each manager will hand out two million.'

'What?' he says, a smile beginning to show on his face. He looks as if his day just got a whole lot more interesting. 'So ... what do I—'

'Just get me the money,' I say, smiling back at him.

'What, is it good to give you the money? I don't ...'

'No. No it's not. Not really,' I reply. 'But that's what I

want. I want them to beef up security. I need this to fail. Michelle, Jonathan and Noah have handed it over and I need you to also.' Ken will do anything for me. I'm sure of it.

'But won't that put me in a bad light with the board? I mean, if … if it's not right to give you two mill … Hang on a minute. It is okay to give you two million though, right? There is no limit we can transfer between banks. So this doesn't add up.'

'They're just testing everybody. Me, you, the other assistant managers. Let's just get this over with and see what they're looking for from all of us. I guess they're testing timescales and … I don't know. I genuinely don't know,' I say, creasing my brow at him as we're buzzed through the second door. 'There's a meeting tomorrow that all of us need to attend. That's all I know. I haven't told you about this, okay?'

'Okay. No problem, Vincent,' he says. His smile still hasn't faded, even though he's as confused as he possibly could be. My improvisation wasn't great. My story is filled with holes. But I did the best I could, thinking on my feet. Ken is leading me into his office when my iPhone buzzes. It's Noah. Holy fuck!

My 'okay' life stayed okay for a number of months, but it started to wane. I'd only have to hear Ryan rustling around in our kitchen for me to get pissed off with him. Everything he did seemed to annoy me. So, I started to annoy him, purposely. I'd ask him about the progress he was making on the book with more regularity.

'It's a work in progress,' he would repeat.

I didn't buy it. I also didn't care. I was just irritating him for the sake of irritating him. I wasn't even snooping when I opened his laptop one Saturday afternoon when he was out. He said he was off doing some research for his book. Maybe he was. I didn't give it much thought, to be honest. I was happy he was doing something different and out of my way for a couple of hours. My laptop was on our bed and Ryan's was nearer to me as I slobbed on our couch, so I picked his up out of pure laziness. There was fuck all on the TV and I wanted to pass a boring afternoon watching shit videos on YouTube.

I searched for the Google Chrome browser but it was nowhere to be seen. I know Ryan likes to use Safari, but I've always found it a weak search browser. It was only when I tried to download Chrome that I realised he already had it. Weird. A search through the desktop led me to it in a hidden folder. It kept getting weirder. The browser history was totally blank. There was only one reason for that. He'd been deleting it. I'm not very tech savvy, but I know that much. As it turned out, I certainly knew more than Ryan. Deleting the history only deletes it from the history section of the browser but not from the entire hard drive. I had to Google how to relocate his activity, but it didn't take long for thousands of URLs to flash up before me. I sat upright on the couch. Ryan had clearly been addicted to a forum called honeypotcommunity. I had to have a snoop. I was gobsmacked. There was an ongoing chat sitting at the top of the first page I opened by two scumbags who called themselves ItalianoStalliano and TeenCum069. They were sharing sick videos of kiddy porn. I could see that from the still screen of one of the videos before even pressing play. Waves of nausea echoed through my body. I couldn't watch. Instead, I read the discussion these two sick fucks were having. One of them was telling the other how to lure kids through Facebook. I knew Ryan's novel was supposed to be dark, but I racked my brain to remember if he had mentioned any paedophile subplots in it. I couldn't think straight. There was a constant pinging sound in my ear. I couldn't shake it off. Why the fuck would Ryan be reading these forums? What would he get from it? He'd been through thousands of pages of this stuff. So many questions ran through my mind, so much so that I couldn't answer any of them. I figured Ryan must be trying to get into the mindset of a paedophile for his book. That was the only logical explanation for this sick shit. He must have been reading these forums to understand how these scumbags work, how they operate. I remember feeling certain that Ryan wouldn't have pressed play on any of the videos. The two cunts exchanging tips on the forum made my blood boil. The discussion was really sick. I scrolled to the top of the page to take note of the home URL of the website. I figured I'd have to ask Ryan about it. That was when I noticed the login details in the top corner. They read: 'ItalianoStalliano signed in'.

Holy fuck. Ryan was one of these sick cunts!

'Mr Butler, Jonathan just rang and said you are taking two million euros from every branch today. Did you lie to—' Noah attempts to ask sternly. I don't let him finish.

'Noah,' I sigh. 'You're sticking your nose in where it doesn't belong. You are actually ruining a very good security examination.'

'I'm sorry, Mr Butler. I don't understand.' Neither do I.

'I'll, eh … I'll call you back in two minutes, Noah. Bear with me. Do not speak to anyone. Not to any of your staff or to any of the board. I will explain everything in two minutes.' This is a mess. I take a look at the screen of the phone after I hang up. 11:41. Holy shit.

'Ken,' I demand like a sergeant in the army. 'Get the paperwork signed. Bring it out to me to sign and then let's get to your vaults as soon as possible, okay?'

'Okay,' he replies. He looks perplexed. I don't have much time to think my way out of this mess.

11:35

Ryan

IT'S HARDER TO PICK AWAY AT THE TAPE ON MY WRIST. BUT I'M doing the best I can. I think the best way to get this off is to loosen it upwards and slide my arm out. Easier said than done. Each tug painfully plucks a hair from my hand. It's like mini torture. I could probably be more aggressive in my approach but I don't want to stir the prick, especially when I'm so close to getting free. If I needed any confirmation that this fucker is as stupid as I felt he was, then having *Jeopardy* on the TV has nailed it. He's swept away by the quiz show, not paying any attention to me as he embarrassingly gets each question wrong. He's a fuckin' retard.

'He is author of *The God Delusion* and *The Greatest Show on Earth?*' asks the host. It's the first question I've genuinely listened to. *The God Delusion* caught my attention. Vincent has a copy. I know he's never read it, but he tells people he has.

'Who is, eh ... who is – what's 'is name?' the prick spits. He keeps pretending he has the knowledge to play along.

'Richard Dawkins,' falls out of my mouth. I don't know why I even bothered. I shouldn't be engaging with him.

'Yeah ... yeah ... yeah, Richard Hawkins,' he shouts at the TV.

Fuckin' idiot. Hawkins. This cunt makes me laugh inside, he really does. He'd make a great character for a book. If only I had the balls to write one. He punches the air with delight when the answer is confirmed. He didn't even get the answer right when given the correct answer. As he's steadying himself for the next question, I manage to force the thumb of my right hand underneath most of the tape wrapped around my left wrist. It's the first time I've managed to get in this far. I stretch it upwards as far as I can and try to squeeze my arm out slowly. It's plucking out every remaining hair on my hand, but I'm making progress.

It's coming out! It's coming out!

I'm not sure if it's relief or nervousness that fills me when I finally find myself free from the chair. It's probably a bit of both. I'd just been concentrating on getting free for the past couple of hours, but now the real test begins. I stare over at the glass table. The gun is about five feet from him, maybe ten feet from me. But he's slouched into the corner of the couch. If I move first, I'll be at the gun before he even notices me. I'm sure of it. I take a moment to play the possibilities out in my head.

When I get to the gun, I'll shoot at his kneecap.

I don't want to kill this cunt. I don't want the mess of a murder charge on my hands. I'm sure I'd be cleared in self-defence, but I'll just down this fucker and let the cops deal with him from there. I allow myself a deep, silent breath before rubbing my thumbs across the palms of my hands to remove the excess sweat. It's now or never. Two more breaths and then I'll leap.

Teencum069 bullied me into believing I was a pussy for not taking advantage of Brady. I knew it was ironic. Somebody who rapes kids calling another guy a 'pussy'. It reminded me of school. And just like school, I gave in to the bully. My obsession with trying to be liked has always got me into trouble. It makes me gullible. It wasn't just Teencum069's taunts that lured me back, it was my fascination with wanting to finally play around with a kid. I watched a hundred different videos of other guys abusing all sorts of kids: fat ones, skinny ones, ugly ones, cute ones, boys, girls. They kept playing in my mind over and over again. I wanted to create my own memory. I couldn't dampen the urge. I continued to message Brady, as Nicole. But I never arranged another meeting with him. I haven't arranged a meeting with any kid since then. An alarm seems to go off in my head every time I get to that point. My fascination with kiddie porn lies in just watching it. I haven't had the balls to rape a child … not yet anyway. I don't trust myself to not follow through with my urges. I've thought about killing myself to end the pain of admitting to myself that I may be a paedophile. I've even written a suicide note.

I don't know why I screech as I leap; it stirs the prick. But he stands no chance. I'm at the gun before him. I end up on my arse, facing him, pointing the gun towards his knees as he tries to get up off the couch. But it won't fire. I pull the trigger twice before he's on top of me, punching at my head.

Have I been held hostage by a fuckin' fake gun?

I know his punches are landing on me, but I don't feel a thing. I'm numbing to the eventuality of being battered to death. I don't want to die. At least I don't want to die today. The cunt pins my shoulders to the ground, using his knees as he straddles my chest. He's shouting at me as blows continue to rain down on my face and chest. I don't know what he's saying. I've become deaf. When he releases his grip to get off me I assume he's done. That's until I see his large boot come straight towards my face.

11:40

Darragh

I STAND OVER HIS BODY, ONE FOOT EITHER SIDE OF HIM, AND click the safety off on the gun. I don't know why I make a point of doing that as loudly as I can. He can't hear me. He's knocked the fuck out. That was some kick to the face. It was like Paul Pogba. I want to shoot him right now. But I can't. I need to wait on JR's instruction. Not long now. Twenty minutes left. I'm out of breath after that. That came outta the fuckin blue, like.

Why the fuck did I leave his right hand untaped?

He musta peeled off all the tape round his ankles and wrist. I duck me head to take a look under the chair he was tied to and see loadsa torn strips of the stuff.

'You're a fuckin idiot, Darragh, a fuckin idiot,' I repeat over and over, stabbing my temple with the barrel of the gun.

I might be goin' mad. Maybe it's the coke. I knew I shoulda stayed sober this morning. At least I have everything under control now. I better get this cunt tied back up to that chair. He's a heavy little fuck. It's not easy liftin' a bare body. His skin's all slippery. Thank fuck he still has his boxer shorts on.

The feeling in the air was quite dead when I returned to JR after killing that rapist. He didn't greet me like The Boss did after I'd got away with the delivery to Limerick. There was no party thrown in me honour. JR takes his business much more seriously. He had exciting news for me when I returned though. He told me he could fully trust me after I'd carried out the hit, and told me about the most exciting plan I could ever dream of. He wanted me to go fifty–fifty with him on the biggest bank robbery in the history of Ireland. And it was genius. He had been looking into this one for over a year. He was researching Bank of Ireland's staff first to see how he could pull off a tiger kidnapping theft through them. But he couldn't find anyone. I didn't know what a tiger kidnapping was. I thought it was fuckin genius when it was explained to me. He told he wanted to kidnap a bank manager's wife and instruct the manager himself to rob the bank. But he said the process of taking money out of the Bank of Ireland was complicated and would have taken a longer period of time. That was when he stumbled onto ACB. Being a smaller bank is exactly what made them perfect for this heist. They had only four branches left in Dublin and we were going to take two million out of each of them. He said he even found some pussy-ass gay couple who we could use for the robbery. 'As easy as taking candy from a baby,' was how JR explained it to me. I couldn't see how it could go wrong. I still can't. Once I keep this fucker tied up, of course. I nearly fucked everything up.

JR has done his research on every aspect of the morning. He followed Vincent and Ryan for weeks, trying to understand their patterns. He even knows the patterns of all the four other bank managers. He's a fuckin legend. Right now, ACB is being robbed of eight million euros and nobody in this whole city has one fuckin clue about it. In the earlier plan, JR was going to do the kidnapping while I followed

Vincent around the banks, just to keep an eye on him. But he was so impressed with how I carried out the murder of the rapist that he felt I was the best man for the more forceful job. He could see it in me that I really wanted to do this part of the job. I told him hundreds of times that I wanted to get me hands as dirty as I possibly could. An eight-million-euro theft, a kidnapping and a possible murder. Me hands can't get much dirtier than that. I couldn't wait for this day to come. It was four months ago when JR first said it to me. I've read every note JR has taken ahead of this mornin'. We've studied every possible scenario. Someday, in the future, I'm going to be just like JR. I'm gonna have me own little apprentice and I'm gonna teach him the genius ways of being a gangster. After all, I'm learning from the best. The Boss was pretty good, I could never deny that, but JR is on a different level. I bleedin' love the guy.

I've eventually got this greasy fuck's body into a sitting position but not even severe slaps across his face are waking him up. I need his head to stop flopping down towards me. I manage to wrap more tape around his wrists, but it's difficult to get his legs steady without his body slouching to one side of the chair and falling towards me. His legs are pointing out and forming a stand for himself. That's the only thing keeping him upright on the chair. I couldn't give a fuck anymore. I wrap the tape around his mouth to the back of his head once again. I never should have removed that this mornin'. I take a look at the microwave as I'm done. 11:45. Fuckin hell. Fifteen minutes left. I wonder where Vincent is. This is getting too close now. I grab at the phone and dial one.

'He's not out yet,' JR whispers into the phone. He knows. He's waiting outside the bank.

'No, I, eh … I'm just wonderin', ye know, it's like eleven forty-five. It's …'

'Darragh,' he says sternly. 'What am I gonna say next to you?'

'Stick to the plan.'

'Exactly. Listen, Vincent will be coming out of here soon, but if he doesn't, you need to get ready to shoot that fuck you have there, okay?'

'No problem,' I say.

'It would take Vincent ten minutes to drive back to you from here, so if he's not out of here in the next five or so minutes, Ryan's fate is decided. You need to be strong.'

'I am strong. I will be strong. I've got it all under control here, JR.'

'I know you have,' he says. 'I trust you to complete the plan, Darragh. Get yourself ready.'

When JR hangs up I let a spray shoot through my lips, causing them to make a fart sound. That's what finally stirs Ryan. That's how much this cunt loves asshole.

'You're about to be fuckin killed, lover boy,' I whisper at him as I reach for the gun.

11:45

Jack

Damn! I missed Vincent going into Mayor Street. I can see his car parked on the opposite side of the Luas tracks. Mayor Street can be a busy-ass street. There's a Luas stop just a hundred yards away and there are thousands of offices around here. My plan was to stand outside the wine bar across from the branch smoking a vaporiser in an attempt to not look suspicious. So many people smoke outside bars and go unnoticed. But there are too many people already here smoking this morning that I almost get into a conversation. I don't know why there are half a dozen guys smoking here already. It's not even midday. They must do a popular lunch inside. I never thought of that as part of the plan. I assumed it would be a quiet bar around this time. I thought they only served alcohol. The last thing I want to do is to get into a conversation with somebody – especially after the Antoinette mess. I ain't taking any chances. The less I'm seen, and especially heard from, the better. I decide to pace up and down Mayor Street very slowly, with the phone to my ear. I don't need call anybody so I just pretend to talk again. I need to steer clear of the CCTV at the Luas stop. I'm waffling some nonsense down the phone when it surprises me by ringing. It's Darragh. He's fretting about the deadline again, but I put him straight. I know he'll shoot Ryan at midday.

I'm starting to get a bit nervy now that I'm not standing where I assumed I would be. I wonder how long Vincent will be in that bank. I need to know. It's a pivotal part of the plan. I look at my watch. It's between a quarter to and ten to twelve. Jaysus, this is so tight. I guess he'll be another ten minutes at least. I already know he'll miss the deadline. There's no way he'll get in and out of there and back to his apartment before midday. But that's fine. That was always part of the plan. Vincent was never meant to make it back home. The wine bar was the ideal spot to stare over at the bank's exit but it's not going to work today. The only option I have to see Vincent come out is to stand on the other corner of Mayor Square. It's busy with pedestrians over there but at least I won't have others standing around me like I had outside the bar. It's not ideal, but there's not long to go. Christ! This is all about to go down in the next few minutes.

I had a few pints on a couple of different occasions in the Deer's Head before arranging to meet Darragh. I knew the barman was aware he sold a bit of weed out of his pub. When I asked him if he knew where I could buy a twenty-euro bag he didn't hesitate in telling me a guy came in around two o'clock almost every day that could fix me up. I wanted to smash my son's killer square in the jaw when I first met him, but I'd already worked on keeping my cool. It wasn't easy. In fact, that's been the hardest part out of this whole process. He thought I was a cop at first, but I soon quashed that idea in his head. I knew straight away he was as thick as horseshit but I had to pretend to like him. I had to befriend him. He was fascinated with my plan to use him as my apprentice. We'd meet up once every couple of weeks in the pub but I made sure to leave no trace. I told him he could call me JR on our very first meeting and he never questioned what the initials stood for. He still hasn't asked. In fact, this idiot has been robbing and murdering for me and he has absolutely no idea who I am. He hasn't even questioned it. He's just been caught up, living his dream. That's what he told me I had done for him – made his dreams come true. He thinks he's Henry Hill in *Goodfellas*. He didn't hesitate in taking money from tills when I ordered him to. We'd split it all down the middle. The money I was getting was being put towards this whole plan. The first wad of cash I spent was on petrol. I sent Darragh off on a road trip to Mayo to test his nerve. He arrived back high as a kite after killing Bob Nugent, a bloke I had researched meticulously to find. He got a thrill from the killing. He told me, 'It was much better than the first time.' That really tested my cool. But I just about managed to pass the test. I've seen Darragh every week for about a year now and I've wanted to knock his lights out each time. I should be rewarded with a medal for remaining so calm and patient. I sat him down one day, soon after he returned from Mayo, and read through the plan for today. He was like a five-year-old on Christmas morning. Giddy with excitement.

'Eight million euro,' he kept repeating over and over again.

Quite odd for somebody who always insisted it wasn't about the money. I bluffed and told him I'd carry out the kidnapping and possible murder while he would shadow Vincent to each bank. I always knew that wasn't going to be the case, but I just wanted Darragh to feel like it wasn't a set-up. I let him naturally tell me he would like to work the apartment. It made it feel like he was plotting and planning with me. He wasn't, of course. I played him.

I don't like where I'm standing but it's either here or outside the wine bar. This street is just way too busy for my liking. I check my watch again. Only three minutes have passed since I last looked at it. I'm sweating. And it's not just because of the sun. I'm not supposed to go over to the car until I see Vincent come out, but I have to bring that part of the plan forward. There are just too many people passing me by. The car's about five hundred yards from where I'm standing now, but I decide to walk around the short block and come back to it from the other angle. That way nobody will see me starting from a standing position and heading straight to the car. If anybody does see me get into it, I want it to look like I'm getting into it because it's mine. Maybe I'm getting too paranoid. I don't like changing my plan, even if it is just bringing something forward by two minutes. It's only a short walk around the back of Sheriff Street. I feel at the back of my trousers pocket to confirm I have what I need. As I approach the car from the pathway I keep my fingers crossed that the doors are unlocked. They should be. John never locks them. Releasing my crossed fingers just ten yards from the car I reach into my back pocket for the taser. John turns around and almost smiles at me when I open the passenger door. He thinks I'm Vincent. His smile turns to confusion just before I stretch my arm towards him and taser his ribcage. He's out cold as soon as I do it, but I follow up with a second blast just to make sure. The car is freezing. He must have had the air conditioning on its coldest setting all morning. Suits me. I've been sweatin'. I turn off the terrible classical music playing on the radio and notice the digital clock as I'm doing so. 11:53. I grip the taser tighter in my hand and sigh loudly. Not long now.

11:50

Vincent

I TAKE A DEEP BREATH AS I SIT DOWN NEXT TO KEN. WE'VE
ordered two of his staff to count out the bundles of cash.
They looked at us as if we'd just landed from another planet.
Ken's assistant manager, Chloe Brannigan, genuinely thought
we were joking. She's only allowed inside the vault with Ken.
They know something odd is going on but they didn't
question us. I press the button on Ken's office phone to dial
out and take the time while the tone rings to wipe my face
with the palm of my hand. I haven't been this panicky since I
collapsed on all fours this morning on Nassau Street. Ken
must be starting to feel my fear. His excitement of minutes
ago seems to have waned. He looks up at me before being
distracted by Noah's voice.

'Hello, Mr Butler,' he booms out. I stretch to the phone to
lower the volume.

'Hi, Noah,' I say, trying to sound calm. 'I've Ken here
with me.'

'Hi, Ken.'

'Hi, Noah.'

'Hello,' another voice screeches.

'Hi, Jonathan,' I answer. 'Bear with us one second.' That's literally all it takes for Chelle to add her voice to the conference call.

'Okay,' I start. 'We're all here. Listen, I have ten minutes to get out of Mayor Street with two million euros or the board are gonna be pretty pissed.'

I've been thinking about what I'm going to say for the past few minutes. I haven't had much time. There are still holes in my story.

'They spoke to me last night after work and said they were going to test each bank's security measures …'

'It doesn't make sense,' interrupts Jonathan.

'Didn't I say listen?' I ask. Nobody answers. I fill the silence with a soft tut before carrying on.

'They are trying to test the withdrawal times. They are claiming withdrawals are taking way too long from both internal and external sources. They want to test internal today and maybe external next week. I don't know …' I stumble. 'I don't know what they're up to. You know yourselves, they probably don't even know what they're up to themselves. It's … it's …'

Noah takes my stuttering as a signal to chime in.

'But, Mr Butler,' he starts, sounding annoying as always. 'I spoke with Mr Sneyd this morning and he had no knowledge of the withdrawal from my branch.' Fuck! Ken stares at me. It elongates my silence.

'You know Clyde,' I say, pushing out a fake snigger. 'He doesn't even know what day of the week it is.'

No response follows. I notice Ken's eyebrows raise. My spine falls back into the leather chair. My mind is lost.

'Vincent …' calls out Chelle.

'Boss …' says Ken into my face, following up after a further silence.

I can't answer them. I'm stumped. My improvisation

skills are normally so good. As they talk over each other, trying to get to grips with what's happened so far this morning, I peel my spine, vertebrae by vertebrae, from the back of the chair.

'We're being robbed,' I sob.

I still couldn't genuinely believe Ryan had been watching kiddie porn even when reading his sick forum discussions with Teencum069. I figured there'd have to be an explanation. Maybe he was trying to get information out of a paedophile for his book? Maybe he was trying to get into the head of a paedophile for his book? But the ringing in my ears wouldn't stop. I clicked on almost every URL link he had hidden in his folder as I tried to come to terms with it all. That was when I remembered there was a Word document called 'note' hidden in the folder too when I first opened it. I clicked out of Chrome, my stomach still turning, and opened the document.

'Dear world,' it started. The ringing in my ears grew louder. 'Today is the day I end my time with you all.' It was a fucking suicide note. I slammed the lid of the laptop down and sprinted for the door of our apartment. I wasn't even dressed. I had an old T-shirt and a pair of boxer shorts on. That was it. I remember a bizarre moment as I stood at the elevator doors waiting for them to open, not knowing what I'd do if another resident appeared in front of me. Luckily the lift was empty. I stood inside staring at myself from all angles in the mirrors that surrounded me. I didn't press any button. I just stood inside for what seemed like ten minutes until the ringing in my ears stopped. Then I strolled back into my apartment and read his suicide note word for word. He left it until the end to mention me, but he did so in glowing terms. He thanked me for all I had done for him, for the life he'd enjoyed with me before he got depressed and turned into a sick man. Tears rolled down my face. But I couldn't sympathise. I couldn't get to grips with what I'd found out over the past hour. My boyfriend was a fuckin' paedophile. The ringing in my ears started again after I'd finished reading the note. It didn't go away until the exact moment Ryan arrived back home that night.

Ken rushes from his chair to grab at me, holding my arms in a hug that confirms he really cares for me. Noah is first to speak.

'I knew it,' he says before the others join in, making the noise from the speaker inaudible.

'Calm down, calm down!' shouts Ken into the phone as he loosens his grip on me. 'Let the boss speak.'

'Ryan is going to die,' I continue sobbing. 'They have Ryan.'

'Who has Ryan?' asks Chelle. Everyone else seems stunned into silence.

'Some asshole broke into my penthouse this morning and told me to come back with eight million in used notes by midday or else he'd shoot Ryan in the head.'

'Call the police,' offers Ken. I look at him as if he's stupid.

'Don't you think I've thought about that?'

'Sorry, Vincent, sorry. I'm just ... I'm just ...'

'No, I'm sorry, Ken. It's me who should be apologising. To everyone. To all of you.'

The line has gone silent again. The other three had been offering something to the conversation but they all spoke over each other. I didn't hear any points or questions they raised.

'Listen,' I say. 'I just need to get back with all the money and Ryan will be safe, okay? I want you guys to ring the cops after twelve o'clock. But only after twelve o'clock, d'ye hear me?'

'It's almost twelve now, Vincent,' Noah pipes up.

'Vincent, are you alright?' asks Chelle, butting in with what I hope is genuine concern.

'I'm fine,' I exhale.

'I knew you weren't right this morning when—' Chelle's sentence is cut off by Jonathan and Noah trying to have a say. The sound grows inaudible again.

'ENOUGH!' screams Ken. He's still on his knees next to me. 'For fuck's sake – Ryan's life is at stake here. There's only about seven minutes left. Vincent,' he says, removing my own hand from my face to look at me. 'Do you have the other six million?' I nod in reply. 'Okay, well let me get the other two mill for you and get you outta here.'

I can hear the panic on the other end of the line but I try not to listen to it as Ken leaves me alone in his office.

'Guys,' I say, shutting the three of them up after a few moments. 'Call the cops. But only after midday, okay? Wait until Ryan is safe. Promise me you'll wait until after midday.'

Chelle is the first to answer. 'We will, Vincent,' she says. 'We promise.'

Noah is still adding to the conversation but I speak over him.

'Please, Chelle. I'm leaving this with you. I trust you so much. Leave it another ten to fifteen minutes until I can get back to him and then call the cops.' I hang up and sit stunned in the silence. The noise of Ken's wall clock brings me crashing back to reality after a few seconds. *Tick, tock, tick, tock.* I look at the screen of my iPhone. 11:54. Fuck me! I have to ring the fucker holding Ryan hostage.

'Here you are, boss,' Ken says in one breath, swinging the two briefcases towards me before I lift the phone to my ear. 'Go get Ryan!'

I don't know why I'm wasting time hugging him and trying to justify all that's gone on this morning. Ken wipes the tears from my eyes before shoving me towards the door.

'Go on, boss, go!'

I can barely see the phone through my moist eyes, but I know I only have to press one to reach the greasy prick.

'I have it, I have it,' I say down the line as I race through the floor of the bank.

'Wow, good man,' he replies. 'With just a few minutes to go. You kept it tight, fag, huh? I bet you like it tight.'

'I'll be back to you in ten minutes. I'm getting into the car now,' I pant down the line as I'm buzzed out of the bank door. He hangs up. I don't have time to care.

I put the phone back into my pocket and race across the tram tracks and into the back seat of the car with the cases. John wasn't by the boot to meet me this time. It doesn't matter.

'My apartment, John, quick as you can.'

11:55

Ryan

Fuck me. My head feels like it's spinning in a washing machine. It doesn't take long for reality to set in. When it does, my stomach spins quicker than my head. The blur in front of me focuses after a few seconds tick by. The prick is standing staring at me, smiling behind a pointed gun.

Holy shit.

My plan clearly didn't go well. The last thing I remember was this exact scenario happening the other way around. I was pointing that gun at him. Then I remember. It's a fuckin' fake gun.

I turn my head towards the microwave even though it really hurts to do so. It's just ticked to 11:56.

Four minutes.

I try to ask if he knows where Vincent is but only a muffled sound comes out of my mouth. I've been taped back up. Fucking hell. I won't be able to talk myself out of this. I can't tell this smarmy little cunt that he's left his DNA all over my TV screen, that he's fucked either way. My mind tries to focus, but it can't. I can't remember where Vincent was when I pounced for the gun, so I've no idea where he could be now. My mumbling is making this prick laugh. He only stops when his phone rings. I know it's Vincent. It's typical Vincent. The hero at the last second.

'Wow, good man,' says the prick down the line.

Vincent has done it! Jesus Christ. This is like something from one of Tom Cruise's shit action movies. The clock stopping with just seconds remaining before the world blows up. I can't believe this is real life. The prick doesn't even bother to look at me after he hangs up. Instead, he dials out. He must be letting his partner know everything is complete. I wonder how Vincent is. He must be in pieces. I try to breathe in a relaxing manner, imagining I'm back at yoga when the prick begins fretting on the phone. Something's not right.

'Sorry?' he asks, puzzled.

Pause.

'But he'll be … Vincent is … he'll be here in a few minutes with all the money.'

Pause.

'But I … Really?'

Pause.

'Of course, JR. I'll do it now.'

What the fuck is going on here?

I thought about suicide for forty-eight hours straight without any sleep breaking up my nightmare. I wondered how I could kill myself in the most painless way. I assumed an overdose of painkillers would be the way to go, but a quick Google search led me to believe that slitting my wrists might be the most sudden ending. Fuck that. That sounded way too dramatic for me. It also sounded tough to do. I wasn't sure where I would kill myself either. Doing it at the penthouse never crossed my mind. That would've been too much for Vincent to bear. He would have had to deal with losing the love of his life, as well as finding his body, and possibly having to move out of his dream home if that was the case. He surely couldn't go on living here if it was where I topped myself. And Vincent has worked so hard to own this home. He loves his penthouse.

After two days, I began to think myself out of it. Maybe I was too much of a coward to go ahead with killing myself. When I finally managed a decent stretch of sleep, I woke up a new man. Why should I give up my apartment, my boyfriend, my life? I had so much to offer the world. I wrote the first two chapters of my novel that morning. It was great work too. A real gripping opening; Chad Sutcliffe was an amateur photographer turned paparazzo who began to obsess about one Hollywood star in particular. I thought about using real Hollywood stars for the story but when I realised I'd have to kill a couple of them off, I figured I'd have to make 'em up. Denise Knight was the name I concocted for my leading lady – a cross between Denise Richards and Kiera Knightly. I envisaged a smiling face with big, beautiful eyes and that was the name I came up with. I wanted my readers to fall in love with her so that when she's killed late on, it's a real shock twist. But it's hard to use the laptop for an extended period of time without surfing the web. And when I go surfing, I inevitably end up in choppy waters. Before I'd even started chapter three the very next day, I was already looking at kiddie porn. I was determined to not enter the chatrooms to converse with TeenCum069, but I only staved that off until lunchtime. The sick fuck kept at me to meet kids. He wanted me to film myself with them. He was beginning to repulse me but then again, so did cocaine the first time I tried it. Now I'm addicted to both. We chat for hours, talking about what strategy we would use for our victims. But there's never been a victim my end. I just can't bring myself to do it. I guess that probably makes me a coward. No matter what I do, I end up being a fuckin' coward.

He seems to have a grin on his face as he points the gun at me. I'm pretty certain, even though I didn't hear, that his partner in crime has just ordered him to kill me. I think about screaming and shouting but for some reason I'm quiet. I believe he isn't really going to do it. He can't do it.

That's a fake gun, right?

'Any last requests?' he asks.

12:00

Jack

HERE HE IS! HE HAS THE PHONE TO HIS EAR AS HE RUSHES towards the car, hugging the final two cases with his other hand. They're not even cuffed to his wrists. He's obviously pleading with Darragh. He jumps into the back of the car without noticing John slumped in the passenger seat.

'My apartment, John, quick as you can,' he says before realising it's not John he aimed that demand at.

I don't hesitate. I dig the taser under his arm and squeeze the trigger. He falls flat into the gap between the front and back seats. Perfect! I turn the key in the ignition and pull away slowly, noticing that nobody has followed Vincent out of the bank.

I've done it! I've fuckin' done it!

The rush feels insane. As I'm pulling away, Darragh calls.

'JR, he's out, he's out. We've done it,' he yelps. 'He said he'll be back here in less than ten minutes.'

'Game over, Darragh,' I say. 'It's midday now and he's not back. Do your job.'

'Sorry?' he asks, puzzled.

I didn't think he'd be. I figured he couldn't wait to blow Ryan's head off.

'I'll look after Vincent from here. I'll get the money. But kill Ryan. Vincent missed the deadline. We stick to our plan.'

'But he'll be ... Vincent is ... he'll be here in a few minutes with all the money.'

'It's midday and he's not back at the apartment. Do your job.'

'But I ... Really?'

'Stick to the plan!' I say, raising my voice a little.

'Of course, JR. I'll do it now.' I know he'll do it. But I'm not taking any risks.

'I'll stay on the line. Let me hear you do it,' I say.

I've always trusted Darragh to carry out the murder. His eyes lit up when I first told him about this whole plan. He kept telling me I was a genius over and over again. Maybe he's right. It is a pretty smart plan. I told him as much as I possibly could. He knows I have two getaway cars parked up in different areas of Dublin. I wanted to sound legitimate to him at every opportunity. I certainly achieved that. He never guessed for one minute that I was setting him up. As soon as I hang up from Darragh, I call the cops.

'There's something huge going down at the penthouse of Arbour Building on Horse Fair. A man is holding another man at gunpoint. He's probably already killed him. You need to get there as soon as possible,' I say in one long breath.

'Okay, sir, please calm down. Can you stay on the line?' It's unbelievable how cool these emergency operators remain in circumstances like these. But I know this woman has already ordered a police car to arrive at Vincent and Ryan's penthouse through the push of a button.

'No, I can't stay on the line. This is very real, ma'am,' I say. 'You need to be quick.'

'A police car is on its way right now, sir,' she says. 'But if

275

you can stay on the line to give me—' I don't let her finish. I hang up. I have to call Darragh back. It's an important part of the plan. I wait two minutes before making the call.

'Darragh,' I say, deliberately sounding panicked.

'Yeah, JR?'

'Where are ya, buddy?'

'I'm just headin' out of the apartment now. Everythin' alrigh'? What's wrong...'

'The cops are coming. I think Vincent, the fag bastard, had somebody call the cops. You need to get out of there as soon as possible.'

'Wha' the fuck? Comin' here, ya mean?'

'Yeah. On their way to the penthouse. You should be fine. Get out as quickly as you can. Darragh, listen to me. Best of luck, buddy, okay. And remember, whatever happens, stick to the plan.'

I can't keep the smile off my face as I drive down Sherriff Street to head towards East Wall. That's where I have my second car parked up. That's my job done. I've no more calls to make. All I have to do is slot this car in behind the grey Toyota Corolla that I have waiting for me and transfer the money into the boot. The cops should be arriving at the apartment any minute now. It's touch and go whether Darragh will make it out before they come. But even if he does, they'll catch up with him within minutes. I've spent a large amount of time wondering whether he'll try to shoot himself out of this situation or just hold his hands up. I'd prefer he spent the rest of his life in prison over a quick death. But I made my peace with both possibilities a long time ago.

As I turn onto East Road, I look at the clock on the dashboard. 12:08. I'm so good with time. I think I have a natural clock in my head. This morning couldn't have gone any more perfectly. I slowly roll the BMW into the space behind the Corolla and take the first two cases Vincent dropped in the back of this car with me as I get out. I take a good look around the street as I do this, but I know nobody will be lurking here. It's too remote. It takes me two more trips from car to car before I have all eight cases flung into the Corolla. Vincent and John are still out cold in their car. They will probably start to come round in another fifteen minutes or so. A flutter of relief runs through my body when I drive away. It's not that I didn't think the car would start, it's just that driving away in this car confirms the robbery went as planned. There's no way I'll be caught from here. Even when the cops are on this case they won't be looking for a grey Toyota Corolla in Dublin. I smile at myself in the rear-view mirror as I pull out onto Alfie Byrne Road and head north. I've one more car stop to do before heading for Belfast.

12:00

Darragh

I shouldn't be surprised that JR still ordered me to kill Ryan. I guess he's right. Vincent's instructions were to be back here by midday, not to be coming out of the last bank at that time. I gotta stick to the plan. I don't think Ryan knows what's comin'. He's very quiet for someone who's about to have their brains blown out. I screw the silencer onto the barrel of the gun after I place the phone on the arm of the sofa with JR listening in. Then I point the silencer between Ryan's eyes.

'Any lasts requests?' I say, really cool, before firing a bullet through his head.

His chin just rests on his chest after the shot. I'm amazed at the lack of blood. It was the same with the sick rapist I killed a few months ago. The small amount of blood from a headshot is really surprising. I always assumed it'd be a mess. That's not the case. Maybe that's the difference between movies and real life. I grab a fistful of his hair to lift his head up, just so I can make sure there are no signs of life.

'Rest in peace, fag,' I whisper into his ear before dropping his head back down.

'Job done, JR,' I say into the phone.

'Excellent, Darragh. I'll see you tomorrow as planned, okay?'

'You got it.'

I feel high as a kite as I begin to pack my bag to leave. I notice the broken tape on the chair under Ryan and tut. That was me only mistake of the day. It's disappointing but I'll learn from it. At least I sorted out the mess. The morning has gone almost perfectly for me. I got the job done. Here I am. It's midday and I'm a multi-fuckin'-millionaire, just as JR promised I would be. I'm almost skippin' out the door with pride when the phone buzzes.

'Darragh,' JR says in such a way that it frightens me.

'Yeah, JR?'

'Where are ya, buddy?'

'I'm just headin' out of the apartment now. Everythin' alrigh'? What's wrong…'

'The cops are coming.'

I can't believe what he's saying to me. I'm so stunned that it almost stops me in me tracks but I gotta keep moving. I need to get the fuck outta here.

'You should be fine,' says JR, tryna keep me calm. 'Get out as quickly as you can. Darragh, listen to me. Best of luck, buddy, okay. And remember, whatever happens, stick to the plan.'

Holy fuck!

I can't help but take a look at Ryan's body hanging off the chair before I slam the front door of their apartment behind me. I can't take the lift. At least getting down the stairs will be easier than comin' up. With me bag thrown over me shoulder I bounce as quickly as I can down each step. I bet it was that Noah what's-'is-name that rang the cops. JR always said he'd be the troublesome one. I started the day feeling a mix of nerves and excitement. That's certainly how I'm feeling now. I've just killed another man. That's three on me list now. But this is the closest I've been to gettin' caught. I have no idea how long it will take the cops to get here.

I'm almost on the ground floor when I get me answer. The sirens ring through me ear. It's the scariest sound I've ever heard. I've been frightened before but this is proper fuckin scary. It's a really, really strange feeling to be properly frightened. Your stomach turns. I can feel fear inside me body. I hold me hand out in front of me to see how much it's shaking. Quite a lot. I'm normally cool. I manage to get meself into the cramped staff area I broke into this morning when I hear the cops screech outside and make their way into the lobby. I don't fuckin' believe this. I'm literally trapped. I have to think my way out of this mess. My only option is to sneak back up the stairs to break into another apartment. I could probably hide out there until the cops go. But surely they'll check each apartment. Staying here is probably me best bet. At least I can hear them from here if I press me ear up against the door.

'Everything okay?' I hear one booming cop's voice say.

The receptionist is quite quiet. I can't hear her response but I get the feelin' she's surprised by all this. So am I. Everything had gone perfectly right up until the last minute, literally. Now I'm about ten feet away from bein' arrested for murder. I stare at the gun in my hand. I know I've five bullets left in the round. That should be enough to get rid of a couple of cops. But I know that's the stupid decision to make. I wonder what JR would do in this situation. He gave me strict instructions to get away from the rapist's house a few months ago but I have no instructions for leaving this place. We never thought it would get to this. I'm just supposed to return home now. I'm conscious of the mobile phone in me pocket but I can't ring JR. If I can hear them talking in the reception area then they would surely hear me.

I'm lookin' for ways of hiding in this small room when I hear another cop car pull up outside. I'm really fucked now. I've gone from being high as a kite to practically shittin' meself. I feel me stomach again. I genuinely need to shite right now. I notice the empty bucket I tripped over this morning. Shitting shouldn't be at the forefront of me mind, but I can't hold it in. Maybe it will relieve some of the tension. Sometimes I do me best thinkin' on the jacks. I hear the ping of the elevator arriving on the ground floor and I know the cops are on their way up to the fags' apartment. They're gonna find Ryan's body and call for more backup. They're bound to search every inch of this place. I loosen me belt, pull down me jeans and squat over the bucket. Me stomach rumbles as my ass practically pukes. I really am sick with worry. Me hole seems to think I'm finished but me stomach has other ideas. It's still rumbling. The shitting isn't helping me relax. It's not doin' the job I hoped it would. I can't think straight. I find meself eyeballing a rack of towels and decide that they'll be great to wipe me hole with. How can I be thinkin' about that right now? Then I notice a janitor's uniform hanging behind the towels. That seems to stop the shitting.

Yes, Darragh! You fuckin' genius.

I kick me shoes off and pull the waistband of me jeans over me feet. The uniform is way too big on me. The sleeves look like a fuckin elephant trunk hanging over my arms. But at least it looks like I work here. I should be able to walk out unnoticed. I'm thinkin' 'bout whether to take the direction of the stairs or whether to brave it and walk out onto the lobby floor and straight through the exit. I can't hear any cops in the reception but I'm sure there's one or two out on the street waiting to see if someone comes out. I'll have to bide me time. I decide I should head upstairs. I'm about to make me way to the stairwell when me stomach rolls again. This has only ever happened to me once before when I got food poisoning. Fear genuinely does seem to make you shit yourself.

I zip down the top half of the uniform towards me knees and squat over the bucket again. Me shit is still wet. It slaps against the rest of the shit in the bottom of the bucket at the exact same time the door slams open.

'Stay where you are,' a fat cop shouts at me before yellin' out for backup.

I pat me hand around to feel for the gun but I don't know what way I've pulled this uniform down. It seems to be inside out. The realisation that I'm fucked makes my stomach roar again. The two of us hear the shite spray outta me hole as we stare into each other's eyes awkwardly. He holds his gun in one hand and his nose in the other as he makes his way towards me. I'm fuckin done for.

SIX MONTHS LATER

12:00

Jack

I don't feel Frank's presence that much around here anymore. Especially not on these rooftop terrace bars. We didn't come up to one of these when we visited together. I did feel his presence the first few times I returned after his death. But ever since I moved here permanently, his shadow seems to have disappeared from every street corner. It's probably the clearest sign that I've started a new life. He's still very much in my heart, of course. My memories of Frank are my most treasured thoughts. They're worth a lot more to me than the millions I possess.

I split the money between sixteen different banks throughout Europe. Four of those are here in Rome. I'm so rich. I'm rich in more than just monetary terms. I couldn't be happier. Which is some achievement given how much of my life has been filled with heartache. I've been living in Rome for over four months now.

I drove to Belfast straight after the robbery, only stopping in Drogheda for another car change. I stayed in the Radisson Blu Hotel for ten days. My flight to London was always booked for May the third. I spent two weeks there, setting up four accounts with two different banks. I don't like London. There's a real lack of warmth on the streets of that city. I've travelled through France, Belgium and Switzerland on the way to my new life and, while they all have many beautiful traits, spending time in them has reassured me that Rome is the most idyllic place in the world to live in. My travels went perfectly well except for patches of boredom. But I got everything done that I needed to without any hitches. It went almost as perfectly as the morning of the robbery itself. I was always certain Darragh would do as instructed. His commitment was never really an issue for me. The little prick was so gullible – gullible and stupid. It was his stupidity that made the whole plan possible. I almost felt sorry for him on occasions. He'd make me laugh. He was so dumb that he became the comedy in my life for seven months. But there was never a moment where I forgot he murdered my son. I was intent on screwing him over, more so than getting the money. I often wonder what he's up to. I know he was brought to Portlaoise prison initially. I'm not sure if he's still there now. They sent him there the day after he was arrested. That's what I read in the *Irish Daily Star*, crashed out on the bed of my hotel room a couple of days after the robbery. His trial can't be far off. He's most likely racking his brain trying to figure out who the hell I am. Then again, he might not be. He probably still thinks we're best pals. Maybe he's still sticking to the plan. The cops must be leaning heavily on him for any nugget of information about his accomplice. He knows nothing. I covered every track I made. I went through everything with a fine-tooth comb countless times and couldn't find any holes in the plan. We executed everything perfectly. The only time I felt worried through the whole ordeal was when I bumped into Antoinette. I often think about her. I never used to. But she became a central figure in my most memorable morning ever. When I was shacked up in Belfast, I worried that I would see a picture of myself in the newspapers. But I knew in my heart that Antoinette had no idea who she was talking to that morning. I was totally unrecognisable. There was another small instance when a police car siren almost made my heart jump out of my mouth after I'd picked up the third car just outside Clogherhead. I had literally just transferred the cases into it and had driven only twenty metres when I heard a blaze of sirens. The cops flew by me, much to my relief. I laughed out loud, banging on the steering wheel.

I'm certainly safe now. There's no catching up with me here. I adore Rome so much. There's character on every street. But it's been slightly lonely, living here for seventeen weeks without much company. I made friends with a Dutch couple, who were staying in the first hotel I was living in, but ever since they went home I've had nobody to share a drink with. That's all about to change. I look at my watch and release an excited puff of my cheeks. Two minutes past twelve. I'm so excited about our new life. My favourite thing about Rome is these rooftop terraced bars. There is no better place on the planet to be on a bright day. It's not hot, but the glare of the sun is making me squint. My eyes take in as much as they possibly can from this height. The Hotel Forum overlooks the Colosseum and the grounds of the Roman Forum. In the distance you can just about make out the steeples of Vatican City. That's a country all to itself. The smallest country in the world. I've walked through it twice now, laughing at the hypocrisy of Christianity. Religion is a joke, but it's a funny joke – ye gotta give them that. The big tourist attractions aren't the reason we've hungered to live here. It's the tiny nuances of this ancient city that made us crave living here. My stroll down Via Margutta and Via Gregoriana this morning still had the same effect on me that it had the very first time I walked it ten years ago. I love the effortlessness of the architecture. Nothing's flashy, but it's all beautiful. It makes Dublin seem really ugly. Rome makes every city unimpressive by comparison, in fairness. I take another sip of Château Petrus as I breathe in the excitement of today through my nose. That's the sort of wine I can drink now. I just paid almost two thousand euros for this bottle. I guess that's what multi-millionaires do. As I place my glass back down onto the table I hear a faint shuffle of footsteps brush the patio ground behind me. My stomach flips over.

12:00

Darragh

PRISON ISN'T BAD. WE'VE A GAMES ROOM HERE. THERE'S AN Xbox 360 and a PlayStation 3 in it. I've been masterin' FIFA over the past few months. Nobody can beat me Man United team.

Prison's a bit like a boys' club. It's fine once your cell door is open, but when you're locked up it can get a lil boring. All you have for company is your own mind and that often plays tricks on itself. I look at the clock on the wall of the meeting room. It's just ticked by midday. Jennifer is always late. I bet she's not here for at least another ten minutes. I'm not bothered. It'll be more of the same. She'll try to get me to plead guilty again. I left so much DNA at the fags' apartment that she feels I've got no chance in me trial. They found me fuckin cum all over the television. Fuck it. I never thought of that. I don't know what I was thinkin'. The cops are tryna get me to rat JR out but I ain't givin' in. I'm sticking to our plan.

This prison doesn't look like anything I've seen on the telly before. It's actually a bit modern. It's clean. It's certainly cleaner than my bedsit. The bed's a bit uncomfortable, but that's me only real complaint. The mattress is so thin it's like sleeping on an ironing board. But I'm slowly getting used to it. The screws are fine. Most of them are keen to get along with the prisoners. They just want to get through a work shift without any drama. There's a couple of dicks, but most of them really couldn't give a shit. I haven't had a run in with any of them. In fact, I haven't had a run in with anyone. The prisoners seem okay to me too. I just keep meself to meself. There are a few guys that I play computer games with but that's about it. It's winner stays on down in the games room so my company can change every ten minutes. I'd like to be known as The FIFA King but that nickname hasn't really caught on. I guess you don't get to come up with your own name in prison. I'm not bitter about gettin' caught. I think we were just unlucky. Me lawyer says there were three phone calls made to the cops at around twelve o'clock on the day of the murder. They know who two of them are. Michelle and Noah from the banks. Vincent caved at the last minute, tryin' to save Ryan's life, and told them everything. But he fucked up. He got his pussy-ass boyfriend killed. I hope he's carrying that guilt around with him. The cops seem to think it was my partner who made the third call. I don't believe them. JR would never have ratted me out. We're too close. They keep tellin' me I can halve the amount of time I'll have to spend in prison if I give him up, but that's just not gonna happen. I'm going to get through this on me own. My trial's supposed to be only two months away but me lawyer seems to think it will be delayed past that. She's not happy with me. I can sense it. She really wants me to rat JR out. She doesn't understand the rules of bein' a gangster.

When I'm alone in me cell I think through the morning of the murder again and again. Sometimes I get a little paranoid about JR's involvement. It often flashes through me mind that he wanted to keep all that money to himself. But why did he give me fifty per cent of every other robbery we carried out? It doesn't make any sense. I've added up in my head that he musta made me over eighty grand in the short few months that we worked together. And why did he set my computer up on the day to make it look like I was home all morning? He gave me an alibi. He gave me the disguise. Besides, JR rang me to warn that the cops were on the way. Why would he do that if he was trying to frame me? None of it adds up. He's hardly an enemy. He's a good friend. A great friend. Probably the best friend I've ever had. In fact, he's definitely the best friend I've ever had. My lawyer and the cops have a different twist on it though. They haven't a fuckin clue. They just want to put an end to this whole thing. One prisoner told me they have quotas to reach anyway. My lawyer would benefit from me taking a plea deal and reducing my sentence. She has a reputation for plea deals and that's how she gets so much business. I like her though. Jennifer must be over fifty but she's hot. Her face ain't great. She's got a few scars dotted around her cheeks. I'm not sure if it's from acne or a knife. But she has that Latino body all men drool over. Big ass, big hips. I like spending time with her even if she does try to bully me a bit. She complains that I don't say enough in our meetings, but that's because all I'm ever thinkin' is how much I'd love to bend her over and fuck her South American brains out. Besides, even if I did want to give JR up, I don't really know that much about him. I know his name, that's about it. In fact, I don't really know his name. I know his initials. Billy, the barman who introduced me to JR, told me once that he thought his name was Jack somethin'-or-other. I think it began with a B or a D. He says JR looked like a guy a mate of his used to play golf with years back. He wasn't a hundred per cent sure though. But even if I went down that road, I have no idea where Billy is now. The last I heard he was moving to Galway to become a barman at some jazz club. I don't even know Billy's surname. I could look into it, I suppose. Maybe I will in the future. But I'm certain JR will contact me at some point. We can hardly talk now. These cunts are trackin' everything I do. JR will have to wait it out, probably for another couple of years. That's a shame. I miss him. We spent so much time together. I certainly have the time on my hands to be patient. I have to shut out the bullying from Jennifer and the cops. I can't let it play on repeat in me head while I'm in me cell alone. I'd probably ask for a less annoyin' lawyer if Jennifer's ass wasn't making me dick hard.

I guess the good thing about prison is me urges to kill seem to have gone away. I still think of the faces of the three men I've murdered. I can only remember the first two from the photographs that appeared in the newspapers over the days after their deaths. But Ryan's face is very clear to me. I can even hear him talkin' to me sometimes. I feel a sense of success over the cops that they think I've only murdered one man. I may have to spend the rest of me life in prison, but I still got away with murder – twice! I'm a proper fuckin gangster. I'm gutted I got caught but I'm fine with how my life's gone. If I had the chance to go back in time to meet JR in the Deer's Head, I'd do it all over again.

12:00

Vincent

I NEVER RETURNED TO THE PENTHOUSE. I COULDN'T.

Chelle and her husband Jake organised the collection of my furniture and all my possessions. I've never set foot in any of the banks again either. My colleagues understood. I told them I was moving to Sydney to live out the rest of my life where Ryan always wanted to live; that I was dedicating the rest of my existence to his memory.

The bank sorted me out with a very handsome redundancy package. They rushed it through as quickly as they could. Half a million euros. Thank you very much. That added to the €890,000 profit I ended up with for the sale of the penthouse. I couldn't leave Dublin until the police finished their investigation, though. There was a period of two weeks where I was under serious consideration of being involved in the crime. Nobody at the bank thought I had any part in it but one of the detectives came down very hard on me. Even my tears of self-guilt didn't give him reason to sympathise with the fact that my boyfriend had just been murdered. I suppose he was just doing his job. The other detective looking into the case was always on my side.

Maybe they were just playing the good-cop, bad-cop card. It seemed that way to me. But after a couple weeks of intense scrutiny and uncertainty, they relieved me of any involvement.

They're still on the lookout for whoever escaped with the cash. Darragh Galligan isn't giving up his partner in crime. That freak wasted no time putting a bullet through Ryan's head. My ex-boyfriend died instantly. I imagined Ryan's face every minute of every day for the next three months. I couldn't get what he would have gone through that morning out of my mind. But I was keen to put that whole life behind me.

The glare of the low sun makes me blink as I push through the glass door. It reminds me of the morning of the killing. A waiter greets me with a friendly smile but I don't need his assistance. I know who I'm looking for. There's no mistaking the back of that head. It's always had more hair on it than mine. He feels my presence and spins around just before I get to him; then grabs me in tight.

'We did it,' he whispers into my ear. I've missed his voice. I've missed his face. I've missed those lips. Jack is the best kisser I've ever kissed. I guess that's down to the years he spent kissing girls before he realised he was gay. I don't know why it took him so long. He's so obviously camp. Much camper than me.

'Yes we did!' I reply before leaning off him so I can stare into his blue eyes. I love every inch of him.

I never felt our plan would fail. Jack had new passports and identifications set up for us through his contacts with his old mates and I set out a plan to spread the money without any suspicion. We're both Canadians now. Stanley Lam and Roy Gagnon.

Fucking Stanley! I've actually become quite fond of it ever since Jack first told me what my new name would be. It's grown on me over the past few months. The paperwork is official. The guys Jack knew from his gangland days know all the tricks with that sort of shit. The real Stanley Lam and Roy Gagnon are dead, but their deaths have never officially been recorded in Canada. We are them now.

I taught Jack how to spread the money throughout Europe. The main bulk of the eight million is dotted around four different banks in Switzerland, but we've bank accounts in London, Brussels and here in Rome. Between us, we possessed the expertise to pull this off. We just needed to make sure the execution of the morning went without a hitch. I knew what the rough tiger kidnapping plan was, but Jack purposely didn't tell me when or exactly how we were going to pull it off. We planned it that way so that my fear would be very much real on the day.

We talked about living in Rome on the very first date we ever went on almost two years ago. Now here we are, multi-millionaires in our favourite place in the world, living out the rest of our days. Hopefully there's a lot of days to come. We're both classed as middle aged, but at almost 50, the chances are we're both over the half-way line.

It was Jack who raised the idea of me robbing my old bank pretty early on. But he was genuinely only joking. We laughed at the thought. We were two genuinely nice guys whose lives got turned upside down at the very same time we started to fall in love. Not long after I'd found out Ryan was fucking kids — and as a result was suicidal — Jack's investigation into the killing of his son Frank was tying itself together. He discussed his search for Frank's killer with me over pillow talk even in our early days of dating and we had long discussions on what he should do when he finally caught up with him. A light bulb went on in Jack's head one day when he revealed the rough plan to me. I thought he was crazy. But the more we talked about it, the more it seemed to make perfect sense. It actually became a no-brainer. We were shocked we could both be so dark.

We figured out a way to get rid of both Ryan and Darragh in one genius swoop while helping ourselves to our dream life. We both genuinely felt that we deserved our dream life. We'd both been served shitty hands up until that point. I try not to think about Ryan at all. I don't feel a huge amount of guilt. He wanted to die. I'm not sure if Bob Nugent wanted to die, but he deserved to. The shit I saw that sick fuck doing to young kids in videos he posted to Ryan as TeenCum069 was vomit-inducing. He left a few hints in the forums about who he was and where he was based. It didn't take long for Jack to track him down and use him as the ultimate test for Darragh. We had to know if he could kill. It all fell into place for us. The serendipity of it all would almost make you believe in fate. Jack and I had always arranged to meet up here on the rooftop of the Forum Hotel at midday exactly six months from the day of the robbery.

Darragh's upcoming trial gave me a big problem though. I was due to be a key witness for the prosecution. My lawyer fought hard to keep me away from the courts. The police weren't happy but I was finally pardoned on the grounds of personal grief. The detective who had come down hard on me during the investigation turned out to be my hero. He told the courts they had more than enough evidence to put Darragh away for life without me needing to take the stand. The little fucker had actually wanked all over our apartment during that morning, spraying his juice all over our TV. You couldn't make it up.

Besides that, there's a mountain of evidence stacked against him. He even had the gun he killed Ryan with in his pocket when he was arrested. He's clearly not a bright little prick at all. Jack nailed it. He got everything spot on. So did I. I was brilliant. Not only during the morning of the robbery, but in the months that followed. I had to play the victim to perfection and I fucking nailed it. Everybody was smothering me with sympathy. Even the board members went out of their way to fawn over me after flying over from America. They have a plaque dedicated to Ryan in each of their Irish branches now. That makes me laugh. The only time I almost came out of character was when Clyde Sneyd snuffled under my arm at Ryan's funeral to cry into me like a little baby. I should've been given an award for the straight face I kept as I patted the top of his head.

And to think somebody once told me I couldn't act!

THE END.

WANT TO KNOW...

- what Jack and Vincent got up to next?
- how Darragh is getting on in prison?
- how Jack and Vincent concocted their plan?
- how David B. Lyons came up with the idea for this novel?

Well, you can watch this exclusive interview with the author right here where he will answer all of the above questions as well as many others.

www.subscribepage.com/middayq&a

DAVID B. LYONS'S NEXT NOVEL IS ENTITLED:

WHATEVER HAPPENED TO BETSY BLAKE?

Facing a life-or-death surgical procedure, Gordon Blake decides to contact a local private investigator in a last-ditch attempt to find out what truly happened to his daughter, Betsy.

But after a seventeen-year search that turned up nothing, inexperienced PI - Lenny Moon - is hardly going to find out any new information before doctors begin Gordon's surgeries in just five hours time.

Or is he?

The clock is ticking…

Find out more information about
Whatever Happened to Betsy Blake?
by visiting TheOpenAuthor.com

ACKNOWLEDGMENTS

This book would not have been completed without the immeasurable support of my wife, Kerry. Thank you for helping me figure out that life is just way too short. To my daughter Lola, I love you so much, but please don't read any of daddy's books until you're over eighteen, okay? A big thank you to my mam, Joan, and my sister, Debra, who - let's be honest - didn't really give two shits when I rang them to tell them I got offered a publishing deal.

To my best friend Barry O'Hanlon, thank you for your always-constructive feedback. Your eyes will always be the first to read my works. Lisa Richards is awesome – I owe you a massive thank you for reading one of the very first (bad) drafts of Midday way back when. Karen Fullam, Margaret Lyons and Charlotte Jones, I owe you all a massive thank you for reading early drafts of this novel and helping me fine-tune it.

I am forever indebted to my publishers Betsy Reavley and Fred Freeman for making my dreams come true. Your constant support, in a multitude of ways, is unmatched in any professional arena I've been a part of. I also owe a debt of gratitude to the amazing Alexina Golding, Sumaira Wilson and Sarah Hardy for their continued presence while, between us, we perfected the publication of this novel.

Made in United States
North Haven, CT
12 September 2022

24021052R00182